BAYSIDE
Escape

Bayside Summers
Love in Bloom Series

Melissa Foster

ISBN-13: 978-1-948868-10-5

Cover Design: Elizabeth Mackey Designs
Cover Photography: Wander Pedro Aguiar

A Note from Melissa

I am truly thrilled to bring you Violet and Andre's story! Violet is one of those complex, mysterious characters who has been teasing me for so long, I was beyond ready to dive in and find out more about her. She's been through a lot with her kooky mother, her disjointed childhood, and the way she was thrust into a new life as an inn owner with her estranged sister. It's about time she found her happily ever after. You might remember hearing about Andre in Bayside Desires. He's back in her life, and he's not about to let her go. I hope you enjoy Violet and Andre's sexy, romantic adventure.

There is a very big cast of characters in this story, and each one plays an important part in Violet's life. You can find a down-loadable character list on my website:
www.melissafoster.com/books/bayside-escape

I have more fun, sexy romances coming up soon. Be sure to sign up for my newsletter so you don't miss them.
www.MelissaFoster.com/Newsletter

If this is your first Love in Bloom novel, dive right in! All Love in Bloom stories are written to be enjoyed as stand-alone novels or as part of the larger series. For more information on Love in Bloom titles visit www.MelissaFoster.com

Love in Bloom FREE Reader Goodies

If you love funny, sexy, and deeply emotional love stories, be sure to check out the rest of the Love in Bloom big-family romance collection, and download your free reader goodies, including publication schedules, series checklists, family trees, and more!
www.MelissaFoster.com/RG

Remember to check my freebies page for periodic first-in-series free ebooks and other great offers!
www.MelissaFoster.com/LIBFree

Happy reading!
Melissa Foster

Chapter One

VIOLET PACED THE floor of her half sister Desiree's bedroom, stealing glances out the window of their waterfront inn. They'd been blessed with a gorgeous September evening, the sky was clear, and the breeze hadn't yet kicked up. Summer House sat high on the dunes, giving Violet a gorgeous view of the beach below, where Desiree's fiancé, Rick, mingled with his brother and friends around the beautiful arbor he'd built for the wedding. The ceremony was supposed to start in ten minutes, but Violet and Desiree's selfish, flighty mother, Lizza, had yet to show up. Desiree had been watching the parking lot like a hawk out the front window, while Violet and three of their closest friends tried to distract her. It was bad enough that their good friend Harper couldn't make it back from Los Angeles for the wedding *or* to help out at their inn while Desiree was on her honeymoon. If Lizza was lucky, she'd have an equally good excuse, or she'd have *Violet* to answer to.

Rick's sister, Mira, was nursing her newborn baby girl, Holly, as the girls chatted about the wedding. Desiree looked anxiously out the window again. If Violet had any hope of getting her down to the beach before she fell apart completely, they had to get a move on.

"How much milk can one baby drink?" Violet asked.

Mira touched Holly's cheek and said, "As much as she needs or wants. As Hagen says, it's not like she can have a hamburger." Hagen was Mira's little boy, who was outside with her husband, Matt. "You might as well call me *Bessie* from now on. I feel like a milking cow."

"You look beautiful," Desiree reassured her.

"Well, *beautiful Bessie*," Violet said, "you'd better hurry up or the sun's going to set."

"Shh," Desiree urged. "Don't rush her. Let Holly eat in peace."

Desiree looked gorgeous with her blond hair tumbling loose over the shoulders of her peach maxi dress. The corset top laced up the front, showing off her hourglass figure, and the skirt had ruffles from hips to ankles. Desiree was as proper as Violet was unfiltered, and after a lifetime of barely knowing each other, they'd spent the last couple of years forming a sisterly bond Violet had never imagined possible. The wedding was exactly as Desiree had wanted, with lots of frilly, flowery shit and sappy, tacky things, like wooden signs leading down the dune that read LEAVE SHOES HERE! YOU'RE ALMOST THERE! and THIS WAY TO YOUR FOREVER!

At least Rick wouldn't let Desiree down. He was determined to make sure all of her dreams came true. Desiree thought their honeymoon was going to be spent at the Monroe House, a remote Upstate New York resort, but they were only spending one week there. Desiree had never been overseas, and once their week was up, Rick was going to surprise her with an additional two weeks in Portugal. Violet couldn't be happier for her.

"Babies need calm environments," Serena said, peering into the mirror and fussing with her dark hair. She had recently gotten engaged to Rick's brother, Drake.

Violet rolled her eyes. "Babies spend nine months getting rocked and rolled as their mommy and daddy bang like bunnies."

"Violet!" Desiree chided her.

Violet set her hands on her hips and said, "Don't even pretend you're embarrassed by that when every one of us knows if you have good or bad sex based on the breakfasts you make for us each morning."

Desiree's cheeks flushed. "But you don't have to *talk* about it!"

"Yes, she does," Mira said with a smile. She pressed a kiss to Holly's forehead and tucked herself back into her dress. "Look how much fun she's having making you blush."

Desiree sighed.

Emery, Desiree's best friend, who had recently moved to the Cape, watched as Mira burped Holly and said, "I think I need a baby."

"Like you need a hole in the head," Violet said. "You can barely feed yourself."

"That's what Dean is for." Dean was Emery's fiancé, and he co-owned Bayside Resort, the property next door to the inn, with Rick and Drake. "And I have an insatiable appetite for that man." Emery waggled her brows, making them all laugh. She looked down at her lean, toned body, a benefit of teaching yoga at the inn, and palmed her breasts. "Besides, if I had a baby, I'd have nice knockers."

"Can we *please* hurry up so Des and Rick's fuckery can finally be legal?" Violet waved toward the door.

Emery bit her lower lip, giving Violet a worried look. Emery had grown up with Desiree in Oak Falls, Virginia, and she knew just how often Lizza had let her down.

Violet glared at her.

"Come on." Violet grabbed Emery's arm and dragged her away from the others. "If you mention *Lizza* I will kill you right here and now."

"I won't," she whispered as the others fawned over Holly and Desiree. "But…" She glanced at Desiree, who was heading for the window again.

"No *buts*," Violet said sternly. "I've got her." She went to corral the others and said, "Okay, *Bessie*, Serena, please go keep the guys company and tell Ted we're on our way."

Ted was Desiree's father, and for the first seven years of Violet's life, he'd also been Violet's stepfather. Until Lizza got bored, divorced Ted, and yanked Violet out of the only happy family she'd ever known. She'd left Desiree to be raised by her father, and she'd whisked Violet away to live a nomadic lifestyle as Lizza taught English as a second language, meditated, and floated through life on a whim.

The girls hugged Desiree, and then Violet ushered them out the door, trying to ignore the thickening of her throat as sadness rounded Desiree's shoulders.

"I can't believe she didn't show up," Desiree said. "I thought she really wanted to see me get married. She even said she was bringing a plus one." Her voice went low and angry. "Why did she bother asking us to reserve the artist's cottage for her for a month if she had no intention of showing up? We could have rented it out. You don't think something could have happened to her, do you?"

"*No*. She has spent a lifetime letting us down. This is what she does." Violet dragged Desiree away from the window, gritting her teeth, when what she really wanted to do was hunt down their mother and give her hell.

Lizza had always changed directions as often as the wind. She and Violet had traveled overseas, never staying anywhere longer than a few months at a time, and rarely returning to visit with Desiree. If not for the few brief, uncomfortable visits, and the time they'd spent with their grandmother every summer at the inn, Desiree and Violet would have been complete and total strangers. As it was, before Lizza had tricked them into coming to the inn a few years ago, leaving them with a mortgage, an art gallery, and a secret sex shop, they'd barely known each other. And now *this*? This was too much.

"I'm sorry, Des."

Desiree's eyes dampened, and Violet cursed under her breath.

"I'm sorry." Desiree snagged a tissue from the dressing table and dabbed at her eyes. "I know you hate when I cry."

"I don't hate when you cry. I hate that *she* makes you sad." Blinking away her own damn tears, she took Desiree by the shoulders and said, "Listen to me. Your father is on the beach waiting to walk you down the aisle to marry the man of your dreams, and God only knows how you managed it, but your badass biker sister is wearing a *dress*."

Desiree's eyes swept over Violet's body-hugging black dress, lingering on the open zipper, which started just below her ribs on her right side and wound around her torso, across her lower back, and over her left hip, exposing a trail of flesh all the way to where it ended at the top of a long slit that ran from thigh to ankle. She smiled and said, "I'm never going to see you in a dress again, am I?"

"Not a chance in hell." If it were up to Violet, she'd have worn a black leather miniskirt, jeans, or cutoffs, with her biker boots, a black tank top, and her leather jacket.

"What if you get married someday?" Desiree reached up and touched Violet's long jet-black hair. Then she touched the ink on Violet's shoulder and arm. "You'll make a beautiful bride."

"Not happening, and more importantly, we are *not* going to let Lizza ruin this day for you. You are gorgeous, Rick adores you, and you have the world at your fingertips, so let's spin this positive. At least you no longer have to stress out over how Ted and Lizza will get along." When that didn't earn a response, she said, "Des, Lizza is always going to be *Lizza*."

"She does the best she can," Desiree said sweetly.

Those six words had become their mantra, and they both knew it was the truth. Their mother tried to do what she thought was right for each of her daughters. But that didn't make Desiree hurt any less. Violet had nerves of steel. She could handle her mother's bullshit. But seeing Desiree in pain? That killed her. With Desiree and their friends, Violet had found the stable family she'd always wanted, and she wasn't going to let Lizza waste another second of Desiree's happiness.

"You know, for a girlie girl," Violet said with a teasing smile, "you sort of suck at this wedding stuff."

Desiree's green eyes—the only trait the sisters shared—widened, and her jaw dropped open. "Why? We planned every detail. You said it was beautiful and perfect!"

Violet reached into the bag she'd brought and said, "It will be. I know you said you wanted a small wedding, and you feel like your life is here, so you didn't invite the friends you have from Oak Falls. But you were so close to the Montgomerys that when Amber reached out to see what they could give you, there was only one thing I could come up with, and her sister did a beautiful job." She fished out the black garter with pearl appliqué and pretty pink ribbon and lace and handed it to Desiree.

"Violet!" She laughed. "Morgyn *made* this? It's so pretty."

"I know you would have asked for something white or pink, but nobody bangs the headboard as loudly as you and Rick without a little naughtiness going on."

Desiree swatted her, her cheeks flaming red.

"I think you also forgot you need something borrowed."

"Oh gosh, you're right," Desiree said, frantically looking around the room.

"I've got you covered." Violet reached into the bag again and handed her a small pink-and-white batik pouch she'd made. "You're borrowing the pouch. What's inside is a gift."

Desiree opened the pouch and shook out a gold necklace with two dainty interlocking yellow and white gold rings. Her eyes dropped to the matching necklace around Violet's neck, and her eyes welled with tears. "Sister necklaces?"

"Don't get all sappy and ruin your makeup. Emery will give me hell if you do." She secured the necklace around Desiree's neck, choking back her own emotions. "It symbolizes infinite strength, protection, and unity. The rings move freely but are forever connected. No matter where we are, we'll always have each other."

Desiree threw her arms around Violet's neck.

"Oh God, more hugging?" Violet teased. It had taken her a long time to get comfortable with Desiree's frequent outpourings of affection, but as she embraced the sister she'd missed for so many years, her heart swelled. "Okay, bridey. Time to put that garter on and get down to the beach to marry your man."

They rushed down the wide staircase. Desiree stopped on the first floor and grabbed Violet's hand. "Wait! Our shoes! We left them in the room."

Violet groaned. "We're leaving them at the top of the dunes anyway. Do we really need them?"

"But what about the Harley-Davidson Tybee boots Donovan special ordered for you?" Donovan owned Swank, the Provincetown boutique where Violet and Desiree had bought their dresses.

"I'll wear them tonight. Come on, before Rick thinks you backed out."

"Like he'd ever think that."

They headed for the back door just as the front door flew open and their mother breezed in, waving her hands and flashing her Julia Roberts smile. Her long dress was tie-dyed in orange, black, and white. It was cut wide and deep at the neckline and belted at the waist, with a long flowing skirt and billowing sleeves. Lizza was tall and slim, and like Violet, her dress was slit right up to her thigh, giving her a youthful appearance.

Her wild chestnut mane swished past her shoulders as she came at them. "Hello, my darlings!"

Violet froze, anger bubbling up inside her.

Lizza threw her arms around Desiree and said, "Happy wedding day, Desi."

"I thought you weren't coming," Desiree said uneasily, her eyes shifting to Violet over Lizza's shoulder.

Lizza released her and embraced Violet equally as eagerly. "Violet, look at you! Why, the Cape has been good for you, hasn't it?"

"Where have you been?" Violet asked curtly, annoyed that the first words out of her mouth weren't an apology for Desiree. "Des has been waiting *all day*."

"It's okay," Desiree said. "I'm just glad you made it."

"It's not okay," Violet seethed. "When you say you're going to be at your daughter's wedding, you show up before the start of the ceremony, which we're now late for."

"Oh, Desi, I'm sorry. Vi's right," their mother said. "It's been a busy day, and I wish I could have come sooner. You didn't think I'd miss your wedding, did you?"

Violet scoffed. Desiree elbowed her, silently chastising her with pleading eyes as the front door opened again. Lizza spun around and said, "There you are!" She ran toward the door, arms up, blocking their view of what had to be a crazy man since he was traveling with their mother.

She lowered her arms to take his hand and spun around with a beaming smile and said, "Girls, this is my plus one!"

Violet couldn't breathe.

Standing before her was the man she'd left behind in Ghana more than two years ago. The man who had asked her to move to Boston and become his *wife*. Beautiful, loving, talented Andre Shaw. His hair was the color of desert sand. It was longer on top than she remembered, cut short on the sides. He must still run his hands through it, because it was tousled, and a few wispy bangs hung over his thick brows. She could still feel his chiseled cheeks beneath her fingers, his warm lips on hers, and the slide of his aquiline nose against her skin. A dusting of scruff covered the devastatingly sexy cleft in his chin, but his loving dark eyes—the ones that still haunted her dreams—bore a mix of shock and pain, as if he'd seen a ghost.

Violet tried to swallow, but her mouth was bone dry.

Desiree's face was a mask of surprise at their mother's younger, handsome date, who looked like he'd come from a summer photo shoot despite the wrinkles in his brown linen pants and tan linen shirt.

Violet closed her gaping jaw, trying to blink away what could only be a mirage.

"*Daisy*," Andre said with disbelief.

The endearment turned her knees to jelly, and she clutched Desiree's hand as his whispers echoed in her mind. *You're sweeter than a Violet. You're my Daisy.*

"Oh no, sweetheart," Lizza said. "It's *Violet*, remember? Andre Shaw, *these* are my daughters, Desiree and Violet." She took his arm and gazed up at him. "Isn't he just gorgeous? I was delighted that he could come with me. Andre is an artist and a doctor. He runs one of the companies I work for."

"Well, um, Andre, it's a pleasure to meet you," Desiree said. "Should we arrange for a room at the inn?"

"Don't be silly." Lizza waved her hand as if Desiree had made the most ridiculous suggestion. "He's staying in the cottage, with me."

What. The. Fuck?

Emery ran through the back door, slowing when she saw Lizza and Andre, and said, "Is everything okay? Rick is about to pull his hair out."

"So am I," Violet mumbled.

"Emery, *darling.*"

As Lizza greeted Emery, Violet grabbed Desiree and hauled her toward the back door. "Let's go. It's your wedding day."

"But what about Lizza? And oh my gosh, *Vi*," she whispered. "Andre must be our age! And he's gorgeous! What's he doing with *her*?"

"I don't even want to know…"

IT DIDN'T MATTER how long Andre stared at Violet, or how many times he caught her stealing glances at him, he simply couldn't make sense of her being there. Not after he'd looked for her for so long and come up empty. It was like the universe was playing a trick on him. As if all the talking about her that he'd done in Paris with his friend Brindle had conjured her. But how messed up was that? The only reason he was there at the Cape was because he'd taken Brindle's advice about getting away someplace new to finally get over Violet—*Daisy. My Daisy*—once and for all. That was why he'd taken Lizza up on her offer to stay at the cottage she'd rented while he was between projects instead of staying at one of his usual haunts. The Cape was close enough to visit his parents in Boston, and he was able to secure a part-time volunteer position at the Outer Cape Health Clinic for the last three weeks of his stay, which was supposed to help keep his mind off Violet. But now his head was spinning, which was nothing compared to the hurt and anger warring inside him.

Applause and cheers rang out, startling him from his thoughts. He clapped as Desiree and Rick sealed their union with a kiss and a scruffy dog with a peach bow around his neck barked as it ran circles around them.

"That's Cosmos," Lizza said. "He's a little matchmaker."

Andre wasn't about to ask what *that* meant. He hadn't heard a word of the ceremony, and until now he'd hardly noticed the sounds of Cape Cod Bay kissing the shore or the scents of the sea surrounding them, things he'd once savored. He was well practiced at keeping busy to escape thoughts of Violet, but she was *right there*, looking beautiful and troubled, making him want to hold her and get the hell out of there at the same time.

Lizza squeezed his arm and said, "Isn't it exciting? My baby is *married*!"

He looked at the carefree woman he'd met overseas more than two years ago. He'd met Violet on the same trip. He'd been working at a clinic through Physicians Around the World, which was similar to Doctors Without Borders. He wondered if Lizza knew what a can of worms she'd opened by inviting him there. He tried to remember her interactions with Violet when they'd all been in Ghana, but she'd come through the village for only a couple of days with some sort of mission group. For the life of him, he couldn't remember the two of them spending any time together, much less Violet calling her *Mom*, or even giving her more than a brief nod. None of this made sense. Violet had told him about her strange relationship with her mother, and now that he knew that woman was *Lizza*, he felt guilty for being there with the person who had caused Violet so much grief. Then again, he'd spent months looking for Violet, and it was only because of this odd coincidence with Lizza that he'd found her again. But seeing her unleashed too many conflicting emotions. He needed to get the hell out of there.

"Congratulations," he said, mentally preparing his exit speech.

"Come on." Lizza pulled him to his feet. "We have to go congratulate them." She held on to his arm, guiding him toward the crowd. "Look how beautiful the flowers are. Desi planned everything with the help of her friends. I want to introduce you to my girls' friends. They're a hoot! But watch out for my Violet. She's a pistol, and trust me, you don't want her to go off."

Actually, he'd prefer if Violet had gone off on him rather than slipping away in the middle of the night and leaving without a trace. He glanced at Lizza's proud smile. It was obvious she had no idea what had gone on between him and Violet. Would she care if he took off?

"Come on, now. Don't be shy," Lizza said, dragging him into the middle of the crowd. "I want to squeeze in there and congratulate Desi and Rick. Excuse me for just a second."

As Lizza pushed her way through the crowd of overzealous men and joyous women hugging and laughing, congratulating the happy couple, Andre couldn't take his eyes off Violet. She stood at the edge of the crowd in a wicked black dress, her colorful tattoos snaking over her shoulder and down her arm. She looked his way, and their eyes connected—and held. His body instantly heated up despite the way she'd disappeared from his life.

Her hands curled into fists, and she turned away, causing the slit in her dress to open, revealing the ink on her thigh. That strategically placed open zipper offered another peek at the tattoos on her back. He knew those tattoos by heart, had kissed and loved every spec of the earth signs on her thigh and the colorful wings that began just beneath her shoulders and flared over her hips and buttocks, covering all but a few inches around her spine. Did she have any new tattoos, as he did? He hadn't had a single one before they'd met.

Memories of Violet traipsing around the village in skimpy shorts, tank tops, and biker boots flooded him. She'd had a major chip on her shoulder, but she was sweet as sugar to the children. She made colorful face masks for the doctors in the clinic so they wouldn't scare them, and she made fun, colorful gowns for the children who had to stay overnight, giving them something to focus on other than their illnesses or the proce-dures they were undergoing. She was always in control around others, and protective as hell of each and every child, even the ones who fought, scratched, and bit. Now she looked anything but in control. Oh yeah, maybe no one else noticed, but he couldn't miss the slight inward turn of her left foot, the way her toes dug into the sand. That was her *tell*, like she channeled all her uncomfortable thoughts into that move. She'd done it a lot when they'd first become close, and it had been inescapable the night he'd confessed his feelings to her.

And then she'd disappeared like a ghost in the night.

The cheers quieted, and people began mingling. A tall, brown-haired guy sidled up to Andre and said, "So you're the guy who's got the girls gossiping." He offered his hand. "Gavin Wheeler."

"Andre Shaw. Nice to meet you." He shook his hand and said, "Why are people gossiping?" He glanced at the guests, noticing what he hadn't before. Two brunettes, one slim, one curvier, and a regal-looking short-haired blonde were watching them intently, talking and giggling. Behind the brunettes, three rather large guys also had them in their sights, only they weren't smiling.

Gavin shrugged. "Everybody's got to check out the new guy."

Andre raked his hand through his hair and looked up at the dunes, thinking about where he could go if he left. He'd seen the large tables that had been pushed together on the patio, draped in peach tablecloths and decorated with gorgeous bouquets of peach, white, and red roses. It occurred to him that this was likely a destination wedding, and Violet was probably leaving after tomorrow. She'd made it clear that she never stayed anywhere for long, especially when her mother was around. Maybe he could stay in the cottage after all.

"Thinking about taking off?" Gavin leaned closer and said, "Better make a run for it fast if you're going to, because here comes the firing squad."

He turned around and saw the three gigglers heading his way. *Shit.*

"Want to introduce us to your new friend?" the blonde asked with a flirtatious smile.

She was gorgeous, all legs and a sweet face in a short blue dress. *Definitely not the type of woman to sneak off in the middle of the night.* He stole a glance at Violet, talking with Lizza and Desiree with an irritated look in her eyes, and his stomach took a nose dive. Would he ever be able to think about another woman without wishing it was *her?*

"Andre Shaw," Gavin said, jarring Andre from his thoughts. "Meet Chloe and her nosy cohorts, her sister, Serena, and Emery."

Chloe waved, eyeing him flirtatiously. "Nice to meet you."

He nodded. "You too." If he weren't so fucked up he might return her flirtation, but it'd been a long time since he'd wanted to flirt with anyone.

"Hi. I'm Emery." The thinner brunette thrust her hand out. As he shook it she said, "I'm engaged to Dean, the bearded guy over there." She pointed over her shoulder. "He's the one who looks like he sort of wants to kill you. That's actually his happy face."

Great. So you're engaged to a dick?

"And I'm Serena. My guy's the groom's brother, Drake." She pointed to the guy beside Dean, who winked at her. Then she smiled at Andre and said, "So, you're here with Lizza? How do you know her?"

"We met on a project. Sometimes she works for my company."

"What do you do?" Emery asked.

"I'm a physician, and I—"

"But Lizza's an *artist*," Serena interrupted with a scrutinizing tone. "What type of company do you own?"

"She could still know him," Chloe pointed out.

"Well, yeah," Serena said, "but it's not likely since she's always traveling."

"They probably forgot you're standing here," Gavin said to him. "You might want to make that run for it now."

"Oh no." Chloe touched Andre's arm. "Don't leave. The party is about to start. So, you're a doctor, and you know Lizza through your company, which is…?"

"Operation SHINE—"

"You're the guy behind Op SHINE?" Chloe exclaimed.

"What's Op SHINE?" Serena asked.

Before he could get a word out, Chloe said, "It's like Physicians Around the World, but SHINE allows doctors to sign on for shorter periods of time than PAW, right?"

"Something like that," he said absently, watching as Violet headed his way with a serious look in her eyes. His heart rate kicked up with her every step. Even barefoot she gave off a tough, seductress vibe. It was Violet who had set him on a different path than the one he'd always known. Both of his parents were physicians, though his mother had only worked part time while Andre was young. He'd followed in their professional footsteps, and his life had always included charitable work, like the assignment with PAW he'd been on when he'd met Violet. Had he not been only six months into the nine-month assignment when she'd taken off, he would have gone after her. But even then he wouldn't have known where to look. She'd told him she'd spent little time in the States, so she could have been *anywhere*.

"I work in the medical field, and I keep up with the industry," Chloe explained.

"You work in *administration*," Serena said just above a whisper.

Chloe elbowed her, whispering something back.

As Violet neared, Andre's jaw clenched as he drank in her sexy curves, her long black hair lifting in the breeze with each determined step. He didn't trust himself not to give her hell for the way she'd left him without a trace. He had to get out of there before he said something he'd regret, but her green catlike eyes pierced his barriers, pinning him in place. *Sweet Jesus, you still hold all the strings.*

Violet stopped beside Chloe, her jaw tight, her eyes a mix of determination and vulnerability.

"Vi, have you met—"

Violet put her hand up. "Stop talking." Her eyes narrowed, still locked on Andre as she said, "Tell me you're not fucking my mother."

"Whoa," Gavin said. "Okay, ladies, that's our cue to get out of here."

"Are you kidding?" Emery complained.

"No." Gavin mumbled, "Good luck, dude." Then he dragged the girls away.

Andre wasn't about to satisfy the plea in Violet's eyes. He glanced at Gavin and the girls, who had joined the rest of their friends but still had their eyes on him and Violet.

"Are you screwing Lizza?" Violet demanded.

He slid his hands into the pockets of his slacks as if his heart weren't hammering against his ribs and said, "Patience was never your strong suit."

She huffed out a breath and crossed her arms. "Are you?"

He stepped closer, catching a whiff of jasmine. How many times had he smelled that scent in the last two years and caught himself looking around for her?

Too damn many.

"Maybe you'd like to start over with something like, 'Hello, Andre. I'm sorry I disappeared in the middle of the night and never thought to let you know I was still alive, much less why I left.'"

She pressed her lips together, sadness washing over her face for the briefest of seconds, softening his resolve a little. She lifted her chin as she said, "I asked you a question. *Are you* screwing my mother?"

He lifted one shoulder. "What if I am? You washed your hands of me years ago."

She grabbed his arm and pulled him toward the dunes. "What is going on? How long have you been with Lizza?"

"If either of us has a right to demand answers, it's me."

She lowered her eyes.

"*Why*, Daisy? That's all I want to know. Why did you take off like we meant nothing?"

She kicked at the sand, her mouth twitching like she wanted to say something, but either didn't want to or she couldn't.

He leaned closer so she had no choice but to look at him, and holy hell, that was a mistake. The vulnerability in her eyes, thinly veiled by a mask of strength, nearly brought him to his knees. He tried to push those feelings down deep, as he'd been doing for what felt like forever, and said, "I've only ever seen you speechless once before, and the next morning you were gone." He couldn't help but add sarcastically, "Will I be so lucky tomorrow?"

"I live here," she said with narrowed eyes.

"Yeah? For what? A week? A month? Two?"

She looked over her shoulder at all the people on the beach, and her expression warmed. "This is *home*."

Home? Boy, he'd like to pick at that word like a raven on roadkill. Violet didn't know what the word *home* meant. But if she was staying for a week, a month, or longer, then this was his chance to get some answers and finally get the closure he needed to move on with his life.

She cleared her throat before turning back to him, the warmth gone from her expression. "How long are you staying?"

"Again, not that it's any of your business, but I was invited to stay for a month, until I leave for my next project."

"A *month*?" She shook her head. "You and Lizza cannot stay here for a month."

He arched a brow. "Oh, but we can. It's already been arranged, and I've already committed to volunteering at a local clinic. I'm not about to let them down. And you know what else? I *like* it here. The sand, the sea, the people I've met. Chloe seems *especially* interesting. Did you know she works in health care? This might be just the break I need to clear my head of *old distractions*." It pained him to speak of their love like that, but not nearly as much as it hurt to see the ache in her eyes.

He looked away so as not to get sucked in again and caught sight of Lizza watching them. He waved and forced a smile. "If you'll excuse me, Dai"—he caught himself before the endearment slipped out; the first step in moving on was letting it go— "*Violet*. I believe my date wants to introduce me to her friends."

Chapter Two

NEVER IN HER life had Violet imagined being jealous of the woman who had wrenched her away from the only people she'd ever felt connected to. But here she sat, nestled in the lap of the green-eyed monster, as her mother hung on the arm of the only man Violet had ever loved. She tried to distract herself from the obvious by focusing on Drake and Rick, playing guitars and singing sappy songs as Desiree danced with Serena, Emery, and Mira beneath the twinkling lights they'd strung above the patio of the inn. But that was like trying not to breathe, because just across the lawn Lizza stood beside Andre, who was holding Hadley, Daphne's baby girl, while they chatted with Daphne and Chloe. Daphne was the very cute, very *single* office manager for Bayside Resort. Her daughter was the most serious baby Violet had ever seen. Her little brows were always furrowed, and she rarely smiled for anyone, and yet there she was, cooing in Andre's arms. There must be an aphrodisiac in the air tonight, because not only were Lizza and Hadley mooning over the prominent Boston pediatrician, but Chloe and Daphne were hanging on his every word, too.

Could life get any fucking worse?

Cosmos darted out from under the table and ran toward

Andre. *Jesus, even the damn dog?*

"What do you think, Vi?" Gavin said as he took the seat beside her. He'd ditched his tie, his sleeves were pushed up, and his glassy eyes told her he'd had a few drinks. He was a good guy. He'd recently moved to the Cape from Boston and partnered with Serena in opening Mallery and Wheeler Interior Design. "Is your mom crazy good in bed, or does Andre just have a thing for cougars?"

Maybe she'd have to reevaluate the *good guy* thought.

She glanced at the other end of the table, where Matt was holding Holly as she slept. Hagen leaned sleepily against his side as Matt talked quietly with Dean. They were otherwise occupied, but close enough to hear her speak. Biting her tongue wasn't something Violet was used to—or good at—but she'd do damn near anything to make sure Desiree's wedding was everything her sister had ever hoped for. Including being sober on the one night when she deserved to be blitzed out of her mind.

"You know what I think?" Gavin asked. "I think if he plays his cards right he can trade in your mother for Chloe. She's all over him."

"Yeah, and one touch away from getting her hands broken," Violet mumbled as she pushed to her feet.

"Vi!" Desiree rushed toward her, but Rick swept an arm around his new wife's waist, hauling her in for a kiss. Everyone cheered, causing Andre and the others to head their way.

Fuck.

Violet couldn't stomach another minute of Andre and Lizza's ridiculously happy togetherness. She headed for her cottage.

Desiree caught up to her and said, "Are you okay?"

"Of course. I just have some shit to take care of."

"Vi…?" She sounded worried.

Violet stopped walking and feigned a smile. "What's up, Des? I'll be back to help clean up. Don't worry."

"Clean up?" Desiree's brow wrinkled. "You've been acting weird all night. Does seeing Lizza with that guy bother you?"

She couldn't look into her sister's eyes and lie, no matter how much she wanted to put Desiree's mind at ease, so she didn't respond.

"Maybe he'll make Lizza more *normal*, you know?" Desiree shrugged and said, "There's always hope. Besides, if he keeps her here for a month—"

"I'll lose my mind." Violet strode toward her front door. She needed to get out of her dress and out of *there*.

"Why? I'm kind of happy for her."

Violet walked into her cottage, and Desiree barreled in after her.

"Don't you like Andre?" Desiree asked. "He's a pediatrician and he knows Dean's dad *and* his brother." Dean's father was a pediatric neurosurgeon in Boston, and his brother Doug, also a physician, worked overseas. "I asked him how he met Lizza. He said he met her in Ghana a couple years ago. I know sometimes you and Lizza traveled in the same circles, but you were in Bali before coming here, right? You said you broke up with your boyfriend and that's why you didn't return my calls, but that you were going to *take your life back to Bali*."

Forget changing her clothes. Violet couldn't do this right now. When they'd first come to the Cape, it had been too painful to even think about being in Ghana with Andre, and *Bali* had been the first place that had come to mind on that stressful day.

She shoved her feet into her biker boots, eyes downcast as she said, "Yeah."

It was easier to lie without seeing Desiree's face, because she remembered every minute of her last trip to Ghana, from the moment she'd set eyes on the man who would fluster her and cause her to blush, and made her feel so much that she thought she'd die, to the night she took off wondering how she'd ever go on and the months of tears that followed.

"Oh my gosh…" Desiree covered her mouth.

Violet grabbed her keys and headed out the front door toward her motorcycle.

"Wait!" Desiree kept pace with her. "Wasn't your boyfriend also named Andre?"

Violet looked away, gripping the keys so tightly they cut into her hand. She'd slipped and mentioned Andre's name only once, when she'd first come to the Cape. She couldn't believe Desiree remembered it.

"Holy cow, Violet. Is that why you're so mad? Is he *your* Andre?" Desiree asked, wide-eyed. She must have seen the answer in Violet's expression, because her eyes narrowed and she clenched her hands into fists. "I'm going to *kill* her!" She stalked toward the party.

Violet snagged her wrist, stopping her in her tracks. "If there's going to be any killing, *I'm* the one who's going to do it."

"But—"

"No, Desiree. Let this go. Lizza didn't know about me and Andre." It even hurt to say his name.

"But the nerve of him, getting everyone to like him when he's a…a…*scoundrel!*"

Violet smiled at her oh-so-proper sister and said, "He's not a dick, Des. I am."

"I don't understand."

"That's okay. Neither do I." She didn't know how Lizza and Andre had ended up together, but Andre was right, and the truth cut like a knife. She'd left him and had never looked back. She had no right to be jealous or anything else for that matter. But that didn't stop the pain from seeping in through her pores like poison.

Desiree tilted her head. "You're *okay* with him and Lizza?"

"Not even a little," Violet said honestly. "I need time to clear my head."

"Of course. Go." She waved at Violet's bike. "But don't you want to put on pants?"

"No. I want to get the fuck out of here. You know I love you, Des, but so help me, if you tell one person about this— even Rick—I will go apeshit on your ass." Feeling guilty for leaving, she gave Desiree a quick hug and said, "Don't give this another thought. Go get your man and fuck him silly."

"Violet!" Desiree whispered, crimson staining her cheeks.

Violet chuckled as she walked back to her bike, hiked up her dress, and climbed on. She took comfort in the familiar hug of her helmet, the powerful roar of the engine, and the sting of the air against her flesh as she sped out of the driveway.

VIOLET HAD BEEN to Justin Wicked's house so many times since she'd moved to the Cape, her motorcycle could probably guide itself there. The knots in her chest eased as she cruised down the narrow road and his pond-front home came into view. She'd met Justin the summer she'd turned twelve, during one of her visits to the inn to see Desiree and their grandmother. She'd taken off down the beach to escape the discomfort of feeling like a stranger within her own family, and she'd ended up sitting on Wellfleet Pier. Justin had been a long-haired, lanky thirteen-year-old with an attitude as big as Violet's. He'd watched her from a few feet away, kicking at the pier with the toe of his black high-tops, an unlit cigarette hanging from his mouth. She'd finally gotten sick of being watched and said, "Sit the fuck down." They'd been friends ever since.

Justin's motorcycle, along with one she didn't recognize, were parked out front of his house. She passed the house and turned down the driveway that led to his studio. In addition to being a stone sculptor, Justin owned Cape Stone, a stone distribution and stonemasonry company, with his brother Blaine. His other two brothers, Zeke and Zander, worked with their father in their family business, Cape Renovators, and had renovated the inn when Desiree and Violet had first moved there.

She parked out front and walked into the large secluded stone and glass building that had been her safe haven since moving back to the Cape and reconnecting with Justin. The familiar, calming scents of clay and stone greeted her. She turned on the lights, set her helmet on the table, and exhaled a breath she felt like she'd been holding for hours. She sank onto a metal chair, still trying to process seeing Andre again and his being with her mother. Her chest constricted, and she pressed her palm to it, futilely trying to ease the pain. The truth was, she hadn't been holding her breath for hours but for *years*. She closed her eyes, but all she saw was *him* and the anger and hurt in his eyes. His accusatory tone cut through her thoughts. *You washed your hands of me years ago.*

She opened her eyes, staring up at the greenhouse-type glass roof. She ground out, "Fuck," and pushed to her feet, telling herself she was *not* going down the pathetic path of a woman pining after a man. She flicked on the stereo and forced herself to focus on the sculpture she was making for the Wilks, whose six-year-old daughter, Erin, had passed away last spring from a brain tumor. Violet volunteered in the pediatric ward of the hospital, and she'd spent a lot of time with Erin, working with art as a means to ease the sweet little girl's anxiety. She'd loved Erin like a younger sister. The Wilks were holding a memorial for her in March, and Violet was making a garden sculpture of Erin for them.

She began unwrapping the plastic that kept the clay moist. Her specialty was pottery and batik work, both of which she sold in the gallery at the inn, but neither felt special enough for Erin's parents. She looked over the partially finished sculpture. She was sculpting Erin from memory, sitting with her knees bent, legs at her sides, her little feet pointed out. Erin was leaning back on one hand and looking up at a butterfly that had landed on her other hand. Her beloved pet cat, Igor, had remained by her side through the worst of times, and he'd been with her when she died, which was why Violet was sculpting Igor snuggled against Erin's leg.

She hadn't begun working on the finer details yet, and she wasn't confident in her ability to create a face as sweet and innocent as Erin's, but she hoped she'd do a good enough job to do Erin justice. This would not only be Violet's first time sharing a sculpture, but it would also be the first time anyone other than Justin and Andre would learn she sculpted. She was nervous about that, but her love for Erin was bigger than her fear of exposing this piece of herself.

She set the plastic aside, and her thoughts moved to her other large-scale work in progress on a neighboring table, where the torso of a man, recently fired, waited to be glazed. Her heart ached, remembering how Andre had helped her take her love of working with clay to a larger scale. When she'd stumbled upon him in a tent behind the clinic in Ghana, standing barefoot and shirtless, his hands covered with wet, murky clay, her heart had nearly stopped. Not only because she hadn't had access to supplies to do pottery for a long time, but also because standing before her was the most beautiful man she'd ever seen, and he was completely engrossed in his artwork. His hair and broad chest were streaked with clay, as were the jeans that rode low on his hips. He was working by candlelight, and she was utterly captivated. She'd been around artists her whole life, but she was drawn in by the energy Andre radiated. She wanted to walk over and put her hands on his as he molded the face of a woman. She didn't know how long she'd stood there, but at some point his gaze found hers, and to this day she still felt the burst of light in her chest that their first glance had caused. She didn't find out he was a doctor until later that evening.

He may have wowed everyone else—in Ghana and at the wedding tonight—with his medical skills, but it was their shared love of art that had first brought him and Violet together, sparking the most intense connection she'd ever experienced.

She looked away from the torso to try to push those memories aside. Her hands were shaking. *Damn it.* Huffing out a breath, she went to fill a bowl with water and organize her tools. Then she set to work smoothing an area on the sculpture that had become too soft, adding and molding clay, willing her mind to become absorbed with the process. The feel of the clay and the concentration it took to get the lines of the sculpture just right usually overshadowed every other thought. But as she moved on, dampening an area on the little girl's leg that was too dry, and began molding the gentle curve of her calf, she was still shaking.

Half an hour later, she was still consumed by thoughts of Andre. She dropped her tools on the table and began pacing. *What the fuck am I doing?*

The door opened, and Justin sauntered in. He lifted his bearded chin and said, "Hey, babe."

"Hey," Violet said as a tall, thin redhead followed him in.

"Hi," the redhead said, strutting toward Violet wearing a T-shirt that had WHISKEY BRO'S emblazoned across the chest, a pair of skintight jeans, and knee-high black leather boots. She had tattoos on both arms and gave off a tough vibe.

Justin came to Violet's side, and she feigned a smile. He was thick chested, hard bodied, and had a chip on his shoulder the size of Iceland, which went nicely with his ice-blue eyes.

His eyes raked down her body, and he said, "Nice outfit, babe. Say hello to Dixie."

"Hello, Dixie," she parroted, holding his gaze and wondering why he'd bring Dixie into the studio when he knew she kept her sculpting private. The last thing she wanted to do was make small talk with some chick he was banging.

Dixie came to her other side and admired her sculpture. "You're making a little girl?"

No. I'm making a snake. What the fuck do you think it is? "Mm-hm."

"Shouldn't you be at your sister's wedding?" Justin asked.

Violet turned back to the sculpture and began using her thumbs to smooth the clay. "Shouldn't you be entertaining your *date?*"

She probably sounded jealous, but she didn't care. Sure, she'd slept with Justin a few times, but the last time was right after she'd returned to the Cape, when she'd tried to *fuck* Andre out of her system. It hadn't worked. She and Justin had gone back to being just friends who liked to hang out, create art, and ride their bikes.

"Ha! Holy shit, Jus," Dixie said. "She thinks we're *dating*."

The edge of his lips curved up as he said, "Not dating."

"Whatever," Violet mumbled.

"He's my *cousin*," Dixie said. "I live in Maryland. I'm just passing through, and don't worry. He told me no one knows you sculpt. I'm not going to spill your secret."

She grabbed a rag and wiped her hands, glad Dixie wasn't a loose-lipped local. "Sorry. I'm not jealous. I've just had a shit day. Your cousin can screw whoever he wants."

"Wanna talk about it?" Justin asked.

"Not really." She sighed and said, "I can't even focus on this." She picked up the sprayer to spritz the clay and rewrap it, but Justin grabbed her hand.

"I'll do it. You're too pissed. You'll fuck it up."

She tried to wrench the bottle away, but he snapped it from her hand.

"Guy trouble?" Dixie asked as Justin began spritzing the clay.

Violet shook her head and headed for the sink.

"You're wearing a killer dress," Dixie pointed out. "Justin said your sister's getting married—"

"Already married," Violet said as she washed her hands.

Dixie joined her by the sink and said, "When my brother got married, it made me realize how *single* I was. So if that's what's going on, I feel your pain."

Violet dried her hands. "I like being single. I just have a thing for my mother showing up at the wedding with my ex as her date."

Justin slammed the spray bottle on the table. "What the fuck?"

"That's shitty," Dixie said. "If I were you, I'd have blood on my hands—from the dude."

Violet began pacing again. "He didn't know she was my mother, and she didn't know we were once together. Nobody did."

"Glad I'm not the only one who's been left in the dark on that subject." Justin glared at her as he wrapped plastic around the sculpture.

Violet snapped, "Nobody knows about you and me, either."

"So you two *are* hooking up?" Dixie asked.

"No," Violet and Justin said in unison.

"Okay, just getting my facts straight. But now he knows she's your mom and she knows he was your guy?" Dixie asked.

"He knows," Violet clarified. "She doesn't."

"And he's still with her?" Dixie folded her arms, her eyes narrowing as she said, "Then it's time for blood, and I've got your back if you want to take care of him right here and now."

Violet smiled. "You're all right, *cousin* Dixie."

"Hey, we Whiskeys put family above everything else," she said. "Justin is family, and from what he's told me, you're one of his closest friends. That makes you family, too. Our great-grandfather founded the Dark Knights motorcycle club in Peaceful Harbor, Maryland, and there are a hell of a lot more bikers who'll come to your aid if you need it."

"*Whiskeys?*" Violet asked.

She knew Justin and his brothers and cousins were members of the Cape Cod chapter of the Dark Knights and that his cousin had committed suicide when she was in college, prompting their first annual suicide-awareness rally, but she'd had no idea about his connection to the original founder.

"Whiskey is my last name. My aunt Reba is Justin's mom," she explained.

"You know my aunt Red and uncle Biggs," Justin reminded her. "They come to the suicide-awareness rally."

"Oh right, the big guy with the cane? She looks like Sharon Osbourne?" Violet said.

"Right. They're Dixie's parents. But that's enough family history." Justin wiped his hands on a rag and stepped closer to Violet. "Listen, you want me to take care of this? Show up at that wedding with you to prove you're over him? Run the guy out of town?"

Violet shook her head, wishing it were that easy.

"You want him *gone*, right?" Dixie asked. "That'd probably do it. No dude wants to see his replacement."

Justin's eyes were locked on Violet and full of concern. She looked away, and he touched her hip, bringing her eyes back to his.

"You don't want him gone, do you?" he asked.

She ground her teeth together, unable to answer.

"Oh shit," Dixie said. "You're not over him?"

"I don't know what I am." Violet stalked away. "I'm pissed at Lizza for bringing him here, pissed at him for *existing*, and pissed at myself for being so pathetic that I'm standing here so messed up in the head that I can't even sculpt."

"There's only one way to figure this out." Dixie headed for the door. "Come on. Justin has a house full of liquor, and I've

31

got a nose for bullshit. There's nothing a night of tequila can't figure out."

Violet looked at Justin and said, "I think I like your cousin."

"She's pretty cool." He draped an arm over Violet's shoulder as they headed up to the house. "Just for the record, babe, tequila's not going to keep me from wanting to fuck that guy up."

AFTER A FITFUL night's sleep, Andre poured himself a cup of coffee in the kitchen of the cottage where he and Lizza were staying. The cottage was nice, with a bar separating the eat-in kitchen and living room, two comfortable armchairs, and a roomy couch. But he'd recognize Violet's artwork anywhere, and the batik hanging on the wall and the small pottery bowls and vases were painful reminders of the things they'd shared.

He carried his sketchpad out to the patio in the side yard and began sketching—and thinking about the messed-up situation he'd gotten himself tangled up in. He'd met many nice people at the wedding, and not one of them had mentioned Violet having had a boyfriend named Andre. He'd thought that type of coincidence might have come up in conversation. He'd stayed up half the night debating asking Lizza if she knew about his relationship with Violet, but he'd stopped himself for fear of exposing what it appeared Daisy—*Violet*—had kept secret. He'd tried not to think of Violet as *his*, or as *Daisy*, but it just wasn't working. Knowing she'd kept their relationship a secret should probably push him even further away, but if he knew his Daisy as well as he thought he did, then ignoring the fact that they'd ever been together was her way of hiding from the way it made her feel.

And that gave him pause.

A long enough pause to push past his own feelings and try, for the millionth time, to dissect her possible reasons for leaving without even so much as a goodbye.

The rumble of a motorcycle broke through his thoughts, and he saw headlights ascending the driveway. He'd seen Violet take off on her bike during the reception, still wearing her dress. Now he watched her climb off the bike wearing a man's dress shirt, which hung so low he could only hope she had something on underneath.

His gut seized. When they'd been together, although they'd done everything imaginable to each other's bodies, it had taken her months to finally make love with him. He knew she'd had her reasons. He only wished he knew what they were.

She opened one of the saddlebags on her bike and lifted out her dress, carrying it, and her helmet, into the cottage next door.

He'd assumed she didn't have a boyfriend since she hadn't been with a date at the wedding, but that shirt, and the time—five a.m.—told him he was a fool.

Chapter Three

LIZZA BREEZED OUT the side door at a little after six, carrying a sweatshirt and two colorful towels and wearing a pair of green elephant-print harem pants, a purple tank top that had YOGA GIRLS ARE TWISTED across the chest, and a pink-and-white tie-dyed headband.

"Come on, Andre. Emery's teaching a couples yoga class this morning on the beach, and I told her we'd take it."

Andre was no stranger to yoga. Violet had convinced him to try it when they were overseas, claiming it would help calm their sexual desperation. It had been as enlightening of an experience as it was enticing, seeing the strong-willed woman he adored in such a state of mindfulness. After she'd left, he'd been swamped by longing and negative energy. Grinding his teeth and snapping at nurses had lasted about a day or two before one of them brought him back to reality when she said, *Whatever this shit is, tamp it down. We've got children who need miracles, not nightmares.* He'd used yoga to try to channel the negative energy that had quickly become his constant companion, but it had only reminded him of Violet.

And now there was couples yoga to deal with.

Lizza hadn't said a word when he'd settled into a separate

bedroom, but agreeing to do couples yoga might send her the wrong message. Last night he'd been so upset it had seemed reasonable to play up the idea that he was with Lizza just to get under Violet's skin. But now it felt all kinds of wrong.

He set down his sketchpad and said, "Lizza, I hope I didn't mislead you by taking you up on your offer to stay at the cottage. You do realize we're not that *type* of couple, right?"

She waved her hand, laughing softly as she said, "Sweetheart, my days for men like you are long gone. Come on." She pulled him to his feet. "Let's go have some fun and work out the kinks. Then we'll whip up breakfast for everyone. Desiree usually cooks, but I told her and Rick to sleep in. That girl does so much for everyone else. They should be off on their honeymoon, but Emery told me last night that she and Rick weren't leaving until after *I* do. What kind of nonsense is *that*?"

"Sounds to me like she wants extra time with you."

"The only thing that would do is mess her up, and she's perfect just the way she is."

He was an only child and had always been the focus of his parents' attention. He couldn't imagine what it would have felt like if one of his parents had taken off when he was young. Loving Violet and learning about the pain she'd endured after being separated from her sister and her stepfather made him want to take a stand and hold Lizza accountable for her actions, but that wasn't his battle to fight.

He looked down at his shorts and sweatshirt and said, "I should probably put on workout clothes."

"No time for that, darlin'." She pulled him off the patio and toward the dunes. "Let's go show these pretty little couples how it's done."

AN HOUR AND a half later, Andre stood before the grill in the side yard of the inn, drizzling chocolate sauce over a plate of strawberry crepes he'd just made, laughing at something Dean had said. He loved cooking, and he traveled to newly developing nations and small villages so often, he was used to cooking on grills and over open fires, making do without the luxuries he'd once been tied to.

"I can't believe my man didn't know you could make crepes on a grill," Emery said as she picked a strawberry off Dean's plate and popped it into her mouth.

Dean stroked his beard, eyeing her as he said, "Where would you rather I experiment, doll? In the bedroom or the yard?"

"*Snap!*" Chloe looked at Andre and said, "The bedroom. *Always* the bedroom."

It was probably time to nip *that* in the bud, too, before anyone got the wrong idea. When Andre and Lizza had arrived for couples yoga, everyone was paired up except for Chloe. Why would anyone show up alone to a couples class? He didn't bother to ask. Lizza insisted Andre be Chloe's partner, and Ted's late arrival for the class had solidified the deal.

"We always had a creative sex life, didn't we, Ted?" Lizza said, causing silence to descend around them. "What?" She looked around the table. "How do you think Desiree was conceived? Immaculate conception? Where's the fun in that? Sheesh!"

Everyone laughed except Ted, whose cheeks reddened.

Eyes trained on his plate, Ted said, "How about these crepes?" and shoved a forkful in his mouth.

Andre served up another plate of crepes, and Drake reached for it.

"Don't even think about it, Savage," Serena said, snagging the plate. "That's mine."

"Seriously, Supergirl?" Drake lowered his voice and said, "What makes you think I wasn't going to serve that *to you?*"

"Aw, you're so sweet." She handed him the plate, grinning as she sashayed over to the table and sat beside Emery.

Drake took the chair beside her and patted his lap. "Over here, babe."

As Serena climbed onto Drake's lap, Andre turned back to the grill, and saw Cosmos making a mad dash toward Violet's cottage. Violet pulled the door closed behind her and scooped up the excited pup, smiling as he covered her face in sloppy kisses. It was good to see her smiling again. Man, she looked hot as sin in a black miniskirt, gray shirt, and the black boots with silver buckles she'd worn often when they'd been together, despite the heat.

By the time she reached the inn, she was scowling. She set Cosmos down as she entered the fenced area and the pup raced to Lizza, who was dangling a piece of crepe for him.

"Violet, honey, grab a plate while the crepes are still hot," Lizza said, lifting Cosmos onto her lap.

"Andre made breakfast for everyone," Emery said. "There is nothing this guy can't do. He partnered with Chloe for couples yoga, and I swear, the man's almost as flexible as I am."

Dean made a growling sound. "I was just about to say if things didn't work out with Lizza, he could move in with me and Emery to cook breakfasts, but forget that. The only man I want my doll thinking about is *me.*"

Violet's jaw tightened. Her eyes moved from Andre's face to his bare chest, lingering long enough for a hungry look to crawl across her face. He'd forgotten he'd ditched his sweatshirt during yoga, and now he was glad he had. Let her see what she'd walked away from. Her gaze moved to the tattoo on his shoulder, FAITH IN LOVE. It hadn't been there when they were together.

The heat in her eyes morphed to something he couldn't read—anger or hurt maybe—but in her next breath her expression went stone cold.

"Well, isn't this domestic," she said sarcastically. "Should I start calling you *Daddy?*"

"Oh shit," Drake mumbled.

Before Andre could form a response, Violet stormed toward the parking lot. He wasn't going to let her do *that* to him again. He took off after her, falling into step beside her. "What the hell was that?"

"You're the one screwing my mother." Her eyes remained trained on her bike as they crossed the gravel driveway.

"Stop running and talk to me." When she didn't stop, he grabbed her wrist and said, "You're the one who left me in the dark, remember? You owe me some answers."

The toe of her left boot pushed into the gravel. "I'm sorry, okay? It was a shitty thing to do. I shouldn't have left without telling you why. Can we just let it go at that?"

"No. I can't." He released her wrist and said, "Damn it, Daisy. If that was some kind of test, I couldn't have passed it. You knew I had three months left on my contract. I couldn't go after you. And when I was finally able to, I looked everywhere. I scoured the Internet for any hint of where you'd gone."

"You knew you wouldn't find me online," she said a little less harshly.

"No shit, but people do stupid things when their hearts are broken."

"I'm sure you got over that real quickly when you went back to your black-tie affairs and private practice in Boston."

"Is that what you think? That my feelings weren't real? That I'd forget us?"

She lifted her chin and said, "Nobody is irreplaceable," but she looked like she didn't believe what she'd said, either.

"You were," he said honestly. "I went back to Boston and tried carrying on with my life. I tried to forget the woman who stayed up half the night making a special gown for a three-year-old boy who was terrified of having surgery the next day. The woman who cried alongside a young mother whose baby died in childbirth." He stepped closer and said, "I tried to forget the woman who implored me to step outside of everything I had ever known and do more for others. But that didn't work, because all I saw in Boston was the empty spot beside me where you belonged. All I heard was your voice in my head every damn day when I entered my plush offices, seeing children who had health care and the best doctors at their fingertips."

He noticed her lower lip trembling, and she clenched her jaw. He didn't want to hurt her, but he couldn't stop the truth from pouring out. "You helped me see a bigger, *broader* picture of myself. A picture that meant risking everything. And yeah, I was scared as shit, and I had no idea how to live my life like you did, moving from one place to another without ever putting down roots. But I took the risk, *Violet*. Operation SHINE exists because of *you*."

Her brow furrowed. "Operation SHINE?"

"That's right. I fucking did it. Maybe I was chasing your ghost the whole time, or rising to the challenge you put before me. I don't know and it doesn't matter. I pooled my resources and connections and bought an international humanitarian organization that had fallen into the wrong hands. I revamped the staff, redirected the efforts, and it was the absolute *right* thing to do."

"Wait…" She shook her head and looked back at the inn, catching her friends watching them. They all looked away, and she said, "Lizza sent a postcard about Operation SHINE months ago. I donate to them."

"Lizza volunteers sometimes," he said. "She and I are *not* what you think we are." He paused, letting what he'd said sink in. Violet looked about as confused as he'd been for the last few years. "Do you have any idea what it was like for me to pour out my heart and soul to you and wake up the next morning not just alone but having been *abandoned*?"

She turned away, but not before he saw tears in her eyes. *Damn it.* Could he have chosen a more hurtful word? "Christ. I'm sorry, Daisy. I shouldn't have said that."

She shrugged and said, "Fuck it. It was a long time ago. Who cares?"

"I do." He glanced down at her left foot pointing inward and digging into the ground and said, "Obviously you still do, too."

She looked down, speaking softly. "It was so long ago, I don't even remember us."

His heart hammered against his ribs as he ground out, "Bullshit."

He hauled her against him and crushed his mouth to hers, kissing her so deeply he felt his love for her seeping out of his skin. She clung to his arms, her nails digging into his flesh, but she didn't fight him, didn't try to pull away. Her tongue swept eagerly over his, but he knew she was still holding back, and damn it, so was he. Because what the hell was he doing? Setting himself up to be slaughtered again?

He tore his mouth away, leaving them both breathless, and seethed, "Remember us now?"

Her hands slid from his shoulders, and she touched her lips as if they were still burning for more, like his were.

"I'm not leaving until I get answers, if for no other reason than to finally get the closure I deserve." Struggling against every iota of his being, he turned and walked away.

VIOLET STOOD ON the gravel watching Andre walk away, feeling just as she had the night she'd left their village, like she'd been sliced open and left to bleed out. And just as it had that night, her body refused to let him go. She could still taste him. His musky scent had rooted itself into her pores, and the hard press of his hands gripping her shoulders remained. She felt possessed by him, by his essence. He was *everywhere*. But hadn't he always been?

She didn't know how long she stood there staring in the direction he'd gone, and she couldn't remember going up to her pottery studio at the inn. But several hours later, she was sitting at her potter's wheel, covered in clay, still thinking about their confrontation. Desiree had come up to talk with her, but the ache in her chest hurt so bad, she'd sent her away. It wasn't fair to take her heartache out on the one person who probably cared most about her, but for the third time in Violet's life, she felt like her world was spinning out of her control, and she didn't know how to stop it any better than the first two times—when Lizza had taken her away or when she'd left Andre.

She realized she was crying and dragged her forearm across

her eyes. She forced herself to focus on the vase she was creating. The only time she ever felt completely in control was at her potter's wheel, when she decided what she was making, how it would look and feel. Sometimes she strove for beauty; other times she went for interesting or meaningful. Today she just wanted to lose herself in the work and forget Andre's accusation. *Do you have any idea what it was like for me to pour out my heart and soul to you and wake up the next morning not just alone but having been abandoned?*

Abandoned…

The clay lobbed to one side, and she realized she was squeezing it. She closed her eyes, and her shoulders slumped as she thought about the truth in his accusation.

Violet had started her life having already been abandoned. She never knew her biological father, who had left when he found out Lizza was pregnant. When she'd asked Lizza about him, her mother had said, *You don't need his ugliness rattling around in your head. It's better if you don't know.* But Ted had loved and taken care of Violet as if she were his own child, and she'd opened up to him, and after her baby sister was born, she'd bonded with her, too. Lizza had stolen that happy second chance away and thrust her into a nomadic lifestyle. Gradually over the years, Lizza had abandoned her, too, even if on a different level. But her mother had taught her an important lesson. Life was easier if she didn't form close bonds, and Violet had become an expert at building walls around her heart.

Except she *had* formed a bond with Andre. A deep, meaningful connection that had been so real it had scared the hell out of her.

And then I left him.

Abandoned him. A tear streaked down her cheek.

"Knock, knock," Lizza said from the doorway, drawing Violet's attention.

Violet swiped at the tear.

Her mother's wide-legged pants swished around her long legs as she crossed the studio floor. She wore a dark shirt beneath an oatmeal cardigan that was frayed along the edges, and looked soft, like an old favorite. Violet had no clue what *an old favorite* of her mother's might be.

Lizza's bracelets clinked as she looked over the pots and vases Violet had drying on various tables. "You still do beautiful work, sweetheart. I'm glad to see you've continued doing pottery. I worried about you having been away from it for so long. You've always been my earth child. Working with your hands fills your soul in ways other things cannot."

Violet scoffed, her blood boiling. "Like you *know* me?"

They'd spent years living in remote villages with sometimes fewer than fifty people, so they were never far apart. But Lizza would go off to teach or meditate, sometimes leaving seven-year-old Violet alone for hours.

Lizza smiled and came to her side. "You're my resourceful girl. The earth has always been your playground—hiking, learning, creating, experimenting…"

"Like I had any other choice?" She spun the wheel, working the clay and hoping for the knots inside her chest to unfurl, but they just kept tightening.

"You had choices, honey, and I listened as best I could."

"You listened?" Violet pushed to her feet, standing eye to eye with her mother, and said, "When exactly did you listen, Lizza? When I begged you to take me back to Ted and Desiree? Or was it when I told you I was lonely and had no friends?"

"Honey, those were the things you said, but I listened to the things you showed me. You would have been unhappy tangled up in classrooms and curfews. Don't you remember how you used to sneak out of your elementary classes when we lived in Oak Falls? I had to go to the school and hunt you down nearly every day."

Violet scoffed and stalked away. "I don't remember that."

"I'm not surprised. You were in first and second grade," she said kindly. "You would wander out of the school. Or rather, you would *scheme* and then wander away from the school. I'd find you in a tree or surrounded by bushes, playing in the dirt, drawing, making flower necklaces for Desiree. You could never be tied down, Violet. You have too much of me in you. I imagined what would happen when you became a teenager, and I wasn't going to lose my girl to drugs or thievery."

"A lot of faith you had in your daughter, huh?" Violet turned on her, unable to keep the rage inside. "Most mothers see the good in their children. But not you. You saw me as a delinquent when I was seven!"

"No, darling," Lizza said with a thoughtful smile, which only pissed off Violet even more. "I saw everything about you— who you wanted to be and what struggles you'd have in that environment. When we traveled, you blossomed into a creative, well-rounded woman."

"Is that what you think of me? That I'm *well rounded*?"

"Violet, you learned from different cultures, picking up skills from every village. You loved working with your hands, and you found your niche doing it. You made your own patterns, made clothing and gorgeous batiks. Why, at eight you learned to make glue and used that instead of wax for the batiks. You are a bright, resourceful woman."

Tears burned in Violet's eyes. "I might have found my way,

but it was because I had no one else to do it for me."

"Sweetheart, staying in a small town with rules and expectations would have stifled you. Look at your hands; look all around you. You learned how to do pottery all on your own, and it has been good for you."

Violet remembered when she'd first learned to do pottery, and hell yes, she'd learned it on her own. What other choice did she have? She'd seen an elderly potter working at her wheel in one of the villages, and she'd watched her for weeks from afar, hiding behind shrubs beside the woman's hut. One day, when she ducked into her hiding place, she'd found a lump of clay wrapped in cloth and a bowl of water.

"I might have done things unconventionally," Lizza said, "but I've always supported your creative endeavors."

Violet had always thought the potter had left that clay for her. But now she wondered if it had been Lizza. And hadn't it been Lizza who had left her art supplies and pottery equipment in this very studio when she'd tricked Violet and Desiree into coming to the Cape? At that point it had been more than two years since Violet had worked with a potter's wheel, and she'd been elated to find her mother's equipment and supplies hidden in the closet, along with paints and canvases, which Desiree used to get back into painting.

"Don't you see, Violet? The life we lived was what you needed. Life is fluid for people like us, and for Desi, life is structured and habitual."

"I'm nothing like you," Violet snapped. "I would never tear a family apart, and I might have done a lot of things in my life that weren't what other people would call *right*, but I'd never in a million years pretend to be my daughter's ex's lover."

Confusion rose in Lizza's eyes. "Your *ex's* lover…?"

"Don't pretend you didn't bring Andre here to upset me."

"Upset you? Why on earth would I ever want to do that? I love you." Lizza's eyes widened in surprise and she said, "Were you and Andre *lovers*?"

Violet huffed out a breath. "You were in Ghana when we were together."

"*Tsk*. My life blurs together sometimes. I can hardly remember yesterday. I had forgotten we were there at the same time. Why, I think I was only passing through back then, wasn't I? But I don't recall you saying you had a boyfriend."

Because I never did.

Shit. She'd forgotten about that.

"Honey, I brought Andre here because when I was in Paris visiting a friend I ran into him in a coffee shop. He had gone there for a medical conference and stayed for a few weeks, and he was miserable. I could see it in his eyes. He had some time off between projects for Operation SHINE, and I had reserved the cottage. He said he needed a place to…" Her brow knitted. "Oh! I remember. He said he needed a place to *decompress*. With the bay right outside your door and you girls and all your lovely friends here, I thought it was the perfect place for him to figure out whatever had him so down. The universe brought us together; why *wouldn't* I offer him the luxury you and Desiree had afforded me?"

Violet leaned on one of her worktables, wishing she knew if she could believe Lizza or not. At this point the damage was done. It didn't really matter, did it?

"Anyway, sweetheart," Lizza said softly, "I came up to hug you goodbye."

"You're *leaving*?" She stormed across the room, stopping inches from her mother, and said, "I am *not* going to let you crush Desiree's hopes *again*."

"Desi knows, and she's okay with it. Emery told me Desi and Rick had changed their honeymoon plans so she could spend time with me over the next month."

"And now you're screwing her, like always."

Lizza reached out and touched Violet's cheek. Violet leaned away from her touch.

"No, honey. I'm setting Desi free to begin the life she's always dreamed of. And I have a feeling you need this time without me, too, to find your own answers."

Chapter Four

LATE SUNDAY NIGHT, long after Lizza had taken off for her next adventure, Andre sat in his cottage finishing a sketch he'd started that morning. He'd been drawing practically as long as he'd been able to hold a pencil. His parents had supported his love of the arts, hiring well-known artists to teach him the intricacies he now taught children when he traveled. In middle school, he'd wanted to create more substantial art, and found that he also enjoyed working with clay. His parents had supported those endeavors, too, hiring an award-winning Czechoslovakian sculptor to teach him over the summers. He never traveled without his art supplies, and they, along with his motorcycle, which he'd stored in a Boston garage while he was traveling, were being delivered tomorrow.

He set the drawing on the coffee table and sighed, unsure if he should cancel the delivery until he figured out if he was staying. He could rent a car, draw rather than sculpt. If Violet had her way, he might be gone before the end of the week.

A knock startled him from his thoughts. He answered the door, and his goddamn heart beat like a jackhammer at the sight of Violet.

"Hey," she said.

She wore a black zip-up sweatshirt open over a dark tank top that stopped short of her hip-hugging jeans, exposing a path of tanned, toned skin with a splash of ink. He noticed her left leg slip inward, and he had the urge to reach for her. But he'd been thinking about that morning when she'd come home just before dawn, wearing some guy's shirt, and reminded himself that he'd spent more than two years searching for her—and she hadn't *wanted* to be found.

He pushed his hand into his pocket and said, "Hi."

"Got a minute to talk?"

He bit back, *About fucking time*, and said, "Sure. Want to come in? Have a drink?"

She nodded and stepped inside. He grabbed two beers from the fridge, and when he returned to the living room, she was holding his sketch pad, studying the image he'd drawn. He handed her a beer and took the sketch pad.

"Was that…?"

He set it on an end table by one of the armchairs. "Just a drawing," he lied. He'd been sketching Violet's naked body from memory for so long, it had become his go-to outlet for his emotions. He'd started the sketch earlier that morning. He was drawing her lying on her side, the same way he'd sculpted her when they were together.

He waved to the sofa. "Have a seat." He sat in the armchair closest to her.

She inhaled deeply as she sank into the cushion. "I know I owe you an explanation." Her thumb moved over the label on the beer bottle, but her eyes remained trained on him. "And I'm sorry about disappearing. That wasn't fair."

"That's one way to put it." He took a long pull on his drink, wanting to say so much more, but more interested in her reasons than in telling her what she'd done to him.

She pushed to her feet and paced, fidgeting with her hands. "While we were together I got an email from Lizza telling me Desiree needed me and that it would help prolong her life if I would come to the Cape."

He went to her, knowing how much Desiree meant to her. "Why didn't you tell me? Is Desiree okay?"

"She's fine. It was a trick." She stopped pacing. "At the same time, Lizza emailed Desiree asking her to come to the Cape to help run her art gallery, and said it might prolong *Lizza's* life. But she wasn't sick, at least not the kind of sick you'd think. She'd hit our vulnerabilities with the precision of a smart bomb. And then, in pure Lizza style, she took off after we showed up, leaving us with a mortgage on the property, a gallery, and a secret sex shop in the back. That's how we ended up running the inn. This is the house I told you about, where I visited with my grandmother and Desiree when we were growing up. I've been here ever since."

"Jesus, Dai—*Violet.* That's…" She'd told him some bizarre stories about Lizza, but to scare her own daughters like that? He shook his head, trying to understand not only why her mother would do that, but also trying to process the fact that Violet had been in the States, right under his nose the whole time.

And did she say *sex shop*? He couldn't get lost in that right now. "You've been here? On Cape Cod?"

She nodded.

"But you knew I lived in Boston. I looked everywhere for you—outside the country, of course, because you said you'd never stayed in the States for more than a week since you were a teenager. Why didn't you tell me before you took off? We'd been together for months. I don't understand why you'd leave without saying goodbye. We'd just made love for the first time—"

"And you proposed!" she snapped, on the move again. "Who *does* that?"

"Who does that?" He closed the distance between them, stopping her from wearing a path in the floor. "*I did*, Violet. The guy who fell so fucking in love with you, I couldn't imagine going back to a life without you in it. Did I totally misread us? Because if I did, then the last two-plus years I've been torturing myself for nothing."

"No—"

"Then what happened? Did I scare you off?"

"Yes. No! *You* didn't scare me. What I felt for you scared me." She was shaking as she set the beer bottle down and crossed her arms.

"Don't you think it scared me? I've never felt anything like what I felt when we were together."

"But I could never be who you needed," she said angrily. "You were a prominent doctor living in a big city, with highbrow friends, attending black-tie dinners, and all the other shit you told me about. Shit I didn't know how to—or want to—be part of, no matter how I felt about you. I'm sorry, but I couldn't do that. I wanted the *you* I knew in Ghana. The man who put the people he helped before everything else in his life. The guy who walked miles to see families and check up on their children, the guy who sculpted and drew in his free time and enjoyed sitting under the stars with villagers and didn't care if his shoes got dirty. Not the guy who was tied to a system that I didn't believe in or tied to his cell phone and worried about attending the right parties or what the society pages say about him."

He opened his mouth to defend himself, and she said, "Don't even try to say you weren't like that. You *told* me you were, that it was what you had always done."

"Fuck." He pushed a hand through his hair, pacing the floor. She was right. His life had been exactly that before he'd met her. "But if you'd come back with me, that would have changed."

"You couldn't have changed those things, and even if you could have, what would have happened when you realized I wasn't everything you ever wanted? That I was too restless to stay put? When you found me sleeping on a hammock in the yard because your place was too confining? Or when I cursed during a fancy dinner with your doctor friends? What then?"

She paused, breathing heavily, and he read between the lines. She'd been abandoned by her father, her mother, and he knew she worried she'd never be enough for Desiree. Christ, she'd left him to avoid being left behind herself.

"And then you would have resented me for being unhappy," she said less vehemently. "And I would have resented you for wanting me to be something I couldn't. If you loved me, you would have *known* I could never be that person."

"You took the choice out of my hands, didn't you? You never gave me a chance to show you what I thought, or what I hoped for."

"Don't you *see?*" she yelled, her eyes pleading for under-standing. "There was never a *choice* to be made. You *knew* that I had never stayed anywhere for any significant amount of time. I couldn't be your *big-city* wife, but I'd waited my whole life to have a relationship with my sister, and that letter from Lizza made me believe I was never going to get that chance! I could be—and I wanted to be—whatever Desiree needed if she was dying. And at that point I thought she *was*."

"So you *chose* to leave me wondering what the hell I did wrong."

She shook her head, tears glistening in her eyes even as she seethed, "If I had tried to say goodbye, I *never* would have left. That's how much I love you! And that makes me an awful person, because who chooses a man over their own flesh and blood? But I didn't know what else to do! I thought my sister was *dying*—and leaving you nearly killed *me*, too. Did you ever think about that?" She threw her arms up in the air and said, "And then you show up with Lizza and you ruin everything."

He wanted to reach for her, to point out she'd said *love* in the present tense, but he couldn't put himself in a position to be sliced open again. He needed to know where he stood. "Ruined *what* exactly?"

Her jaw clenched.

"*What*, Violet? Whatever's going on with you and whoever you had a date with last night? If you have a boyfriend, give the word and I'll leave you alone. I came here to get *over* you, not all mixed up like this again."

"I *don't* have a boyfriend! I was just...*out* last night." She crossed her arms again and said, "Do you have someone special in your life?"

He shook his head, gritting his teeth and wondering whose shirt she'd worn home that morning.

"Then what did I *ruin*?" he asked. "That you wanted to put down roots, just not with *me*? Because that stings like a motherfucker, but I'm a big boy. I can deal with it."

"No! I didn't know I was even capable of putting down roots. All I knew when I came here was that everything hurt. It hurt to think about you, to say your name, to know that I'd left behind the only man I'd ever loved. God, Andre. It hurt so much I could barely speak to people most of the time without being a bitch. But Desiree *needed* me. She couldn't run this place alone. We'd both been hurt and tricked by Lizza, so I learned to bury my feelings for you, to function again. I learned how to be a friend, how to be a sister, and yeah, maybe I still suck at it sometimes, but I finally know what it means to be part of a family."

She lowered her eyes, speaking softer. "And while I was learning all those things, I wondered if I'd made a mistake. If I could have been the person you wanted." She lifted her gaze and said, "But I know I couldn't have. *Look* at me." She tore off her sweatshirt and held her arms out. "I'm not doctor's wife material. I'm the girl who curses and says shit nobody wants to hear. I cannot stand fake people, I hate dresses and heels, and I'd never give up my bike for *anyone*."

He set his beer on the table and took her hand, unable to keep his distance a second longer. Maybe he should be more upset, but knowing all she'd been through brought a level of understanding that helped ease the pain. "You think you're not enough because of everything you've been through and the shitty people who have made you feel that way."

She lifted her chin and said, "I'm enough for *me*. And I'm enough for Desiree."

"*Daisy...*" He gazed into her eyes, admiring her strength, even though it was that strength that had allowed her to walk away from him. "You were always enough for me just as you were. And yeah, you're right. We wouldn't have made it in Boston."

She lowered her eyes with a pained expression.

He lifted her chin so she had to look at him and said, "But

not just because you dislike everything I had been brought up to respect, or because you think you wouldn't have fit in. You wouldn't have liked being a big-city wife, and I should have seen that. But there's another reason we wouldn't have been able to stay in Boston. I changed while we were together. I know you thought I couldn't change without resenting you, and maybe that would have been true if I had changed *for* you. But you changed the way I saw the world, and that changed who I wanted to be. When I founded Operation SHINE I sold my practice, my house in Boston, and all the material shit that went with it. I got rid of the Beamer and bought a bike. You've put down roots, and I've torn mine out." He breathed deeply, struck by their new juxtaposition, and said, "SHINE will be opening two medical clinics every eighteen months. I plan to be there when each clinic opens for three to four months to make sure they're appropriately staffed and operating effectively. When I'm not in the field, I work with my staff to coordinate ongoing fundraising efforts, recruit medical staff, prepare for the next location, and try to forget the woman who had such an incredible impact on my life."

HE'D CHANGED HIS whole life, given up everything to create a garden from seeds *she'd* planted. She didn't know what to do with that information any more than she knew how to handle the pained confirmation of how much she'd hurt him. Violet grabbed her beer from the table and guzzled it, wishing she could dive in headfirst.

Andre laughed softly. "That's one way to deal with it."

"It doesn't help. Trust me; I've tried." She sank down to the arm of a chair and said, "Well, if this doesn't take the fucking cake. You've become a modern-day Patch Adams and I'm an inn owner."

"Tell me about it." He looked around the cottage and said, "So you own this place, too?"

She nodded.

"And you're living here full time?"

"I haven't left the *state* since I arrived." She hadn't realized that until just now, but not only hadn't she left; she didn't have the itch to take off like she used to.

"I can't even imagine it. You were my *gypsy*, wanting to do so much for so many, content to live with nearly nothing. And now you have all this."

"I didn't think I was capable of sticking around, but I didn't want to lose the only family home I'd ever really known. When Desiree said she was going back to Virginia, I said I'd stay. And once she said if I stayed, she was staying, I knew I had made the right choice. I don't think I ever knew how badly I wanted to be with her, and *know* her, until Lizza tricked us into coming here and then took off."

"Was it hard? Staying at first?"

She nodded. "I missed you so much I wasn't sure I'd survive." *It still hurts, a hundred times as badly now that you're here.* "Desiree fell in love with Rick the first summer we were here, and that made it even harder. I was happy for her, but it was like tearing open a wound. I thought about reaching out to you once your contract was over, when I knew you'd be back in Boston. But even though I was here, I still couldn't be the woman you needed." She didn't tell him that when her friends had all gone to Boston during the brief period in which Serena had lived there, she had stayed behind. It would have been too hard knowing he was there *somewhere.*

"Thank you for explaining it all to me."

She shrugged one shoulder. "I don't know if it did any good or not, but I feel like a fucking truck has been lifted from my chest."

He laughed. "I think that truck took a few rides across mine."

God, she'd missed him. She wanted to throw her arms around him, to strip off his clothes and love his body the way she'd dreamed about for so long. But he wasn't like any other man she'd ever been with. She knew what would happen if they made love…

"I don't know where we go from here," she finally admitted.

"We could try to start over, but how do I know you won't bolt again?"

She smiled and said, "Where would I go? I'm *home.*" She paused, sure he could hear her heart thundering in her chest. He had no reason to trust her, and that scared her as much as being close to him again did. "I'm not sure I know how to do this."

He stepped closer, his dark eyes imploring her, but for what she wasn't sure. He smelled familiar, and when he brushed a lock of hair from her shoulder, his touch sent heat skittering along her skin.

"Do *what*, exactly?" he asked softly.

She could barely breathe, but after years of hiding from her feelings, she didn't want to hide anymore. "Be near you without wanting to be yours."

"Then maybe we need to find a new beginning, because it sounds like the very heart of who we each are has changed, and we both have some trust issues to work on."

She wasn't sure what that meant. A new beginning as

friends? Or a new beginning that might lead them to separate worlds? She was too afraid to ask.

He took a step back, putting space between them, and her heart sank. He was quiet for a long moment, looking at her with a mix of emotions, which she was also afraid to define. And damn it, Violet hated being afraid.

Fuck it. There was only one way to get past fear. She needed to face it.

"Isn't now when you're supposed to kiss me?" she challenged.

The edge of his lips quirked up, and he said, "Actually, I don't believe we've been properly introduced. I'm Andre Shaw. I travel most of the year providing medical care to families in newly developing nations."

Tears burned again, and she hated that, too, even though these were happy tears.

"Damn it, Andre—"

She went up on her toes and crushed her lips to his, praying he wouldn't turn her away. When he kissed her back, the knots in her chest loosened. And as he took the kiss deeper, everything else failed to exist except his mouth loving hers, his strong hands holding her. All she heard, all she *felt*, was blood rushing in her ears, her heart pounding against her chest. And then it happened, just like it always had. Her legs weakened, her insides softened, and her entire body melted against him. She needed to get a grip, but he tasted so good and *right*, and *oh*, how she'd missed him! She never thought she'd have another chance at seeing him again, and here he was, kissing her back.

But if she didn't stop, she wasn't going to. And then what?

Fuck. Fuck, fuck, fuck.

She didn't know how to have a new beginning. She wasn't

like most women who knew exactly what to do in relationships. What if she fucked it up again?

What if I don't?

Holding on to that thread of hope, she reluctantly broke the kiss, breathless and wanting. She licked his taste from her burning lips and managed, "I'm Violet Vancroft. I own Summer House, and the cottages." *Don't stop there. Say something. Anything. Just don't let it end.* "I live next door, and I haven't traveled for more than two years. You can walk me home if you'd like, but you're not coming inside my cottage."

"Aw, *Daisy*—"

"*Violet.*" It killed her to correct him, but the way he said *Daisy*, laden with love, hadn't changed one bit. If he said her name like that she'd have no chance at going slow.

"Violet," he repeated, reaching for her hand. As they walked out his door he said, "Why can't I come in?"

"Because I like you too much. But if you don't piss me off, I'll give you a fucking mind-blowing good-night kiss at my door."

Chapter Five

"HAVE YOU MADE any decisions yet?" Andre held his cell phone to his ear as he stepped out his front door, feeling refreshed after finally having a good night's sleep.

"Sort of," Brindle said. She was still in Paris. "I think you were right. I need to face this pregnancy head-on."

Brindle had planned her vacation to Paris to figure out what she wanted out of life, and then she found out she was pregnant. She and Andre had connected while there, commiserating over love, life, and what it really meant to be happy.

"Good. I'm glad, babe." He headed for the inn, instantly spotting Violet's silky black hair. Relief swept through him. Even though she'd said she had nowhere to run, he wasn't sure if she'd had second thoughts and would ditch him this morning. She didn't need any particular place to run to. She was the queen of finding her way. After all, she'd had to do it her whole life.

"By the way," he said, "thanks for your advice. I took it and came to the Cape with Lizza."

"And...?"

Violet was eating breakfast at the table in the side yard at the inn with Desiree, Serena, Chloe, and Emery. Her new *family.* He was glad she'd found them, even if it had caused him years of grief. "The woman I told you about owns the cottage I'm staying in."

"*Owns?* I thought you said everything she owned could fit into a duffel bag and that she never stayed anywhere long?"

"Everything she owned *used to* fit in a duffel." Violet's eyes met his, hitting him with the electric jolt of a defibrillator. "But I guess people change." He walked into the fenced-in area and waved to Rick, Dean, and Drake, who were coming up from the beach, shirtless and sweaty. "Listen, Brindle, I've got to go, but I think you made the right decision, and I'm here if you need me. Let me know what happens when you get back to Oak Falls."

He ended the call, and as he slipped his phone into his pocket he noticed Violet was scowling and pointedly avoiding his gaze.

"Did you say Oak Falls? As in Oak Falls, Virginia?" Desiree asked as she poured syrup over her waffles.

"Yes. I was just catching up with my friend Brindle. She's from Oak Falls."

"No way. Brindle *Montgomery?*" Emery said as she glanced at Desiree, who was watching him and Violet like a hawk. "Desiree, Gavin, and I are all from Oak Falls. Violet lived there too, until she and Lizza moved away."

"Gavin was just there for a weekend over the summer," Serena said.

"Wow, small world. I met Brindle while I was in Paris attending a conference. She'd never been there before, so I showed her around." Andre realized Violet had never mentioned the name of her hometown. He looked over, but she turned away and shoved a piece of a muffin in her mouth.

Chloe handed him a plate and patted the chair beside her.

"Sit down and have some breakfast. We have *lots* of extras. Des and Rick might not have left for their honeymoon yet, but it is officially *on*, if you know what I mean." She winked, and Violet glowered at her. "What? Everyone knows Desiree makes fabulous breakfasts when she and Rick have a great time the night before."

He couldn't react to that strange explanation. He was too busy wondering if Violet was jealous over Chloe. If she was, that was new too.

"Breakfast fit for a king," Rick said as he and the guys came through the gate. He leaned down and kissed Desiree. "Hey, beautiful wife. This looks delicious."

Dean pulled out the chair beside Emery and said, "I'd say fit for *several* kings, right, doll?" He leaned in for a kiss.

Andre got up and sauntered around the table.

"Several *hot* kings," Serena agreed, holding a forkful of waffle up for Drake as he took the seat between her and Chloe.

"There is a lot of extra food," Emery agreed. "Matt, Mira, and the kids almost never come to breakfast during the school year, Gavin had an early meeting with a client, and Daphne couldn't make it because she's organizing something for her book club."

"I'm in the book club," Chloe said, watching Andre. "Daph's putting together the itinerary for our next in-person meeting."

"I had no idea you knew how to read," Serena teased.

Emery waved at the food, "Andre, grab some breakfast and tell us how Brindle's doing before these two start bickering."

He knew Brindle hadn't told anyone about the pregnancy yet, so he said, "She's doing well. Enjoying her vacation." He piled fruit and eggs on his plate, and then he sat beside Violet and said for her ears only, "Good morning, gorgeous. Did you sleep well?"

"I don't know," she grumbled. "How did *Brindle* sleep?"

He chuckled. *Oh yeah, you're jealous all right.*

"How close were you and Brindle?" Desiree asked.

"Did you two hook up in Paris?" Emery asked. "I'd imagine she'd be all over a good-looking guy like you."

Now Chloe, Desiree, *and* Violet were giving Andre the stink eye. *Shit. What did I do?*

A motorcycle roared up the driveway, drawing everyone's attention.

Violet mumbled, "Oh shit," as the guy climbed off his bike and pulled off his helmet.

"Oh my gosh!" Emery pushed to her feet. "That's him! That's Vi's *long-dong* naked man! He's the guy from her kitchen!"

Dean grabbed the back of her shirt, pulling her down to her seat as he rose to his feet and the others gawked at the big dude walking up from the parking lot. "Justin Wicked? *He's* the guy you saw naked?"

"You banged Justin?" Chloe asked Violet. "Where have *I* been?"

Andre ground his teeth together. *No guy in your life, huh?*

Violet pushed to her feet as Justin walked through the gate and said, "What are you doing here?"

"Hey, babe. I just wanted to make sure you were okay." Justin glanced at the table.

Andre stood up beside Violet, holding Justin's gaze. He was a muscular guy, and the way he was looking at Andre told him he was possessive of Violet. Hell, who wouldn't be? He was a fool to think she wouldn't have replaced him after so long. He strode past Violet and said, "It was nice catching up."

Violet grabbed his arm. She pointed at Justin and said, "You. Sit down and eat breakfast. I'll be back in a minute." She dragged Andre out of the gate and away from the inn.

"You don't owe me any further explanation," he said.

"Shut up." She let go of his arm and said, "That's the guy I told you about when we were together. The one I've known since I was *twelve*."

"Great. And he's in your life in a bigger way now. Just own up to it, Violet. Emery seeing *long-dong naked man* in your kitchen is a dead giveaway that I've been played."

Her nostrils flared. "I never played you. Yes, he's in my life in a bigger way, but not the way you think. He's been part of my life longer than almost anyone. He was consistently there for me as a kid, and we reconnected when Lizza tricked me into coming back. And *yes*, we slept together a hundred years ago as teenagers—and again that first night I came back to town, when I tried to *fuck* you out of my system. But you know what? It didn't fucking work. *Nothing* worked."

"Is that supposed to make me feel better?" he seethed between clenched teeth. "That you fucked him to forget me and *failed?*"

"Does it matter? So, Justin and I have history together. If you can't deal with that, then that's on you, because I can't change it. I get that you don't trust me to be honest with you, and I don't blame you because I was the asshole who left without a word. But I didn't lie last night, and there's no way in hell I'll let you think I'm lying now when I'm not. Justin and I are *friends*."

"It took you three months to make love to me, but you

came back and jumped right in the sack with that guy?"

"I trust Justin. What would you rather I did? Fuck a stranger?"

"Hardly. I was a fool. All that time we were together, and I thought you trusted *me*."

"It's different! I trusted Justin to protect me from *myself*. I trusted *you* with my *heart*. I haven't had sex with Justin since then, and yeah, Emery saw him in my kitchen naked. Big fucking deal. You of all people know I don't have hang-ups about naked bodies. They"—she waved toward her friends and lowered her voice—"don't even know I can sketch a naked body, much less sculpt one. They sure as hell don't understand the idea of sleeping next to someone naked without fucking them. The night before Emery saw him, I was having an especially hard time and he ended up sleeping over. *Sleeping*, not *fucking*. Don't you get it, Andre? Sex has never meant *anything* to me beyond…I don't even know what. It's been a means to try to feel *something*, or maybe to feel *nothing*. I don't know."

"Then why did it take you so long to open yourself up that way to me?"

"Because being with you, sharing everything that has ever meant anything to me—things I've never confessed to anyone about my family, about *me*—and just *kissing* you, holding your hand, sleeping wrapped up in your arms without even having sex, turned me inside out. If that makes me a loser, then it does. When we finally made love, it was more than I could handle. The emotions were too big. It scared me. I didn't even know who I was, melting at your touch. *Literally* turning to mush inside like a weak, ridiculous girl. *That's* how much I love you!"

Fire flamed in her eyes. She threw her shoulders back as she jammed a finger into his shoulder and said, "And who are you to judge me? How about *Brindle*? Is she the reason you have *faith in love* tattooed on your shoulder?" She poked him again. "You professed your feelings for me last night, pretended you'd never gotten over me, and meanwhile you were fucking some chick in Paris? How does that make you any better than me?"

"I didn't sleep with Brindle," he said sharply. "She's a friend going through a hard time. She's the one who convinced me to take Lizza up on her offer to come here, and an hour ago I was thanking her for doing just that."

"And now…?" She lifted her chin, but that goddamn foot was turned in, diminishing the fight left in him and drawing out the truth.

"Now I'm wondering what other shit we should lay out between us so we can stop fighting and put all this hurt behind us." He was breathing too heavily to regain control of his emotions, so he went with it and laid it all on the line. "I tried being with other women to forget you, but *no one* could replace you. It's been a long time since I even tried. And I have a tattoo that says *faith in love* because of *you*. It was supposed to be a reminder every time I look in the mirror not to let what happened between us turn me into an acidic, virulent man who doesn't believe in love or happiness. But all it did was remind me of *you* and how much I wanted to be with you and *only* you."

He exhaled loudly, feeling like a balloon that had lost all its air. "Damn it, Violet." There was no more anger to spew, no more hurt burning inside him. He swept his arm around her waist, pulling her closer, and said, "You love me, too."

Her eyes widened a fraction, as if she couldn't believe he knew the truth, and just as quickly, acceptance settled in the beautiful green eyes he'd seen in his dreams for so long.

"You said it twice," he reminded her. "Once last night and again just now. You said, 'That's how much I love you.' *Love*, not *loved*."

She swallowed hard, looking so soft and vulnerable he wanted to protect her. "We never fought when we were together. I don't know if this is some sort of sign that we need to walk away from each other, or if it's years of hurt and anger that needed to be expunged. I don't fucking *care* which it is. I'm *not* walking away, because you, Violet Vancroft, own my heart, and like it or not, I think I own yours, too."

Violet looked over at Justin heading their way and sighed, taking a step back.

Andre met Justin's steady gaze and bit back the jealousy tearing through him. He lifted his chin in greeting, earning a curt nod in return.

Justin hiked a thumb over his shoulder and said, "Sorry to interrupt, but um...*we're* not a secret anymore, babe. Y'all are pretty loud."

"Shit," Andre muttered. "Sorry, Vi." He drew his shoulders back and thrust a hand toward Justin. "Andre Shaw."

Justin shook his hand. "Justin Wicked."

TENSION ARCED BETWEEN the two men as they sized each other up. Justin had never come to see Violet at the inn, and she had no idea why he'd chosen today of all days to show up. But she had enough to deal with.

She stepped between the badass biker and the possessive man who was an enticing mix of artist and physician and put her hands up. "Stop the chest-pounding bullshit, okay?"

Neither one moved.

"Jesus, you guys. Cut it out, okay? What the hell?"

Andre and Justin both cleared their throats and then they muttered something under their breath.

"*The Real Housewives of Wellfleet* are gossiping a blue streak," Justin said. "Once Dean and the guys realized Violet was okay, they took off." He eyed Andre, though he was talking to Violet as he said, "You're okay, right?"

"Yes," she said sharply. "Fine."

A delivery truck pulled up the driveway, and Andre said, "That's my stuff." Touching her hip in an obviously claim-staking way, he said, "Let's catch up later." He nodded at Justin, who did the same.

The second Andre stepped away, Justin stepped closer.

She held up her hand, watching Andre walk away, and said, "Give me a second to breathe."

"So that's the dude you told me and Dixie about?"

"Yeah." She looked at Justin and said, "The one I screwed over. I'm such a bitch, Justin."

Justin put his arms around her, squeezing her tight. "You're not a bitch. You're just not used to letting someone love you." He pressed a kiss to her forehead and stepped back.

"What kind of loser does that make me?"

"Only the best kind." He winked and said, "You're damn lucky to have friends like the ones you've got here." He eyed Andre, talking with the delivery guy as they unloaded boxes. "The guys were all up in arms about you and Andre."

"It's not their shit to deal with. I already told you he's a good guy."

"I was telling them that when you started arguing. Then

you said it all for them to hear. Sorry if our shit got in your way with him."

She shook her head. "It didn't. I mean, I'm sure he hates that we screwed around, but all that anger you heard is because of me. If I weren't so fucked up, I could have said goodbye to him like a normal person. Who knows what would have happened."

"If you were like everyone else, we never would have connected. You're the coolest chick I know, and I wouldn't change a thing about you." He nodded toward Andre and said, "I heard everything he told you, and I gotta say, the dude's hurting. But it didn't sound like he wants, or needs, you to change. It sounds to me like he just wants and needs *you*, Vi. Period." He dug his keys from his pocket and said, "You sure you're going to be okay?"

"Aren't I always?"

"Yeah. I'm around if you need me." He arched a brow and said, "*Long-dong* naked man, huh?"

She laughed. "Maybe that'll get you a date with Chloe."

"*Shit...*If Dixie has her way, I'll be taking a trip to Maryland to hook up with one of her friends who works for her family's bar. I'll see you later."

She held her breath as Justin approached Andre, exhaling when he extended his hand with a hint of a smile. She'd never expected to see Andre again, and seeing him with Justin, the only person to whom she'd ever confessed her feelings for Andre, did all sorts of uncomfortable things to her. She wanted to protect Andre from Justin's big-brother-like leers, even though she knew Andre didn't need protecting from anyone. And she wanted to protect Justin from Andre's need to show his dominance. But she wouldn't do that either. She knew them both well enough to realize they needed to do those things as much as she needed to go deal with the gossip girls.

She couldn't hear what the men were saying, but when they both looked over at her with serious expressions, she headed for the girls to deal with the fallout from her past.

As she came through the gate, the girls jumped up from their seats and surrounded her—like a cavalry, not a gossiping brood of hens, as she'd expected.

"Are you okay?" Desiree asked, putting her arm around Violet's shoulder.

Emery pushed in closer. "That was intense. I thought you were going to fall apart, and that was *terrifying*."

"They love you, Vi," Serena said. "Both of them. In different ways, obviously, but, *girl*, you have been keeping secrets from us. What's up with *that*?"

"I didn't mean to hit on your man! Please don't kill me," Chloe pleaded.

Violet threw her arms up and out, breaking free from their grasps. "I'm *fine*. I'm not falling apart, and I'm not going to kill Chloe."

"Thank God." Chloe slapped a hand over her heart.

"So, did you *know* he was coming here?" Emery asked.

"The queen of *fuckery* has a lot of explaining to do," Serena said. "You were all over us about our love lives. Time for some payback. You had two dudes wanting to protect you. I was waiting for a brawl."

"Or a threesome," Emery said with a laugh.

Violet glowered. "You're not getting any more details about my sex life, so dream on. And no, I didn't know Andre was coming here, and he had no idea I was *here*, either." She explained what she'd already told Desiree about Ghana and

Andre's arrival on the Cape.

"Damn, Lizza sure knows how to stir the pot," Emery said. "And we all thought you were in *Bali*."

Violet rolled her eyes. "That's because y'all gossip and get things all twisted up. I told Desiree I was *moving my life back to Bali*. That doesn't mean it's where I was before I came here. It means it's where I would have gone if I'd left instead of staying here."

"Well, now that he's had his say, he'd better be done yelling at you. Or he'll have *us* to deal with," Emery insisted.

As the others jumped on the protect-Violet bandwagon, she wondered how they didn't know they were already there. They were her saving graces, but she owed her sanity to Desiree most of all.

She took Desiree's hand and guided her a few feet away from the others. Gazing into her sister's worried eyes, she said, "I'm okay. Really, Des."

"I wanted to go to you, but Rick wouldn't let me. He said it was better to let you hash it out. I've never seen you like that. You looked like you wanted to cry, run away, and hit something all at the same time."

Violet smiled. "It turns out you *do* know me pretty well. Rick was right, but yesterday *I* was wrong. When you came up to the studio to talk to me, I took out my frustrations on you. I'm sorry. The truth is, I couldn't have found my footing after I left Andre if it weren't for you."

"You also wouldn't have left him if it weren't for Lizza using me as an excuse."

Violet lowered her eyes and said, "I would have, eventually." She looked up again and said, "I couldn't have gone to Boston and survived the life he used to live. I would have lost my mind and he would have regretted ever knowing me."

"I don't think that's true. No matter what you might have faced there, you would have made it work. You made it work here with me, and you stayed when you weren't sure you could. That's love." Desiree opened her arms and said, "I'm going to hug you, and I might tear up, so just go with it." As she embraced Violet she said, "How come you didn't even flinch when Justin hugged you?"

Violet groaned. "Don't start. I have no idea why I do anything."

"So, Emery," she heard Chloe say, "just how long *is* Justin's you-know-what?"

And just like that, Violet knew things would go back to normal, at least around the inn. She had yet to figure out what *normal* meant where she and Andre—and the people they had become—were concerned.

Chapter Six

ANDRE STOOD IN front of the gallery where Violet had been working for most of the afternoon. From the outside it looked like the other three cottages on the property of the inn, except it had a hand-painted sign above the door that read, DEVI'S DISCOVERIES, surrounded by snaking vines boasting orange and purple flowers. His mind traveled back to what it had been like working at the clinic overseas. Violet had been in and out of the facility, visiting with children and dropping off little clay and cloth animals she'd made for them. He couldn't imagine her being happy working in a gallery and not surrounded by children who needed her, or so lost in concentration while doing her artwork that nothing else existed.

The late-afternoon sun cast shadows across the driveway, the tips of which touched the gardens Desiree was weeding. She looked cute with her blond hair pinned up in a ponytail, her jeans tucked into bright green rubber boots, and a Summer House Inn sweatshirt that hung past her waist. He'd noticed her keeping an eye on him, and he wondered when she and Rick were leaving for their honeymoon. Lizza had told him she was leaving so Desiree wouldn't feel the need to stick around, but clearly Desiree still did.

She glanced over, catching him watching her. "Are you going in, or just checking out the architecture of the cottages?"

"I'll let you know when I figure it out." He smiled and crossed the driveway to her. "I'm sorry about making a scene this morning."

Desiree stood up and smiled. "We're used to scenes around here, just not scenes involving Violet. She usually keeps her private life to herself."

"Like I said, I'm sorry."

She wiped her hands and said, "It's okay. We couldn't help but overhear you guys. I think I learned more about my sister during your argument than I have the whole time we've lived here." She stole a glance at the gallery. "She's so mysterious. I don't know where she goes or what she does most of time. None of us knew about her and Justin, and I'm the *only* one who knew she had a boyfriend she'd broken up with before coming here. Or rather, *left behind*—sorry. I hate that she did that to you, but I know Vi well enough to realize she never meant to hurt you. But I'm wondering…" She fidgeted with the basket and finally said, "Was she always tough as nails when you guys were together?"

He couldn't stop the smile tugging at his lips. "She was tough as nails and soft as silk. I don't think there's another woman like Violet on this earth. I know she's mysterious to most people, but she's also an open book. You just have to know how to read between the lines, and that's never easy."

Desiree's brow wrinkled. "I was a teacher, and reading between her lines is totally out of my bailiwick. But there's one thing I do know about her. Even though she acts like she doesn't care, she really does. She's the reason I stayed on the Cape when Lizza left us holding the mortgage to the inn. And when she first met Rick? Even though she barely knew me, she was suddenly my *protector*." She laughed softly and said, "You should have seen her stand up to him. She's pretty amazing. When Rick was going to propose, Violet got in touch with Emery and Lizza and arranged for them to be there as a surprise for me. Things with Lizza are complicated, but Violet knew how much having her there would mean."

"She's got a big heart behind those steely gates," he said. "I don't know if Lizza knew what she was doing or not when she brought me here. But I hated seeing Violet so upset."

"We never know what's behind the things Lizza does," Desiree said. "And trust me, nobody likes seeing Violet upset. She's important to all of us. The thing about my sister is that she sees what other people need in their relationships, and she pushes them toward it. But she doesn't seem to have that same vision for herself."

"Maybe because what she needs isn't typical." How could it be with the way she was raised? He had a feeling Violet knew what she wanted *and* what she needed, but not only didn't she trust people to give her those things; she also didn't seem to know how to put herself, her needs, her desires, first. "Are you worried about her?"

"Of course. She's my sister."

"I don't know what she's told you about us, but what you heard from me this morning is true. I'm still in love with her, and I know we have a lot to work through, but the argument you heard was fueled by hurt and love, not hatred. So if you and Rick are sticking around instead of going on your honeymoon because you want to make sure she's okay, you should know that Violet's well-being is my concern, too."

Desiree sighed and glanced at the gallery again. "She'll pull away from you even if she doesn't want to."

"I know that now," he said.

"She'll make you feel ridiculous for worrying about her, and she'll—"

He put a hand on her shoulder, silencing her concerns, and said, "I know. We all have baggage, and I'm not here to kick hers around. I'm here to help her carry it."

Desiree threw her arms around his neck, hugging him tight as she choked out, "Thank you. She deserves to be cherished." She drew back and said, "But *don't* tell her that—"

"Or she'll run the other way. I know. I've got her, Desiree." He waved to Rick, who was walking across the grass from the resort next door with Cosmos trotting happily beside him. "Looks like someone's ready to have you all to himself. Go enjoy your honeymoon so your mother knows she left for a good reason."

As Rick came to Desiree's side Cosmos tried to climb her legs. She scooped him up and he immediately started licking her face.

"What does our honeymoon have to do with why Lizza left?" Desiree asked. "She said she was leaving so you and Violet could finally find the answers you've been searching for."

He must have looked as confused as he felt, because Rick said, "Looks like Lizza's up to her old tricks again. Her matchmaking worked for us. Maybe you'll get lucky, too." He kissed Desiree's cheek and said, "I think we can leave soon, sweet girl. Daphne said she thinks her sister might be able to help Violet with the gallery since Harper isn't coming back until filming wraps up on her project in three or four weeks."

"Didn't I tell you? This morning Violet and I decided to close the gallery while we're away. She said she wanted to spend time building up her inventory. We had a huge summer, and we don't need the cash…" Desiree smiled at Andre and said, "Besides, I think we all know it's not *inventory* she wants to give her attention to." She laced her hand with Rick's and said, "Let's leave tomorrow morning. I'll call the Monroe House and see if they have space for us to arrive early, and if not, we can find a B and B along the way."

As they discussed their travel plans, Andre went to see Violet. He stepped inside the gallery, taking in the knotty-pine floors, yellow walls, and exposed rafters, both of which were painted bright yellow. Beautiful paintings with Desiree's signature in the corner hung on the walls. He wondered why Violet had never mentioned her sister was such a talented artist. Interspersed with the paintings were batik wall hangings in varying sizes, pottery plaques, clay planters, and a plethora of other items. Each item was different, with beautiful earth-toned glazes and Violet's signature designs of trees and bushes, waves, and other natural elements. Tables covered in vibrant batiks held hand-painted cards, shells, and decorated driftwood. More of her pottery filled shelves and a bookcase. His eyes caught on several tiny clay animals, like the ones she'd made for the children at the clinic, and his heart warmed. He picked up one of the animals and wasn't surprised that Violet hadn't signed her name anywhere on it. She'd once told him that she didn't create so others would give her recognition. *Every piece of art is different, as are the emotions it evokes. I'm not part of the equation.*

Except she *was.* He knew how much of herself she put into every piece of art she crafted. As he admired her handiwork, he remembered standing behind her while he taught her to sculpt the human form. He could still feel her hands beneath his, her back against his chest, as they molded the clay, falling in love one touch at a time.

A door in the back of the gallery opened, and Violet walked through, wearing exactly what she'd had on this morning—a black boatneck tank top and snug jeans that had ragged tears on one thigh and just below the opposite knee—but as she closed the door behind her, she looked *completely* different. Gone was the scornful, troubled look in her eyes, replaced with the challenging look he knew well. It was the look she'd hidden behind for the first week they'd known each other. The look he knew others translated to, *Don't even try to fuck with me.* But he'd become adept at reading between Violet's lines, and her message came across loud and clear—*I've been hurt enough. Let me remain invisible and we'll get along just fine.*

He'd never been good at following orders. And he knew she didn't really want to be left alone. At least not by him.

"I see you're still not signing your pieces," he said as he set the animal down and went to her.

"I doubt that will ever change." She crossed her arms, watching him approach.

"I had a nice talk with Desiree and Rick just now. I'm wondering, what did Lizza tell you about why she left early?"

"She left so Des and Rick could go on their honeymoon. Why?"

He gently unfolded her arms and said, "Because I'm starting to see a clearer picture of the way Lizza works. She doesn't like to take credit for the things she does, either."

"What do you mean, *either?*"

He waved around the room at her artwork. "Does anything in here have your signature? Your unique stamp? A hidden *V* somewhere?"

"No, but what does that have to do with Lizza? She signs all of her artwork."

He lifted one shoulder, thinking that the apple hadn't fallen far from the tree, and said, "Maybe nothing." He guided her hands around his waist.

Amusement rose in her eyes. "Pretty sure of yourself right now?"

"When it comes to you, I'm sure *only* of myself, but that's not going to slow me down. Have you ever heard that song that talks about not making things harder than they have to be?"

"Nope." She smirked and said, "Is this when you *sing* to me? Because in case you've forgotten, I hate sappy shit."

"You don't hate sappy shit, but since you don't like to admit that, this is when I suggest we get out of here for the evening. My bike was delivered today. Let's go for a ride. You can show me your favorite haunts. Let me discover the *new* you. The you that puts down roots and tried unsuccessfully to forget me." He brushed his lips over her cheek and felt her breathing quicken as he said, "What do you say, Violet? Want to see if we're as good together here as we were overseas?"

"My haunts, my bike," she said without moving a muscle, and damn he loved seeing her take control.

He slid his hand down her backside, holding her closer as he nipped her earlobe, and she moaned. "I see you're still a control freak."

"And I see you're still pushy," she said heatedly.

He drew back so he could see the fire in her eyes and said, "I look forward to breaking you of that habit...*again*."

THIS IS A *mistake*, Violet thought as she cruised down the

highway toward Harwich with Andre pressed against her back. How was she supposed to concentrate on anything other than how good it felt to be close to him again? Even through her leather jacket his body felt familiar and safe wrapped around hers. She had almost forgotten how much he called her on her shit, too—and how much she liked it. Some guys were all brawn and bullyish tactics. They were cold steel, while Andre was soft, worn leather, the kind she'd wanted to sink into from the first time she'd set eyes on him. His appeal had little to do with how he looked, regardless of the fact that he was hot as fuck, and she was totally digging his longer hair, and the ink that reminded him of her. It was the understated strength and confidence he resonated that had drawn her in. His ability to soothe or take control with a single glance, a single sentence. When they'd met he was a busy physician with no time for bullshit—*Trust me or trust me. There is no other option.* It had taken him no time to strip her of all her defenses, though he'd done so with such artfulness, she'd never even seen it coming.

As they cruised along one of her favorite stretches of road forty-five minutes from Wellfleet, with woods on both sides and the man she craved like a drug wrapped around her, she was already lost in him. She'd tricked herself into believing they weren't as real or powerful as they were, but he'd opened the gates, and now those emotions flooded her. She was riding a raging river of *Andre*, and she wanted to let go of everything that grounded her and give herself over completely.

Fuck.

He'd done it to her again, and he hadn't even tried.

As she turned off the road and drove down another narrow street, her mind spinning, her body thrumming, she knew only one thing for sure.

She was *not* driving home.

She cruised down the one-lane road that led to Common Grounds Coffeehouse. She parked out front of the unassuming café feeling a mix of nerves and relief. Like Justin's studio, the coffeehouse had become another safe haven, one she'd kept private. Her friends at the inn didn't even know she went there, but she'd never hidden anything from Andre. Well, until that fateful night when she'd left him behind. She hadn't thought she was hiding then. She'd thought she was setting him free. The *hiding* had started only once she'd left, when she'd found the only way to keep her head above water was to keep herself busy enough and bury her feelings deep enough to hide from the thoughts of them that had the power to drown her.

Andre climbed off the bike, looking sexy as hell in dark jeans and a simple white T-shirt beneath his leather jacket. He offered his hand as she climbed off the bike. Habit kept her from immediately accepting his unnecessary, though thoughtful offer, but desire brought her hand to his. It felt strange having him help her from the bike when her entire existence before and after him had been one of never looking for, asking for, or wanting help with a damn thing.

He pulled off his helmet and his bangs tumbled to the edge of his brows. He raked his hand through his thick hair, brushing it casually away from his handsome face. As Violet removed her helmet, she wondered how she was going to do this. How could they start over when her heart and body wanted to dive in where they'd left off? She felt exposed and vulnerable, as if he could read her thoughts, and she hated that feeling. But no part of her wanted to run. She had a second chance with the man she loved, and God only knew if he'd ever fully trust her again, or what would happen at the end of his stay, but she'd missed him too much to give up a chance at even a few weeks of happiness.

She set her helmet on the bike and reached for his.

"You don't want to bring them in or lock them up?" he asked.

"No need. It's not that kind of crowd around here." She set his helmet beside hers.

As they headed inside, he didn't take her hand or drape an arm over her shoulder. That made her even more nervous, but she knew this wasn't going to be easy.

He held the door open as she walked inside, and they were greeted by Elliott Appleton's broad smile. Elliott was twenty years old, with longish sandy-blond hair, wire-rimmed glasses, and a personality that was bigger than life. He also had Down syndrome, and he'd worked at his sister's coffeehouse for several years, along with several other people with disabilities.

"Violet!" Elliott gave her a high five.

"Hey, handsome. How's it going?"

Elliott pushed his glasses to the bridge of his nose and said, "Great. Are you going to take the mic tonight?"

"I'm not sure," she said, wondering if she'd have the courage to get up and speak in front of Andre.

Elliott leaned closer and said, "The guy behind you is checking you out. I'll take care of him." He stood up taller and glared at Andre.

Violet touched Andre's arm and said, "It's okay, El. He's with me. Andre, meet my friend Elliott, *host extraordinaire*. He also bakes like a pro."

"It's nice to meet you." Andre offered a hand.

Elliott ran a scrutinizing gaze over him as he shook his hand and said, "Violet usually comes alone and leaves alone."

"Well, I'm honored to be here," Andre said as he put a hand

on Violet's back.

"Will *you* be taking the mic tonight?" Elliott asked as he picked up two menus.

"They have an open mic from six to ten every night," Violet explained. "People get up and read poetry, sing, or sometimes they just chat with the other customers."

"We call it Say Anything," Elliott added.

"Ah, I see," Andre said. "I think I'll skip it tonight, but maybe another time."

Gabe, Elliott's older sister and the owner of Common Grounds, hurried toward them. Her long red hair billowed over the shoulders of her pastel maxi dress. "Sorry to keep you waiting, Vi." She was a curvy gal with a heart of gold and had a solid three inches on Violet.

"Violet brought a friend," Elliott informed Gabe as he handed her the menus.

"I see that," she said with a smile. "I'm Gabe, the owner of this joint and Elliott's older sister."

"I'm Andre. Nice to meet you."

Gabe motioned for them to follow her. Andre leaned closer to Elliott and said, "Violet's lucky you're looking out for her."

Elliott grinned proudly, and Violet melted a little inside.

Gabe led them toward Violet's usual table just outside the open doors to the patio. Flames danced from the masonry fire pit, and several familiar faces sat around tables listening to Gabe's brother Rod playing the guitar.

"Hey, Vi!" Rod called out as he played.

She waved.

"That's my brother Rod," Gabe said to Andre. "Live-in entertainment."

"Hey, what does that make us?" Cory Blaze asked as he

pushed to his feet and came around the table, where he was sitting with two more of Violet's friends.

"Groupies," Gabe teased.

Cory grinned and embraced Violet. His shaggy dark hair brushed against her cheek as he said, "Got something good for us tonight?"

Violet had been known to take the mic and ramble about whatever happened to be on her mind. "I might skip it, actually. Cory, this is Andre. Andre, these are my friends Cory, Steph, and Dwayne. Cory's a glassblower, Steph writes poetry and runs an herbal shop in Brewster, and Dwayne—"

"Needs no introduction," Dwayne said. He was Justin's cousin, a stocky ex-Marine with closely shorn blond hair and the ability to size a person up in two seconds flat, though you wouldn't know it by his laid-back demeanor. From what Justin and Steph had shared with Violet, the suicide of Dwayne's younger sister, Ashley, had changed him. He acted like he didn't give a shit about much of anything, though they all knew that wasn't true.

Dwayne eyed Andre and said, "How's it hanging?"

"If you don't say something like *to the left* or *long and hard*, he'll ask again," Steph warned. "So *please* say something like that."

"Hey, I'm just being your wingman, sweet cakes." Dwayne winked at Steph. "Wouldn't want you wasting your time with men who aren't well endowed enough for you." He lifted his cup as if toasting, then took a drink.

"Ignore him. He's like a tick you can't pull off. He's been attached to my hip since I was six, and I have a feeling he'll still be there when I'm sixty," Steph said as she came to Violet's side. She was a curvy brunette with big brown eyes and purple streaks in her hair. "How was Desiree's wedding?"

"The wedding was gorgeous, but Lizza caused a shitstorm, as usual." She glanced at Andre and said, "But it's all good now."

Steph wrinkled her nose. "That sucks about Lizza, but I'm glad things are cool. Did you see Rowan inside? He was looking for you last night."

"No. He must have left already. Is everything okay?" Violet asked.

"Yeah. He just wanted to talk about Joni."

"Joni is our friend Rowan's daughter," Violet explained to Andre. "He lost his girlfriend to cancer when Joni was a baby and he's raising her alone. Joni is amazing, but she's an anxious kid. I've been working with her, using art to try to ease her frustrations." Art had always been a big part of Violet's life. When she was little it had given her something to focus on other than their next move.

He smiled and said, "I'm glad to see you're still working with kids."

"I've never stopped working with children," Violet said, then to Steph she said, "Andre's a pediatrician and an artist. We met overseas a couple of years ago."

"Awesome. I like you already," Steph said with a wide smile. "We're all pretty kid-and-art-centric around here."

Steph went back to her seat and Gabe sidled up to Andre as they headed for their table and said, "Everyone wants a piece of Vi."

"I don't blame them." He shrugged off his leather jacket and hung it on the back of his chair.

When he moved to help Violet with her jacket Gabe raised her brows in approval. "Must' be someone special," she whispered.

Andre pulled out a chair for Violet and hung her coat on the back of it, then sat beside her.

"What can I get you to drink?" Gabe asked.

"The usual," Violet said.

Andre set his warm dark eyes on Gabe and said, "I'll have whatever she's having. Thank you."

"I like a man who knows what he wants," Gabe said, before leaving them to look over the menus.

"You don't even know what I ordered," Violet said.

"Don't I?" He reached for her hand and said, "Why are you so nervous?"

She bit back the urge to lie and say she wasn't, but there was no use denying it. It may have been years since they'd seen each other, but he *knew* her, the *real* her.

"Andre." She sighed. "I don't know how to do this. How do we start over when we were so close before? I have no idea if you'll ever trust me again, and that makes me feel like I'm walking a tightrope—"

He pressed his lips to hers, silencing her worries with a sweet, reassuring kiss. It did the trick, calming her nerves and reminding her just how good he was for her. As their lips parted, he pushed his fingers into her hair just above her ear and brushed his thumb over her cheek. He'd held her face like that so many times, she wanted to stay right there, gazing into his eyes forever. She didn't want to think about hurt of the past, or if he'd ever trust her again, because the way he was looking at her, touching her, made her feel like everything was exactly as it should be.

"*God...*" she said under her breath. "You and your magic fuckery mess with my head every time we're together."

"My *magic fuckery*? It was a kiss, Violet," he said in a low voice. "A kiss to tell you we're on this rediscovery tightrope together. Let's just be ourselves and take it one step at a time."

"Easier said than done."

When Gabe returned with their drinks, Andre leaned closer and said, "Ginger chai. 'Anything else is either overdone or not worth the time it takes to drink.'"

You remembered.

"Hey, that's what Violet says about it, too," Gabe said as she set their drinks down. "Have you had a chance to look at the menu, or do you want Vi's usual for dinner, too?"

"I think I can skip the fish tacos," he said with a cocky grin.

Gabe laughed. "Where have you been hiding him, Vi? The guy obviously knows you well."

"I don't know all her secrets yet," Andre said. "But I've got a month to try to weasel them out of her. I'll have a chicken panini with swiss and a side of fries, please."

"A month, huh? Guess we'll either be seeing a lot of you, or a lot less of Violet." Gabe winked and walked away.

"You have changed," Andre said. "When we were at the clinic, you were edgier. Now you're a social butterfly."

She scoffed. "If you said that to Desiree or the others, they'd laugh in your face. They don't even know I hang out here."

"No? With all those friends at the inn who clearly care about you, why have you kept this place a secret?"

"I don't know. Why do I do anything?" she said, hoping to discourage more questions, although the truth was, he made her want to figure the answers out. But that came with its own dose of fear.

"That's what I intend to find out." He sipped his drink and said, "Your ginger chai is better."

"Thanks."

His eyes found hers again, and he said, "What do you usually do during open mic night?"

"I don't know. Whatever comes to mind at the moment."

"Such as…?"

She shrugged noncommittally and glanced around the patio, remembering what he'd said at the gallery about rediscovering each other. It wasn't fair for her to avoid his questions, but revealing her truths had never been easy. As Rod played another song and a woman got up to sing, Violet mustered the courage to try to at least answer some of them.

"You asked why I haven't told anyone about this place," she said softly. "When I first decided to stay here with Desiree, I was pretty much a mess. I was out riding one night and I saw a food truck on the side of the road with a flat tire, and Rowan, the guy Steph mentioned, standing there with a casted arm. I pulled over to help him out, and as I changed the tire we got to talking and ended up here. I don't know if you noticed the sign above the door? The one that reads COMMON GROUNDS, LEAVE YOUR BIASES AT THE DOOR? Well, that spoke to me before I even walked inside. Then Rowan introduced me around, and I sort of fell in love with him, Gabe, Rod, and Elliott. They're just so warm and welcoming, and their hearts are in the right place." She looked down at their teacups and said, "They don't serve alcohol here, which means the people you meet aren't hiding behind it, and as I got to know their friends—Steph, Cory, Dwayne, and the others—this became my go-to place."

"They obviously love you, but I still don't understand why you haven't brought your other friends here."

"Do you always have to ask such hard questions?" she said

with a smile. "When I'm at the inn, I have all these conflicting emotions. I love it there, and you know I love Desiree, but she's the reason I came back and the reason I stayed and helped bring the inn to life again, all of which is great. But she and the inn are also a constant reminder about leaving you behind and the hurt I caused both of us. I don't have that here, and I guess I've tried to keep my two worlds separate."

"I guess I can understand that."

"Thank you. That makes me feel a little less guilty for doing it. From the moment I walked in here, I felt like I belonged in a way I didn't at first with Desiree or our friends at Bayside. I just *fit*."

"Which you don't often feel," he said thoughtfully. He reached for her hand and squeezed it. "I remember that, too."

"And I remember how you fit in with everyone, no matter what their backgrounds were or how they acted."

"Because I was groomed for that, Vi. You were left to fend for yourself as the newcomer in foreign lands every few months and had to teach yourself to be resilient and resourceful so you didn't fall apart like many young girls would have. From what you told me, you were more of an adult at sixteen than I was at twenty-five. It's one of the things that makes you so special."

"I think the word you're looking for is *broken*."

Gabe brought their meals, and Andre kept his eyes on Violet until Gabe walked away. Then he said, "We're all broken. So what? None of us get through this life without bumps, bruises, and a few shattered dreams. What matters is what we do with the unshattered ones."

His words had always soothed her roughest spots, but now they stirred the guilt and loneliness she'd been burying for a very long time. "I'm sorry I shattered your dreams for us, and I want to help us both heal from my mistakes. I was an idiot, Andre."

"Then what does that make me? I'm the fool who proposed to you three months after meeting you."

Her heart was beating so fast, she needed a distraction before she climbed into his lap and kissed him like she was dying to. She picked up her fish taco and said, "Yeah, you're right. You are a fool. Not because you proposed, but because of *who* you proposed *to*. Didn't you know I'd freak out?"

She took a bite as he picked up his sandwich and said, "Hell no. You were the toughest woman I had ever met."

She arched a brow. "That's not why you called me Daisy."

"True," he said. "That's the dichotomy of loving you. You are the strongest and the softest, sweetest, most alluring woman I have ever known."

"Stop it. No sappy stuff."

"Okay, but we were amazing together, and you know it. I probably knew in the back of my head that you couldn't fall seamlessly into my Boston lifestyle. But I was crazy in love, and I didn't think through any of that. All I knew was that I wanted a life with you."

She took another bite, trying to concentrate on Rod setting down his guitar instead of her sprinting pulse or the way Andre was watching her longingly. Cory stepped up to the mic and said, "I…uh…I wrote a little something for my mom. Many of you know she's been gone for a long time, and for those who don't, well, she was the one who taught me to blow glass and to kick ass if anyone got in my way."

A rumble of low laughter and murmurs rolled through the patio.

"This is for you, Mom," Cory said. "You sat on the edge of

my bed when you thought I was asleep, and that's when I got to know you best. In those dusky hours, when your voice was craggy and your fingers moved softly over my back or my forehead…"

Cory's voice blurred in Violet's head, drowned out by her own thoughts. He had such loving memories of his mother, and Violet could count on one hand the number of similar memories she had of her own. More plentiful were the memories of Andre's whispered words, his touch as he walked past her in the clinic or the yard in Ghana. The feel of his breath on her cheek as he taught her to sculpt. Her heart was full of memories of lying beneath the stars talking about why he'd gone into pediatrics—*To help those who are too little to help themselves*—and why he enjoyed sculpting people—*Because people are shaped by love, hatred, choices, strengths, and insecurities, and capturing their essence is a beautiful thing.*

A round of applause pulled her from her thoughts.

"One day I'd like to see you up there," Andre said, still holding her hand. "I want to hear what you share with others."

She wanted to share that with him, too, but a new reality was dawning on her, and it brought another wave of trepidation. She was used to facing unsettling things with fierce determination, but when it came to Andre, she wasn't quite as brave.

"We're at opposite ends of the spectrum again," she said hurriedly. "My life is here, with Desiree, and you're…Where are you living?"

He shrugged and said, "'Wherever the wind takes me.'"

She smiled. "Smart-ass. That's what I said to you when we first met, and you asked me how I decided where to go next."

"I wish I'd known it had blown you here."

"Well, you know now. Doesn't this—where we are right now in our lives—scare you? What happens in a month?"

"I don't know what'll happen tonight or tomorrow, much less a month from now. But even if this is all we'll ever have, it's already more than I ever thought possible." He leaned closer and said, "I learned my lesson with that proposal. From now on it's one step at a time."

One step at a time. How was she going to manage that?

Steph and Dwayne moved to the mic, and Steph began strumming Rod's guitar. Dwayne pulled out his harmonica and joined in.

Andre pushed to his feet and hauled Violet up against him. "Except right now," he said as he pressed one hand to her lower back. His other slid hot and heavy beneath her hair, keeping their bodies flush from her hips to her chest. "Right now I want dance *steps*," he said seductively. "Lots of hip-swaying, body-rubbing dance steps…"

THE EVENING SLIPPED effortlessly by as Violet and Andre danced, talked with her friends, held hands, and stole kisses. When Steph asked how they'd met and reconnected, Violet was glad Andre took the burden of answering off her plate by saying, *We met overseas when I was volunteering at a clinic in a village where Violet had been staying, and fate recently dropped me on her doorstep.*

How could a man who made things easier be the same person who pushed her into revealing her truest self? He was as good at pushing her out of her comfort zone as he was at finessing her into doing things she'd avoided forever, like dancing. Before they'd met, she'd never danced with any guys. She hadn't attended a regular school since she was seven. After that she'd been homeschooled by Lizza until her mother had lost interest and Violet had been forced to take charge of her own education, turning to online information when she could. There were no high school parties or proms to attend, or other means by which a typical teenager might have attended dances. But one evening Andre had taken her into his arms and suddenly she was slow dancing. There had been no music, no couples around them to watch or learn from. There was only the two of them and the desire in his eyes. She'd never known she could feel so close to a man, but that night had sparked a love of dancing *with Andre*.

"Ready, babe?" Andre asked.

She realized everyone else was preparing to leave. She wasn't ready for their evening to end. As she said goodbye to her friends, she was glad to see them embracing Andre, giving him warm pats on the back, and hearing them say they hoped to see him again. On their way out the door, Elliott gave Andre a high five, and her chest felt full.

"I like your friends," Andre said as they walked to her bike hand in hand.

"I'm glad." She pulled her keys from her pocket and inhaled a deep breath before holding them out to him—and it wasn't because he'd driven her crazy on the way up. She'd never trusted anyone to drive her bike before, but she trusted Andre, and this was the best way she knew to show him how much.

"What's wrong? Afraid you can't handle my roving hands?"

"Something like that," she said, because some things were too hard to admit.

Chapter Seven

ANDRE WAS GOING to lose his mind. Violet's warm body pressed against his on the way home. She wasn't groping him or trying to make him want her, but she'd never had to rely on tactics other women used like bait. Just the feel of her had always done him in, and after spending hours holding her hand, kissing her beautiful lips, and hearing the voice he'd missed so much, being apart was the last thing he wanted. As he pulled into the driveway and parked in front of their cottages, he thought up a million excuses to extend their evening. A walk on the beach, stargazing, hearing more about her life. *Hell*, he'd take any excuse he could find. But he'd screwed up by going too fast once, and he wasn't going to make her feel boxed in now.

He parked the bike and helped her off. "She rides like a charm." He knew how big a deal it was for her to trust him with her bike, and that made saying good night even more difficult, because he knew trust didn't come easily to her.

As they carried their helmets toward her cottage, she said, "I've never let anyone drive her before."

"Thank you for trusting me."

He set his helmet on the stoop, and then he placed hers beside it and gathered her in his arms. This time he didn't have to guide her hands around his waist. She gazed up at him with a mix of longing and trepidation, bringing a rush of memories. Even after three months, she'd still been nervous when they'd finally made love. He'd never forget the sounds of her breathless whispers, the feel of her hot hands on his flesh, or the intensity of being buried deep inside her and feeling like his whole life had led up to that very moment—all of which only made him want to be that close again.

"I had a great time tonight." *And I don't want it to end here.* "Think we can spend some time together tomorrow? I'd love to see your pottery studio."

"Yeah," she said. "I'd like that."

He touched his lips to hers, taking her in a slow, deep kiss, reveling in her soft curves pressed against his hard frame. Kissing her was heaven; having to stop was hell. He brushed his lips over hers and whispered, "I've missed you."

"Me too." Her fingers pressed into his back, as if she was having trouble saying good night, too.

He traced the bow of her lips with his tongue and she pressed for more, as hungry for him as he was for her. Her mouth was warm and sweet, and as he intensified the kiss, her hands pushed beneath his leather jacket and up his back, and she moaned. *Fuck.* That sensuous, needy sound wound through him, taunting, drawing him deeper into her. He threaded his fingers into her hair, his kisses rougher, painfully more intense, as he made love to her mouth the way he wanted to make love to her body. It was *torture* not being able to claim her the way he wanted to, but the thought of going too fast and losing her again was too much for him to handle.

He reluctantly eased his efforts.

"Tomorrow?" he said between kisses.

She made a noise that sounded like a whimper and an affir-mation, and he couldn't help devouring her again. Their tongues tangled, and he ground his cock against her belly. She made another wicked sound, sending heat coursing through him. His thoughts spun as he explored the recesses of her mouth in deep, penetrating kisses, exactly the wrong way to kiss her after promising to go slow.

Damn it. Reality slammed into him, and he tore his mouth away. "Tomorrow" came out like a command.

Her cheeks were flushed and scratched from his scruff, her eyes glassy. "Tomorrow," she said with a seductive smile that told him she *knew* she'd sent him into a tailspin—and she fucking loved it.

He pressed a quick kiss to her lips before picking up his helmet and taking a step back. She arched a brow and held her hand out. Only then did he realize he still had her keys. He pulled them from his pocket and set them in her hand, feeling like a lovesick, horny teenager.

She unlocked her door, and then she glanced over her shoulder and those gorgeous eyes slid down his body like a caress, causing his cock to throb behind his zipper.

"Night," she said. She picked up her helmet and slipped inside, closing the door behind her.

His head fell back with a groan and he closed his eyes, let-ting the cool air wash over him. How the hell was he going to make it through the night, much less through several weeks?

When he stepped inside his cottage, he swore he could still smell her perfume. He leaned back against the door and debated throwing caution to the wind and marching right back over to her place. What was the worst that could happen?

She could be gone in the morning.

That reality sent him away from the door. He stepped around the boxes containing his art supplies, set his helmet on one of them, and shrugged off his jacket. As he tossed it on the chair by his laptop, he was surprised by a knock at the door. When he pulled it open, Violet launched herself into his arms, and their mouths crashed together. After a second of confounded shock, relief and desire soared through him.

"I just need this," she panted out between urgent kisses. "To be in your arms."

"That's where you've always belonged."

He pushed off her jacket while they made out with reckless abandon, as if they might never get another chance, groping and nipping. She pulled at his shirt, and he tore it over his head. Then he made quick work of stripping off hers. All that colorful ink against her creamy skin took his breath away. Her breasts heaved behind her sheer black bra, and damn, he wanted to strip that away, too, to take her as his. To touch and love every inch of her body the way he'd fantasized, the way he *craved*. But he forced himself to slow down, gripping her hand instead.

"*Daisy*, you're killing me," he said on a long exhalation. "I thought we said one step at a time. I can't lose you again."

"I just want to lie in your arms like I used to. Just kissing."

They'd slept together naked for months without making love. But now that he knew how good they were together, how right their bodies and hearts fit as one, it would be ten times as difficult to hold back. He had no idea how he'd manage, but he wanted her in his arms more than he wanted his next breath, and he'd sure as hell figure it out.

He kissed her again languidly, deliciously sinking into her mouth, until those sounds he loved so much slithered into his own lungs, and then he led her toward the bedroom, weaving around the boxes.

"What is all this?" she asked breathlessly. "It looks like you've moved in for good."

"Art supplies," he said as they entered the bedroom, but boxes were the last thing on his mind. He'd walk through a minefield to be with her.

Moonlight spilled over her beautiful body, and he took a second just to drink in her softness, the neediness in her eyes, and the slight tremble of her hands. He stepped in so close, his cock practically climbed out of his jeans to get to her. God, she was so gorgeous, so *his*. This time he wasn't going to fuck up. He cradled her face in his hands, kissing her deeply. How long had he wished for this moment? For a chance to *see* her, touch her, *kiss* her again? To *love* her the way she deserved to be loved? He should be terrified that she'd bolt, and maybe he was, but he was too greedy for her, too in love with her, to let it push past his elation.

He took his time, kissing the graceful length of her neck, slowing to gently suck the tender skin at the curve of her shoulder as he unhooked her bra. He felt her shudder against him, and as he slid the straps from her arms, freeing her gorgeous breasts, the air rushed from her lungs. He dragged his tongue over the ink that stopped just short of the swell of her breast and pressed a single kiss there. He palmed her breasts, brushing his thumbs over the taut peaks as he pressed feather-light kisses down the creamy ink of her cleavage. He didn't stop there, needing more. If all they had was kissing, he was going to kiss her to the moon and back. He lavished each breast, blazing a path down her belly and along the ink covering her ribs. She touched his shoulders with trembling fingers, and when he glanced up, her eyes were closed and a blissful expression curved her lips. He unbuttoned her jeans, kissing her warm flesh as he drew them down. He ran his tongue along the edge of her black lace panties. She smelled like his favorite memory, and the lower he went, the harder she breathed. He dragged her jeans all the way down her legs, kissing her thighs and running his tongue along the lines of each beautiful tattoo. Then he took her hands and lowered her to the edge of the bed, where he removed her boots, socks, and jeans.

Her keen, catlike eyes locked on him as he stripped down to his briefs. She went up on her knees on the mattress, reaching for him as he reached for her. He bent to kiss her, and she leaned slightly to the side, pressing her lips to his cheek, his neck, and finally to the *faith in love* tattoo on his shoulder. Heat slithered down his chest, pooling in his balls.

"I'm sorry," she whispered. "I never meant to hurt you."

"I know," he said, and took her in another smoldering kiss. Her breasts brushed against his bare chest, and his entire body throbbed with need. "I never meant to scare you," he said against her lips.

He eased her to the mattress and came down over her. His hard length pressed against her center as he slanted his mouth over hers, kissing her painfully slowly and diabolically deeply. Her fingers played over the scar on his left flank, which he'd gotten three years earlier on another volunteer mission. He'd awoken to a woman's shrieks and flames shooting out of a hut. He'd sprinted into the fire, and though he'd saved the woman and her four-year-old boy, the boy had hidden from the flames beneath a table. When Andre was down on all fours reaching for the child, a piece of the burning roof had fallen, catching his flank. In the months before he and Violet had finally made love, when they'd lay together naked, doing everything except allowing their hearts and bodies to truly become one, she used to touch him just like she was now.

Her hips rose, rubbing all her sensual softness against him. He gazed into her lustful eyes and said, "Just kissing?"

She nodded with the sexiest grin he'd ever seen.

"I must be a glutton for punishment."

He kissed his way down her body, slowing to love her breasts. He circled her nipples with his tongue, earning one needy noise after another. He rolled one nipple between his finger and thumb as he loved the other. She arched and moaned as he teased and tasted. When he lowered his mouth over the taut peak, sucking *hard*, she fisted her hands in his hair, writhing against his mouth.

"Andre—"

"It's a *French* kiss," he said with a grin, and moved to her other breast, giving it just as much attention. He groped and sucked, rocking his hard length against her center.

"Fuck," she panted out.

"Nope. Just kissing…"

"Stop talking and get to it." She guided his mouth back to her breast and held it there. "Why was it so much easier to stop at this before we had sex?"

He moved lower, pinching her nipples as he kissed her belly, earning another lustful moan. "*Fear*. You were afraid of the emotions having sex with me would unleash."

He clutched her hips and lowered his mouth to her inner thigh in a series of openmouthed kisses. She spread her legs wider, an invitation he wasn't about to ignore. He ran his finger beneath the edge of her panties, lifting the damp center and moving it to the side. The sweetness of her arousal sent bolts of lightning to his cock.

"Fuck, baby. I have never forgotten the taste of you."

He kissed the sensitive skin just beside her glistening lips, and she inhaled a sharp breath. The sexy sound brought his mouth to her again and again, in one greedy kiss after another. He knew how to make her come with a slip of his finger or a suck in just the right place, but he couldn't let go of the fear of waking up to an empty bed.

It was that unsettled monster inside him that made him release her panties, climb over her, and gaze into her confused eyes.

Need radiated off her as she panted out, "Why'd you stop?"

"If we go further, if I fall asleep with you in my arms, how do I know you won't be gone in the morning?"

"Because this time I know the consequences of loving you." Her brow wrinkled and she said, "I'm a nervous wreck, but only because I *know* how I'll lose myself in you, and I don't want to slow down."

His head fell forward with her confession, and her name slipped from his lips like a prayer. *"Daisy..."*

"That's normal, right? To be nervous about that?" She looked away and said, "Fuck me sideways. Did I just ruin this?"

He turned her face so he could see her eyes and said, "No. You just made it even better."

"Jesus. I thought I fucked up. Maybe you should love me until I'm too tired to move."

He laughed and kissed her deeply. "You know how I love a challenge."

"But I need you to do me a favor first."

"Break your kissing-only rule? *Done.*"

She shook her head and pushed at his chest. "On your back, big boy."

He rolled onto his back and she pulled off his briefs. His arousal sprang up to greet her. There was no more beautiful sight than watching Violet love him. The memories of the look of pleasure that came over her as she loved him with her mouth and hands had played in his mind so many times while they were apart, the scent of jasmine could conjure them.

She settled her legs between his and perched above him. Her hair fell around their faces. Her brow wrinkled and she said, "Stop looking at me like that."

"Like what?"

"Never mind. Just close your eyes."

He did, and she began kissing her way down his chest and abs. Her fingers circled his shaft, and she licked him from base to tip, drawing a moan from deep inside him. His eyes opened, and he watched her. Her eyes were closed as she lowered her mouth over his cock, sucking and working him with her hand. The sensual sounds she made drove him mad.

He fisted his hands and ground out, "Fuck, baby. You feel so good." She sucked harder, and he said, "That's it. God, baby, your mouth is magic."

She withdrew his shaft from her mouth and said, "Stop saying sweet shit."

"Why?"

Her eyes flamed. "Because it turns me to mush, and I can't drive you crazy when you do that to me."

"I'm hard as stone, babe. Apparently you drive me crazy when you're mushy, so we're good."

She glared at him, and he chuckled.

When she lowered her mouth over his shaft again, taking him to the back of her throat, his hips bucked and he buried his hands in her hair. "That's it, baby. Jesus, you feel incredible."

She stopped cold, glowering at him.

"I can't help it," he said with a laugh. "Sweet shit just comes out. What do you want me to say—*take it all, bitch*?"

She shot him a death glare.

"There's no middle of the road, babe. I love you, so you get what you get."

"Fuck it. Whatever." She grabbed his shirt from the floor and said, "Am I going to have to gag you?"

In one swift move he swept her beneath him and came down over her, both of them laughing.

"You blew it with all your *nice* talk," she said with a laugh. "I wanted to rock your world."

"You rock my world by just *being*. No more hiding. I like my *mushy* Violet as much as I like my fierce Violet. Now, sweetheart"—he kissed her hard and deep—"I'm going to make love to you good and hard, and I'm going to say sweet shit until you surrender to your inner softness. Got it?"

VIOLET TRIED TO suppress her smile, but it broke free as she said, "Surrender my ass."

His eyes darkened and he said, "Careful, babe." He dipped his head, teasing her breasts again. "That sounds an awful lot like an invitation."

She opened her mouth to give a snarky response, but it turned into a stream of indiscernible sounds as he stripped off her panties and loved her with his mouth and hands, taking her right up to the peak of madness, whispering as he held her there, "You're so sweet, my love. I missed you."

His tender words made everything feel more intense, more

loving, unfurling the knots of aggression that had been her constant companion, her *armor*, for as long as she could remember.

Except when she was with Andre.

She struggled to hold on to the edginess she'd hidden behind for so long, but his love was too powerful, her desire for him inescapable. He feasted on her quivering sex, his emotions pouring out heatedly like a beautiful cascading river, "I love the way you taste, the way you move," and her need for control fell away. She surrendered to their love, fisting her hands in the sheets. Her heels dug into the mattress with every slick of his tongue, every tender word he said. And when he stroked over the hidden spot that made her cry out his name, her thoughts shattered and she rode the waves of their passion. She clawed at his shoulders as he masterfully took her from one orgasm to the next, staying with her through the very last tremor.

She fell limply to the mattress, breathing hard as he kissed her thighs, and panted out, "Andre, I can't wait. Make love to me."

When he moved to the side of the bed and opened the nightstand drawer, she put her hand over his, feeling him trembling a little, too, as she said, "What are you doing?"

"I bought condoms—"

"We didn't use one before. Do I need to worry that you'll put me at risk?"

"Fuck, *no*. I'd never do that to you. I just didn't want to assume you were okay going without one."

She pulled him down over her and smiled up at him. "You're the only man I've ever been okay with *not* using a condom. Now, hurry up and remind me why."

"I've waited years for a moment I never thought would

come," he said huskily. "There's no way I'm rushing through anything with you."

The loving look in his eyes made her tingly all over. He aligned their bodies, leaning on his forearms as he cradled her head in his hands and kissed her deeply. She lifted her hips, and as he pushed into her, all her broken pieces came back together. When he was buried to the root, she felt her entire body exhale.

She wrapped her arms around him and said, "Stay right there. I missed you so much. I just want to feel you, feel *us*, for a minute, like this."

He brushed his lips over hers and said, "You're never going to be able to escape the feel of us again."

A LONG WHILE later Violet lay in Andre's strong arms, listening to the peacefulness of his breathing. Even after all their time apart, his sounds were comfortingly familiar. She moved carefully out from his arms and sat on the edge of the bed, taking stock of her emotions. She eyed their clothing strewn across the floor, his shirt bunched up at the head of the bed where she'd dropped it after threatening to gag him. She smiled, looking at the patient, determined man who was unwilling to let her hide behind her aggression. He really was beautiful, inside and out. She pressed a kiss to his cheek, and then she climbed off the bed and padded softly to the bathroom.

When she returned, he was still fast asleep.

She glanced at the bedroom door, and her pulse quickened. *How did I ever leave you?* She slipped into bed beside him and pulled the covers up over them. He made a sleepy sound as his arm circled her waist, pulling her tight against him.

"You didn't leave," he said sleepily, lacing his fingers with hers.

She snuggled deeper into the curve of his body and said, "Why would I leave when I finally realized this is the one place I belong most?"

Chapter Eight

VIOLET LOOKED UP from the fruit she was cutting in the kitchen of the inn and watched Andre flip a pancake. He looked delicious in a pair of jeans and a forest-green shirt. She still couldn't believe this was really happening—*he* was real, and *there*, and he didn't hate her. That was good, because she probably carried enough self-loathing for both of them. She must have been out of her mind to leave him behind.

He glanced over as he placed a heap of bacon on a stack of paper towels and winked, unleashing a flutter of butterflies in her stomach. She hadn't stopped smiling since she'd woken up at dawn to his tender kisses and his cavity-evokingly sweet whispers. *God, how I love them.* They'd lain in bed kissing and talking for more than an hour before deciding to surprise Desiree and Rick with breakfast before they left for their honeymoon.

She set the plate of fruit aside, thinking about the boxes of art supplies in Andre's cottage, and said, "After breakfast I'll show you my studio upstairs. Maybe you can put your stuff up there and we can share the space." She heard Desiree and Rick talking and grabbed two mugs from a cabinet.

"Good morning," Violet said as they came into the kitchen

holding hands. They looked happier than she'd ever seen them, which said a lot, because they were two of the happiest people she knew.

"Whoa." Desiree's gaze drifted over the platters of pancakes, fruit, bacon, and eggs. "Am I in the right house?"

Rick grinned and lowered his voice as he said, "I don't think I've ever seen Violet cook," as if his comment were meant for Desiree's ears only.

"I'm not cooking." Violet nodded at Andre and said, "That's what he's for."

"Violet wanted to surprise you before you left for your honeymoon," Andre explained.

Violet looked away, but not before noticing the sentimental look in her sister's eyes.

"You wanted to surprise us?" Desiree walked into Violet's line of sight, studying her face. "You're *smiling*, too. Oh, Violet!" She threw her arms around her and said, "Your happiness is the best wedding present ever!"

Violet wriggled out of her arms, and Rick chuckled. Violet glared at him. "You're egging her on. You know that, don't you?"

"She loves you, Vi. It's a beautiful thing. Besides, we're leaving right after breakfast, so I have to get my pestering in now." Rick snagged a piece of bacon and leaned against the counter beside Andre. "Buddy, this is awesome. Thank you. And thank *you*, Violet, for being so thoughtful."

Violet rolled her eyes. "How about making yourself useful and carrying breakfast out to the table before the vultures arrive."

"Too late!" Emery said as she and Dean came through the kitchen door, both wearing workout clothes. "We're here and...*Holy moly.* Violet hasn't scared Andre off yet?"

Violet thrust the plate of fruit into her hands. "Fill that trap with fruit or *knuckles.* Your choice."

"You're all bark, no bite." Emery giggled as she carried the fruit outside.

"Hey, man," Dean said to Andre. "Does the whole delicious-breakfast-incredible-sex thing carry over to *everyone* who stays at Summer House?"

Rick and Desiree laughed.

"Fuck," Violet mumbled, noticing the confusion in Andre's eyes. She handed Dean the platter of pancakes and said, "No, it does *not.*" She handed Rick a plate of eggs and pointed to the door. "Out."

"I'm going," Rick said, and then he and Desiree carried platters of food outside, leaving Violet and Andre alone. *Finally.* She hadn't counted on taking shit from the gossip girls.

Andre wrapped his arms around her and said, "You look hot in purple."

She looked down at her dark purple tank top. "Thanks."

"But pink looks better on you." He kissed her cheek, and only then did she realize her cheeks were warm and probably flushed. "What did he mean by delicious-breakfast-incredible-sex thing?"

"Desiree loves to cook, but when she and Rick take fuckery to the next level, she makes breakfasts that could make a dead man weep."

A slow grin spread across Andre's face. "In that case, I'll have to up my game."

"You up your game any more and I won't be able to walk." They'd made love three times last night, and she was sore in places she didn't know could hurt.

His eyes narrowed and he said, "I meant my *breakfast* game." He grabbed her ass and slanted his mouth over hers.

"Get a room," Chloe said as she came into the kitchen. "I'm just grabbing coffee. Hey, Andre, you don't happen to have a single brother hanging around anywhere, do you?"

"Not that I'm aware of. But I hear Justin is single."

Chloe poured her coffee. "No thanks. I've done the bad-boy thing. I'm holding out for someone who smiles once in a while."

Andre laced his fingers with Violet's and said, "Sometimes you've got to fight for smiles, but that just makes them that much more special."

"Oh *God*," Violet said as Chloe took her coffee out the door. "Can you please not say that sappy stuff about me?"

"Who says I was talking about you?" He chuckled at her deadpan stare. "Like I said last night, you're not going to scare me off, and I'm not going to change how I show my love for you. So you'd better get used to being mushy most of the time."

"*Most* of the time? Sounds horrifying."

"You love it. Besides..." He backed her up against the wall and boxed her in with his hard body. His eyes turned raven black as he ground his hips against hers and fisted one hand in her hair. "I said *most* of the time. I've seen your softer side, and it's as much a part of you as the badass woman you show everyone else. Once you stop fighting what you really feel and allow yourself to be mushy and loved like you did when we were overseas—when I know you're *all in*—we're going to let rough-and-wild Violet out to play—gags, silk ties, whatever you want, baby. I'm all yours."

ANDRE LOVED HAVING breakfast with Violet and her friends. The girls were hilarious, relentlessly teasing her about how *domestic* she'd become, which of course parlayed into jokes about their sex life. Violet took it all in stride, ignoring most of their comments and tossing in enough snarky barbs of her own to put them in their places. Rick and Desiree shared their honeymoon plans, and Drake and Dean asked Andre if he'd like to go running with them in the mornings. Emery insisted he and Violet join her for yoga at some point—unless it interfered with their ability to make breakfast, of course. It was easy to see why Violet had finally been able to settle down enough to stay put.

It was one of the most enjoyable mornings he'd had in a very long time, made even better because it had started out by waking up with Violet in his arms. But this morning had also brought to light things about Violet that he hadn't recognized when they were overseas, like the fact that she didn't seem to like to be hugged by anyone other than him and—he reluctantly admitted—Justin. And she didn't take credit for *anything* she did. It went much further than simply not signing her artwork. He felt bad for Rick and Desiree. Violet had given them each a quick hug when they were saying their goodbyes, and she acted like she wasn't going to miss them. Then she'd stood at the end of the driveway with a mix of happiness and longing in her eyes, watching them drive away. She didn't leave that spot until their car had disappeared around the corner. She wasn't fooling him. She was definitely going to miss them, despite the way she'd announced, *Finally. Now we have the inn all to ourselves for three and a half weeks. Except maybe for breakfasts, when the moochers will be back.*

As he followed her upstairs to her pottery studio, he thought about how she hadn't taken credit for planning to surprise Desiree and Rick with breakfast. That brought his thoughts back to something Steph had said last night at the coffeehouse. She'd told him that Violet had dropped everything to help Rowan with Joni many times and that she had become a surrogate sister to Steph. Steph had explained that her younger sister, Bethany, had been Ashley's best friend, and when they'd lost Ashley, Bethany had lost herself in drugs. Steph's sister had been in and out of her life ever since, and apparently Violet had been a godsend, stepping in to help her deal with the roller coaster of emotions her sister's visits evoked.

As much as he would have liked to have learned those things from Violet, he had a feeling it would take an act of God for her to pat herself on the back. Trusting him enough to bring him into the secret world she kept hidden from everyone, including her own sister, had been a huge step. Even after just a few days it was clear how much her friends on both sides adored her. He just wished their breakup hadn't caused her to create such a divide in her daily life.

"Here it is," she said as he pushed open the studio door.

Bright light flooded the large, high-ceilinged studio. Incense hung in the air, mixing with the smell of clay and paint. He followed her into the unfinished room. His gaze was immediately drawn to the chaos of works in progress to his right, where several wooden tables were littered with clay vases, cups, pencil holders, tools, and sketches. They were as familiar as the woman who made them. Old newspapers and magazines were scattered about tabletops and on the hardwood floor beside a mass of canvas tarps. Fabric was piled high on a round table by a bay of nearly floor-to-ceiling windows overlooking the beach, and batiks were draped over long wooden bars that hung from ropes tied to exposed rafters in the ceiling. A few wooden chairs were strewn throughout that side of the room, each one boasting dried clay streaks left behind by the artist's hand.

He wanted to know the stories behind those streaks and wished he'd been there to witness them coming to life. He pictured Violet working at the pottery wheel, crouching before the kiln in the corner of the room to carefully set her artwork inside. But his heart ached at what was so blatantly missing.

There wasn't a sculpture in sight.

The opposite side of the room told a different story, one where paint cans and tubes were organized by color. Canvases and paintbrushes separated by size and type. An easel displayed a half-finished painting of the back of a man standing on a dock, the outline of a boat visible in one of the slips.

The only commonality between the two sides of the room was the unfinished floor, marred and scratched, speckled with dried paint and clay. This history of Desiree's and Violet's lives coming together.

He picked up a beautiful pottery bowl with fluted edges. "It's all so familiar, and yet it's not."

"It's been a long time." Violet waved at the left side of the room. "That's Desiree's side. She paints, obviously. We share the studio." She pointed to a closed door and said, "That's a supply closet." Then she pointed to another door across the room and said, "That's the bathroom."

"Did you give up sculpting? You were a natural. I always pictured you crafting beautiful sculptures of the kids you helped."

She walked to the windows and looked out at the water. "I still sculpt, just not here."

"Why not here?" he asked, joining her by the windows.

She shrugged, fidgeting with the edge of her tank top. The deep purple made her hair look even darker and her eyes even brighter. He wondered if her moods still influenced her clothing.

"Sculpting was *our* thing," she said. The strain in her voice told him that revealing as much wasn't easy for her. "It's private, something I do for myself."

He pushed his fingers into her hair and cupped her cheek, wondering if she knew how much that meant to him. "I'm glad you didn't give it up. Where do you sculpt? I'd love to see that studio, too."

Her eyes flicked toward the window, then back, with a hint of apology lingering in them as she said, "At Justin's."

That felt like a punch to the gut, but he pushed past it to try to understand. "You keep secrets from your sister and all your friends, but not from Justin? Does he know about the coffeehouse, too?"

She shook her head. "We know some of the same people, but he doesn't hang out there or anything. Dwayne is his cousin."

He took a step back and said, "I'm trying to understand, babe. I really am. But if there's more to you and Justin, please tell me."

"There's not." She crossed her arms. "When I came here, I barely knew Desiree. She was like a figment of my imagination. The sister who was put in front of me for a few brief, uncomfortable days at a time. I had no idea if we'd get along or if we'd ever feel like real sisters again. She was the one my father chose to keep."

The hurt in her voice slayed him. "I'm sorry, babe. I thought that was Lizza's decision."

He reached for her and she shook her head, but she didn't step away.

"If you had a stepdaughter, would you let someone just take her away?" She didn't wait for an answer. "But that doesn't matter. You wanted to know why I don't sculpt here. I had enough going on with Desiree and the inn and the fucking shitstorm Lizza had created. I didn't want my memories of you added onto that. But I also didn't want to forget you or what it felt like to be with you. When I told Justin that, he offered his studio where he does stonework. Our schedules worked out perfectly. In the spring and summer, he does most of his studio work during the day and on weekends. My summer schedule is the opposite. Between the gallery and the inn, I don't have time to sculpt until late at night. This year we didn't take any reservations after August because of the wedding, but we usually take them until late fall. And then mine and Justin's schedules flip-flop."

The sting over how much she'd shared with Justin took a back seat to the heartache she'd just revealed about her feelings toward Ted. Andre had met him at the wedding, and the guy had talked about Violet like a cherished daughter, not like a castaway. As much as he wanted to tell her that, the way she'd thwarted the conversation told him she had no intention of talking about that situation right now. He could only hope she'd open up more about it soon, as she had about other parts of her life.

He was in awe of his strong, resilient woman who had found a way to keep him in her heart while also dealing with rekindling her relationship with Desiree, dealing with the inn, and everything else she'd had to handle.

"I'm glad you have a place to sculpt where you feel safe, and

I hope your creativity flows freely there." He lowered his lips to hers in a tender kiss.

"I was serious before, when I mentioned bringing your landmine of boxes up from your cottage and sharing this space. We can move some things around, make room for your sculpting supplies?"

"Whoa, girl. Slow down. Are you asking me to *move in* to your studio with you?" he teased. "That's a pretty big step."

She smiled and said, "Bigger than letting myself go all mushy while you're fucking my brains out?"

He kissed her again. "You had no choice in that matter. My sexual prowess was stronger than your badass exterior. So yeah, it's a bigger deal. Although I'm not sure it's bigger than letting me drive your bike."

"Damn it," she snapped. "You're right. I should have led with that."

He took her hand and headed for the door.

"Why are you rushing?" she asked, hurrying to keep up.

"Are you kidding? I want to seal this deal before you change your mind."

Chapter Nine

AS THEY SET up Andre's art supplies in the studio, the coming together of their belongings reminded Violet of the night he'd set up space for her to share his crafting tent and art supplies in Ghana. It had felt just as good then as it did now.

"I couldn't help but notice that the rest of the house looks like it's been updated. Why did you leave this room unfinished?" he asked as he carried fluted bowls to another table.

"When we first arrived here, Lizza had arranged for renovations to be done by Justin's family's company, Cape Renovators. Of course, Lizza's ideas were off the wall and would have completely ruined the character of the house. Rick is an architect, and with his help, Desiree and I redirected their efforts, but we couldn't bring ourselves to renovate Lizza's studio."

"I thought she didn't stay at Summer House with you and Desiree when you were little."

"She didn't." Violet set her sculpting tools down and said, "But she had a studio in our house in Oak Falls."

"What was it like back then?"

"I was only seven when we left, but from what I remember, it was what most people probably call *normal*. We played, went to school, had family dinners…"

"With Lizza and Ted? She was around more then?"

"I think so. My memories are mostly of what I lost when we left—sweet, perfect Desiree and Ted, the only father I had ever known. What I remember about Lizza is very different from what Desiree remembers, so I'm not sure if my memories are fabricated from *wanting* to believe them or not."

"You were both so young, I'd imagine you've both spun some of your memories in one direction or another. Kids do that as a means of denial or survival. How do yours and Desiree's memories differ?"

She stifled the urge to shrug. As much as she disliked revealing her memories, each hidden piece of herself she shared with Andre brought a lightening all around her.

"Desiree's memories revolve around trying to get Lizza's attention and Lizza being so absorbed in her artwork, she'd get upset when she was interrupted. I lived with Lizza for many years, and she *does* disappear into her artwork. But don't most artists?"

"Somewhat probably. But when we were together, you were at your calmest and most centered while we were working with fabrics, drawing, or sculpting."

"I still am."

"Actually, that calm was second only to the peacefulness that came over you when you were with children."

It was true, but she hadn't realized he'd noticed. "I do enjoy working with kids. The thing is, while I remember Lizza being consumed by her art, I also remember her leaving art supplies out for us to try whatever she was doing. If she was painting, she would set out blank canvases nearby with paintbrushes and paints open, inviting us to join her without verbally doing so."

"You realize that could be the same memory perceived differently."

"I know, and it's *so* frustrating. I swear people should have thought bubbles over their heads so those things don't happen."

"What would yours say?"

"*Fuck off*, usually." She laughed and said, "My whole life all I wanted was to be with Desiree, and then when we were kids and spent a few weeks here with our grandmother, we clashed *all* the time. She was a huge reminder of everything I'd lost *and* missed. I took off on my own a lot, avoiding the obvious. She says she wanted to be freer, like me, and I would have given anything to be less free and *with* her. But even as a kid I couldn't muster the courage to stick around the inn. I know Lizza thought she was doing the right thing for each of us, but she put us both in our own emotional jails. Luckily, Ted helped Desiree learn to love and be loved."

"Then who taught you?" He drew her closer, and she wound her arms around his neck as he said, "You are a loving person, babe."

"Yeah, but I'm not so easy to love. I do mean shit, like disappearing from Desiree's life, from your life, and being snarky, and I curse and—"

"You *protect yourself* in the only ways you know how because you've always had to, and you *protect others* with sharp words and threats, because you're a loving, strong, *generous* woman. It just takes the right stubborn people to earn the keys to unlock the *Daisy* in you." He pressed his lips to hers. "I've met a lot of your friends, and I think you've given away more keys than you take credit for. I'm one of the lucky ones."

She felt her cheeks burn and said, "I'd hardly call you lucky. There are plenty of women who would have jumped at your proposal and not been afraid of disappointing you or losing themselves."

"You could never disappoint me, and the only place I'll let you lose yourself in our relationship is in the bedroom."

She was glad for his levity. "You *are* wicked in the fuckery department."

"Speaking of fuckery..."

Heat rose in his eyes, and he pulled her tight against him. His mouth covered hers, unexpectedly tender. His tongue swept and probed in an intensely slow, erotic rhythm, claiming a little more of her with every stroke. She held her breath, hoping he'd take even more, but his efforts remained soft and sensual. Just when she felt herself melting against him, he kissed her harder, more demanding. She went up on her toes, her body vibrating with desire as he fisted his hands in her hair, angling her mouth beneath his, and took the kiss even deeper. His tongue thrust against hers as their hips ground together, and he pushed one hot hand beneath her shirt, cupping her breast. She moaned into their frantic kisses, as he brushed his thumb over her nipple and eased his efforts.

She whimpered, and he smiled against her lips as he said, "Remember when all we did was kiss?"

He didn't give her time to answer, taking her in another intoxicatingly rough and possessive kiss. His hands were everywhere at once, fisting in her hair, groping her ass, palming her breasts. Heat seared through her veins, filling her chest, and pooling in her core. She shoved her hands beneath his shirt, needing to feel closer to him, and he eased his efforts again, creating a dizzying rhythm. It was exquisite torture, and she didn't want it to end. When he reached one arm out and swept his drawing supplies off the table without ever breaking their connection, she knew it wouldn't have to.

He held her tighter, pressing all his hard heat against her, as he reached beneath her leather miniskirt and tore down her panties. Her skirt came next, followed by her shirt and bra. She kicked off her boots as he stripped himself bare. Good Lord he was *hot*. His thick cock bobbed between them as he hoisted her onto the table. She grabbed his head, holding their mouths together as he drove into her in one hard thrust, sending scintillating shocks racing up her spine. She wrapped her legs around his hips, clawing at his back and shoulders, as he pounded into her. They devoured each other's mouths, and she grabbed his ass, helping him drive in even deeper. The tease of an orgasm hovered just out of reach. Her limbs tingled and her breathing shallowed, anticipation mounting inside her. He reached between them, finding her magical spot with deathly precision, and catapulted her up to the clouds. She tore her mouth away and sank her teeth into his shoulder, and he followed her over the edge, surrendering to his own powerful release.

"Fuck baby," he panted out as they came back down to earth. "Christ, I love you."

She finally lifted her mouth from his shoulder, leaving tiny punctures around his tattoo.

He brushed his scruff along her cheek and said, "Do you remember biting me like that the first time we made love?"

"I didn't until just now," she admitted.

She thought she'd remembered every second of the night they'd finally made love, but now more bits and pieces were trickling in. She'd been so overwhelmed by the intensity of her emotions, the practically out-of-body experience of making love with him—of loving him so much—everything had blurred together. But she'd never *bitten* a man before. How could she not remember that?

"The first time we made love, you went soft in my arms. You were so open and loving, I remember thinking that I would never let anyone hurt you again." He kissed her neck, holding her so close his heart thudded against her chest. "And then you said, *Don't ever stop.*"

"I did?" She did *not* remember saying that, though she remembered hoping he never would.

"Yes. Then it was like you cut yourself free, and you went a little wild. We both did. And you bit me so hard you drew blood."

"Damn," she said, smiling against his shoulder.

"It was the most intense experience I'd ever had. Seeing you let go like that made me let go, too. That's when I proposed."

He lifted her off the table and lowered them both to the mass of canvas tarps. She lay in his arms, sated and happy, as he kissed her so deeply her body started getting all tingly again.

When their lips finally parted, he chuckled and said, "I'm an idiot."

He gave her a chaste kiss and then pushed to his feet, pinning her in place with a scorching stare, causing her heart to stumble. He stared so long, the air between them sizzled and popped. Just when she was about to go to him, he turned and strutted scrumptiously naked toward the bathroom, as if he hadn't just turned her world upside down.

You're a whole lotta sexy. I'm the idiot.

AS THE MOON rose over the water, they lay together on a

blanket in the studio surrounded by flickering candles, incense, and sketches they'd drawn of each other. Cosmos was fast asleep on the tarps. A cool breeze whispered through the open window, chilling Violet's legs. She snuggled against Andre's bare chest and put her leg over his. Her panties and his shirt were not enough to warm her, but his body heat helped. The hair on his legs tickled, but she'd never been more comfortable or happier. They'd spent the whole day in the studio, making love, talking and sketching, leaving long enough only to grab blankets from the linen closet and retrieve snacks from the kitchen. A box of crackers, a tray of fruit and cheese, and half a loaf of Italian bread sat off to the side, along with some water and a half-empty bottle of wine.

Andre kissed her temple. "Are you too cold? Want to go back to the cottage? Or downstairs to get some tea?"

"No way. I want to stay right here forever. I miss this so much. Not just being with you, but *just being.* Remember how we would sit outside our tents at night listening to the sounds of the village?"

"I do, and sitting around the fire with the villagers when I was teaching you to sketch people. Do you still do that adorable nose-wrinkle thing when you're drawing faces?"

"I never did a nose-wrinkle thing." She leaned on his chest and said, "Wipe that smirk off your face."

"Okay, nose wrinkler." He leaned up and kissed the tip of her nose. "You know, there were nights when I'd try to convince myself that meeting you was all a dream. That I imagined everything. But then I'd remember the feel of your body next to mine or the taste of your skin on my lips, and I knew I couldn't have imagined something so beautiful."

She rested her cheek on his shoulder and ran her fingers

over the hair on his chest. There were times she'd wondered if he'd been real, too. But then the pain set in, and she knew he'd been as real as the water in the bay. "I haven't done this, *just being*, without the stress of guests at the inn or trying not to think about how much I miss you, since I came here. I never realized how *empty* I could feel. But I feel so *full* right now, I have no idea how I survived without this. Without *you*. Not that I need a man to make me feel whole."

As she said the words, she knew they weren't true. It was a knee-jerk reaction to define autonomy, but with Andre she'd never needed to. She lifted her face so she could see his and said, "I always thought I was whole, but the truth is, when I left you, I left a piece of myself behind. A big piece. One that I didn't even know I possessed or could give away."

A small smile lifted his lips as he said, "I've carried it with me ever since. When I woke up and you were gone, my first thought was that one of the village kids came to get you to tell them a story, go for a walk, or make one of those little clay or cloth animals you used to make them. I always thought I was whole, too. But after I realized you were really gone, emptiness consumed me. I thought I'd be busy enough when I returned to Boston that I would eventually get over us, but that was even worse. Then I thought maybe Operation SHINE would fill that gap. But being in the field just reminded me of what I'd lost, and I realized being whole doesn't have to do with strength or capabilities. It comes from here." He placed his hand over his heart. "I carried you in my heart for all this time, and I thought I would never be whole again. It's not surprising that we both tried to replace each other and couldn't, because what we shared wasn't just sex and great conversation. It was *this*."

He waved his hand at nothing in particular. "We wanted

the same things in life, to help others, to enjoy whatever the days and nights held. When other people were trying to get *likes* on social media or find the best iPhone, we were walking three kilometers in the pouring rain, bringing supplies to another village, or lying in the silence of our tent just being together."

He kissed her softly and said, "Do you miss traveling?"

"Yes. I miss experiencing other cultures and learning from them." When they met, Violet hadn't been a volunteer with Andre's group. She'd traveled to the village with a family from another remote community. She'd been raised not to follow the herd, but to take the path less traveled, to help those who weren't on the map. Sometimes she'd volunteered with certain groups, but mostly she tried to help on her own so her time with each community wasn't limited in scope or duration. "Many of the villages I've been to didn't have access to enough food, much less modern medicine, relying on healers and natural remedies that had been handed down through generations. Not that I would want to keep anyone from having sound medical help, but I miss *not* having everything at my fingertips. I liked having to be resourceful, to think about what I could forage for a meal or use to patch a leak in a hut."

"Do you think you'll ever return to that lifestyle?"

"Leave Desiree?" Her pulse quickened at the thought.

He brushed his hand down her back and said, "Not for good, just for a time?"

"I don't know," she said honestly. "I finally have a family, friends, a real home." She sat up and snagged a cracker, needing a distraction. "Tell me about Operation SHINE. I know what your company does, but how do you have so much time off? Don't you need to be in a corporate office, stressing over who to hire or arranging deliveries of supplies to the clinics or something?"

"A wise woman once spent three months telling me that I could help thousands of people outside the system instead of *wasting my life* in my plush offices helping only those who had been born in the *right* areas."

She buried her face in his neck and said, "It's embarrassing that I could have been so obnoxiously preachy. Why did you even like me?"

He laughed and rolled them onto their sides so they were face to face. Then he grabbed her butt and said, "You had a cute ass. Nothing else really mattered."

"Whatever..."

"Babe, you were right. Giving up basic necessities might not be the right thing for everyone, but when I went back to Boston, I saw the *privileged* through new eyes. Young kids packed in my waiting room with phones and video games while their parents checked emails and posted on Facebook. Every day I recognized more of the things you called out, things that were such a big part of my daily life, I never really noticed them before. The parents who complained because I was twenty or thirty minutes late for their appointments, without giving a thought to the reasons why I was late—which was always because I was dealing with another family that needed extra time because their kid received a scary diagnosis or they had questions and concerns that needed addressing. Meanwhile, across the world there were families who traveled for a full day to reach a clinic, and sometimes that day meant the difference between life and death. Your *preaching* saved who knows how many people."

He brushed his thumb over her cheek and said, "You told me that I could do more good in the field than in an office, and you were right about that, too. Operation SHINE is run by smart, capable, experienced professionals who take care of the business end, freeing me to do what I should be doing— practicing medicine where it is needed most."

"So, you bought the company, and you leave it up to others to manage it. That doesn't drive you crazy with worry?"

"No, babe. I trust my directors explicitly, and trust is very freeing." He pressed his lips to hers, and then he said, "As for my time off, it will vary between projects. I might have two months, or six months, or somewhere in between, depending on the timing of the next clinic opening. And I'm never just hanging around doing nothing. Take this week, for example. I have calls to make and reports to read, and I'm meeting with a colleague on Thursday. Next week I start working at the Outer Cape Health Clinic part time. I'll be working Monday, Wednesday, and Friday until I leave for my next project. We're opening a clinic in Cambodia. I'm leaving October fifteenth."

Just that morning three and a half weeks felt like a long stretch of time. Now it felt like it could pass in the blink of an eye.

"What about you?" he asked. "Desiree said you closed the gallery and the inn, and that you were going to work on a few things."

"I, um…" *Can't really think beyond the fact that our time together has a deadline.* "I'm working on a sculpture for the family of a little girl who passed away, and I have things to take care of Thursday, which works well since you're busy. I need to track down Rowan, too. And if Joni needs me, then I want to make time for her."

"Track him down?"

"Rowan runs a food truck, and he hates cell phones even

more than I do. He has one, but he doesn't leave it on or check messages very often. I was hoping to catch up with him at Herring Cove on Saturday. There's an appreciation day to celebrate the Provincetown Soup Kitchen volunteers, and I'm pretty sure he'll be there. I'd love it if you'd come with me."

"Hang out with my girl on a beach and meet the guy who introduced you to Common Grounds? I wouldn't miss it for the world."

She lay on her back, staring up at the ceiling. "We *only* have three and a half weeks?"

He moved over her and laced their hands together. His weight had already become familiar and comforting again. He brushed his lips over hers and said, "No. We *have* three and a half weeks together. See how different that sounds without a question mark?"

She caught his lower lip between her teeth, and his eyes flared.

He stretched her arms as far above her head as they would go and said, "Repeat after me. We have three weeks."

"We have three weeks."

"To fall madly in love with each other."

She couldn't stop grinning. "To fall madly in love with each other."

"And then…"

Violet's heart took over, and she said, "We won't run or hide." *Holy crap, that felt good.* She craned up to kiss him, but he drew back with a coy look in his eyes.

"*Daisy?* Is that you?"

She narrowed her eyes, playing right along with her smart-ass, patient man, whom she was falling even deeper and truer in love with than before, and said, "Daisy's busy fretting over a time limit. It's *Violet*, and she can be a real pushy bitch. I suggest you make good use of having full control over my hands before she realizes how goddamn terrified she is of losing you again and says or does something stupid."

"Don't worry, babe. I've got us covered." He pressed a kiss to the edge of her mouth, and as he loved his way down her body he said, "I'm getting you chipped with a GPS tracker."

Chapter Ten

"I SWEAR, ONE of us needs to learn to cook," Serena said as she pushed her spoon around in a bowl of Frosted Mini Wheats. "I have to meet Gav in forty-five minutes at a potential new client's office. I was hoping to *power up* for the pitch."

It was Thursday morning, and the girls had come over for breakfast, but Andre had gone running with the guys and they weren't back yet. Violet watched the path in the dunes, waiting for him to return, thinking about yesterday. They'd slept in, taken a walk on the beach, and spent hours working in the studio with the windows open, music playing, and Cosmos meandering about. Violet had worked at her potter's wheel while Andre sketched an idea for a sculpture he hoped to start this weekend. Then they'd gone to the coffeehouse and stayed until closing. She loved falling asleep in his arms and waking to his kisses, but the best thing about spending time with Andre wasn't *what* they did; it was simply being together. He calmed her in ways she'd never known she needed, and she had a feeling she settled him in ways he hadn't imagined either.

Emery stood up, drawing Violet's attention as she adjusted her yoga pants, and said, "You should get Abby to deliver a few Perpetual Bliss doughnuts every morning." Serena and Drake had befriended Abby Crew, the owner of Kane's Donuts in Boston, and Abby had been so inspired by their love, she'd created the Perpetual Bliss doughnut just for them. The delicious doughnut was filled with Belgian chocolate pudding, frosted with Taza chocolate, and topped with creamy white and dark chocolate crispy pearls, and Serena was addicted to them.

Violet gazed out at the water, wondering if Cosmos was driving the guys crazy. The ragamuffin had taken a liking to Andre, and Andre had told her last night that he was taking the pup with him on his run this morning.

"Great, Em. Now I want doughnuts." Serena lifted a spoonful of cereal and said, "Daph, you're a mom. Can't *you* cook?"

Daphne bit into her toast and shook her head. "But I can throw Cheerios on a tray really well."

"That's a skill that'll hook a husband," Chloe teased.

"I'm not looking to hook a husband. But I wouldn't be opposed to a little romance in my life. We're reading an erotic romance with the book club this month, and *oh my God...*" Daphne mouthed, *Hot!*

"Erotic romance?" Serena asked. "I thought book clubs read literary fiction."

"Not ours." Daphne pushed to her feet and brushed the crumbs from her sweater and jeans. "But then again, I'm not sure we're considered a *regular* online book club since we meet once a month at different locations."

"Whoever's turn it is to select the book chooses the place we meet," Chloe explained. "The only requirement is that there has to be a beach wherever we go. That's why it's called Oceanside Book Club."

"What if you meet at the bay, or a river or cove?" Violet said absently. Cosmos darted up the path, and she sat up straighter, watching as Andre came into view.

"She speaks?" Emery said with a joking smile.

Violet turned an unamused stare in her direction.

Emery rolled her eyes. "Oh please, Vi. You've been staring at the dunes since we got here."

"I've got to take off," Daphne said. "I want to make a few calls before I open the office." She headed out of the gate and said, "Chloe, we might have to talk to the girls and rethink our book club name. I think Vi has a point. I'll see you guys later."

"I'm on it," Chloe called after her. She looked at Violet and said, "Thanks, Vi. It took us a *month* to come up with that name."

Violet was busy watching Andre pull off his shirt. Cosmos darted back toward him, and Violet wanted to run to him too. But she could just hear the gossip girls if she did. She'd never live it down. His broad chest and shoulders glistened in the sun as he dragged his arm across his forehead. He glanced over and her insides went hot.

"Violet!" Serena tapped the table.

Violet shook her head to try to focus. "What?"

"I was suggesting book club names—*beachside, waterside, dockside*—but you're all googly-eyed over Dr. Dreamy. I never thought I'd see you this way." Serena picked up her glass of juice and said, "I do believe our tough-as-nails Violet is *cock whipped.*"

"Then we're due some incredible breakfasts." Emery reached across the table and snagged a piece of toast. "She does have that well-fucked look."

No shit, Sherlock, Violet thought, smiling to herself. There was no hiding her feelings for Andre, or how he made her feel. *Well fucked* barely touched the surface when love was brewing all around them. She'd miss him today. He was catching up on phone calls and reviewing reports this morning and seeing a colleague this afternoon, which was perfect since she'd be gone for most of the day.

The guys came through the gate, and Andre set his dark eyes on her with a look hot enough to smolder metal.

"Dr. Do Me Right looks like he stepped off the pages of *Men's Health* magazine," Chloe said quietly.

Emery leaned in and said, "Why do you think Vi is drooling?"

He's so far above Men's Health *pretty boys. You have no idea what a man like him is really like.* Violet pushed to her feet and lowered her voice as she said, "Hands off, bitches. He's *mine*." She strutted over to Andre, who swept her into his arms, and she kissed him good and hard.

"Damn," Dean said as he walked past. "Someone's got Vi's attention."

Serena shouted, "It's about time."

"Then why are we eating cereal?" Drake asked as he sat beside Serena.

Violet dug her keys from her pocket and said, "Subject change, please."

Andre laughed. "I'll make something hot and delicious tomorrow."

Chloe giggled and whispered something to Emery.

"His body is *not* on the menu," Violet snapped, and then she turned a softer tone to Andre and said, "I've got to take off. Are you sure you're going to be okay with the vultures?"

"He's fine," Dean assured her.

"Seriously?" Serena asked. "You're going off on one of your *mysterious* outings? You guys closed the inn *and* the gallery.

Where could you possibly go?"

"My world is bigger than this inn," Violet said, and Andre squeezed her hand.

Emery made a *tsk* sound. "I can't believe you're taking off when there's a hot guy here for you. I need to give you relationship lessons, and that really says something about you, because before Dean, I sucked at them."

"I have things to take care of today," Andre said. "Besides, I think I can handle being without Violet for a few hours. She doesn't need a leash."

"Says the guy who took relationship advice from *Brindle Montgomery*, the queen of the on-again-off-again relationship." Emery shook her head. "You and Vi really are perfect for each other."

"Whatever." Violet turned an apologetic gaze to Andre and said, "Catch ya later?"

"Absolutely." He gave her a long, passionate kiss, earning a few loud sighs and several *get-a-room*s.

A little while later Violet was greeted by the competing sounds of loud music and the whining grind of Justin's saw as he cut through a block of stone in his studio. She tossed her keys on the table, grabbed a big metal bowl, and headed for the sink. As she filled the bowl with water, she thought about glazing the sculpture of the torso.

She gathered her tools, and as she wet a piece of sandpaper she realized how rote the steps of sculpting had become and took comfort in them. Before she'd settled down at the Cape, nothing in her life had ever had structure, and she'd taken comfort in that, too. Was it possible to gain comfort from such totally different ways of life—one where she had every modern convenience at her fingertips and another where she often had no idea where she might end up next?

She began gently sanding the neck of the sculpture and worked her way over the shoulders and down the back, pausing only to rewet the sandpaper. She sanded around the rough scar on the left side of the lower back, leaving the palm-sized area jagged and marred. She paused, a chill running through her as she recalled the story he'd told her about saving a little boy and her mother from a burning hut.

"Hey, babe. You okay?" Justin asked.

Violet blinked several times, realizing she'd zoned out. "Yeah. Fine." She should be used to the vivid memories by now. She saw it every time she sculpted a torso. "Is Dixie up at the house?"

"Nah. She took off a few days ago."

"Will she be back for the suicide-awareness rally?"

"No. She's got stuff going on. I didn't think you'd be in for a while since your guy's in town." He crossed his arms, and his expression turned serious. "You sure you're okay? You look a little pale."

"Yes, and stop looking at me like you're trying to analyze me."

He flashed a cocky grin. "Just making sure you didn't get your steel heart broken."

"I didn't." If anything, being with Andre was putting the pieces of her shattered heart back together. "I'm sorry about everything that went down the other morning."

"That was kind of weird, huh? Are we still cool? I'm sorry I came over, but—"

"No. We're good. Don't be sorry."

He uncrossed his arms and then crossed them again, and she knew something was bugging him.

"Spit it out, Jus."

"It's nothing, really. I just hadn't realized I had never been to see you during the day. Do Chloe and all those people come over for breakfast all the time?"

"Crazy, right?" she said with a smile. "Yeah, they do. After Des and Rick hooked up, we met everyone else, and then Emery came up from Oak Falls, fell in love with Dean…"

"Yeah, I know." He cocked a grin. "*Long dong?*"

They both laughed.

"*That* was a fun morning," Violet said sarcastically, although she was grateful for the night Justin had stayed with her.

The night before Emery had seen him in the kitchen, Violet had gone to Undercover with their friends. But there was so much lovey-dovey shit going on, she'd left to sit at the bar, and later that night she'd gone to Justin's studio. As always, working with clay had brought memories of Andre. The longer she'd worked, the sadder she'd become. It had been more than a year since she'd seen him, and she didn't know why the guilt and longing had consumed her so deeply that time. But the bone-deep pain had been excruciating and inescapable, exactly like it had been the day Lizza had taken her away from the life she'd adored. Her thoughts were like a monsoon, unstoppable and terrifying. As if a higher power had known she'd needed him, Justin had walked into the studio. He'd taken one look at her and then he'd taken control, helping her clean up and wrap the sculpture she was working on. He'd wanted her to go up to his house so he could watch over her, but she needed to be in her own bed. He'd driven her home and had sat beside her bed as she'd tried to sleep, but by then she was a sobbing mess. And though she knew there was no substitute for Andre, she needed to feel something other than pain. Safe? Loved? Even now she wasn't sure. She'd asked her most trusted friend to lie with her and hold her like Andre used to.

"I was glad I was there with you, despite Emery's freak-out," he said. "I was so tired, I didn't even think about the fact that I was naked when I saw her."

"You didn't think it was strange that she was staring at you and pouring milk all over the counter? I love my friends, but they definitely have hang-ups about seeing people naked."

"They didn't grow up in villages where women went topless and men wore butt floss."

"Neither did you."

"I'm a dude. It's different. Being nude is way more comfortable than wearing a ball hammock."

She looked at the man who had been there for her since the time she was twelve, feeling blessed. Not only for Justin's friendship, or that he could be the kind of friend she needed without wanting more or judging her, but also that Andre had been able to look past what she knew many guys might not be able to.

"I have no idea how I ended up with two great men in my life, but thanks for not being an asshole."

He chuckled. "Hey, you *know* I can be an asshole."

She held up her finger and thumb about an inch apart and mouthed, *a little bit*, with a smile. Then she went back to sanding and said, "Would you mind if I brought Andre here sometime? I'd like to show him where I sculpt."

He arched a brow. "Would you mind if I came over for the breakfast party sometime? Seems like a hell of a lot more fun than choking down a bowl of cereal by myself."

"You mean can you come over and try to get in Chloe's pants?"

He grinned. "Is that a yes?"

"Breakfast, sure. Chloe's pants?" She set down the sandpaper and stared directly into his eyes as she said, "She's a cool chick and I care about her, so you'd better think twice before putting your snake in her grass, got it? Because I *will* make you regret ever coming over if you hurt her. Or Daphne, for that matter. We both know your snake likes to wander."

He strutted back to his table and said, "Got any other single friends I should put on my potential-hook-up list?"

"Ha! You wish." She picked up the sandpaper and turned back to her project. "Maybe you should take that trip to Maryland after all…"

The rest of the morning passed with smart-ass comments and long stretches of silence as they each focused on their artwork. After glazing the torso and cleaning up, Violet grabbed her keys and said, "I'm taking off."

"Meeting your man for a little afternoon delight?" Justin teased.

"Hardly," she said, heading for the door. "I've got shit to do."

"See you bright and early tomorrow morning. What can I bring to breakfast besides the anaconda in my pants?"

Violet glared at him. "Remember what I said or you'll be sorry."

His chuckles followed her out the door.

ANDRE SAT ACROSS from his colleague and long-time family friend, David Posillico, the chief of pediatrics at Hyannis Hospital. In addition to knowing Andre since he was an infant,

David had worked at Massachusetts General in Boston while Andre was doing his transitional-year internship there. He was as much of a mentor to Andre as Andre's own parents had always been. Andre tried to stop in and say hello whenever he had the chance, which equated to only once or twice a year.

"I still can't get over that you walked away from the security of the practice you worked so hard to build." David was in his early sixties, with thick gray hair and wise brown eyes. He pointed his finger at Andre, the same way he used to when Andre was just a boy, with the proud smile of a favorite uncle. "You're an inspiration, you know. I want all the news about SHINE. Where are you headed next? What are your projections for the future?"

"Thanks, but you're just as much of an inspiration. Just in a different direction."

"Cut it out. Give me the goods on SHINE. Gloat a little."

Andre laughed. "I leave in a few weeks for Cambodia, and I'll be there for anywhere from three and five months, depending on how things pan out. As far as the future goes, for now I'm sticking with the original business plan of opening two clinics every eighteen months. But if recruiting continues to go well and fundraising efforts are successful, who knows what the future will hold. Thank you for your generous donation, by the way. When are we going to get you out to one of the clinics?"

A deep laugh rumbled up from David's chest. "I'm too old to be gallivanting across the world. I'll let you young kids handle that."

"Come on, David. You've got more life left in you than most thirty-year-olds. Come out for a few weeks, see what your money is paying for."

"I'll think about it. Your old man has been after me for

years to go on one of those missions he and your mom love so much." Andre's parents had been volunteering with PAW and other organizations for as long as Andre could remember. "He's amped up his nagging ever since he visited you in Brazil last year. But I'm not like you and your parents. I like my creature comforts."

"Field work isn't for everyone, but if you ever change your mind, the door is always open for you." David knew the score with field work. Depending on the location, volunteers might stay in huts or in tents, or if the clinic was near a major city, they could get lucky enough to stay in the homes of host families.

"I spoke to my father this morning," Andre said. "I'm heading into Boston next weekend to have lunch with them. I'll tell him to stop bugging you about it. Or," he said with a teasing lilt to his voice, "I could ask him to give you some field tips."

"Yeah, you do that." David laughed.

"How's Mary doing? Is she still quilting?"

"My wife will be quilting until the day she dies. She's well. Thanks for asking. You know, my youngest daughter, Alicia, is still single." He waggled his brows.

Andre held up his hands and said, "I'm officially off the market."

"Son, you've never been *on* the market. So, you have a special little lady?"

"If she heard you call her that she might end your life," he said with a smile, thinking of the death glare Violet would probably give David.

"Good for her. She's got to be strong to put up with a mongrel like you." He chuckled and said, "I'm glad to hear you're happy. Maybe you can give your parents some grandbabies so they'll stop spoiling mine."

"I'm in no rush for babies, but I'll keep that in mind."

They had a nice visit, and David was pleased that Andre was volunteering at Outer Cape Health Clinic while he was in town. Andre promised to give his father grief about losing to David in their last golf match.

"Let me walk you out," David said as he came around the desk. "I almost forgot to tell you, we've instituted a new addition to our therapy program for our long-term peds patients. We're using art therapy to help reduce anxiety, and we're seeing remarkable results." He pointed to a child's drawing framed on his bookshelf. "A little boy gave me this when he left the hospital. That's me." He pointed to a stick figure with an oversized head. "Gotta love kids."

"That's wonderful." Andre's gaze drifted to the shelf below, where a little clay giraffe was peering out from between a book and a larger clay elephant. The giraffe was painted yellow with purple spots, and the elephant was made of green Play-Doh. He thought of Violet making animals for the children when they'd been together. He was tempted to ask if they were hers, but he imagined every art therapist had Play-Doh and clay in their bag of tricks. "Are those from the program, too?"

"Yes," he said as a knock sounded at his door.

He opened the door and his assistant, Shelley, said, "I'm sorry to bother you. I just wanted to remind you that you have a meeting with oncology in fifteen minutes."

"I'll be there right after I walk Andre out. Thank you, Shelley."

They followed her out of the office, and Andre said, "I can walk myself out."

David put a hand on his shoulder and said, "I only see you

once or twice a year. I can make time to walk you to the door."

They took the elevator down to the lobby, and Andre was surprised to see Violet coming down the hall. She looked up just as David said, "There's one of our art-therapy volunteers now." A flash of surprise crossed Violet's face as they stepped into her path.

"Hello, Violet," David said.

"Dr. Posillico, hi." She glanced at Andre with a curious expression.

"I was just telling my friend Andre about you and the art therapy you're doing with our patients. Violet helps the children decorate their gowns, and she worked with the little girl who made the animals you saw in my office. The children adore her. Andre is an old family friend. He's a pediatrician and he studied art under some very talented artists."

Andre held out his hand and said, "Andre Shaw, nice to meet you."

"Dr. Shaw, it's a pleasure," she said, playing right along with his ruse.

"I was just on my way out," Andre said. "Maybe we can grab some coffee and you can show me where all that ink peeking out of your sleeve leads."

David's face blanched. "Andre...Um..." he stammered. "My goodness, you can't...I'm *sorry*, Violet—"

Andre chuckled and patted David's back. "David, Violet is my girlfriend. I'm sorry. I had to get you back for the prank you played on me with Mr. Patterson when I was an intern."

David exhaled loudly. "I think you might have just taken ten years off my life, you little bugger."

"I'm truly sorry." Andre extended his hand.

David bypassed his hand and pulled him into an embrace,

smacking him hard on the back. "You're a jackass, but I love you." He turned a playful expression to Violet and said, "I should tell you what a great guy Andre is, but if dating him means we're going to lose you as a volunteer to chase him overseas, then for the first time in my adult life I'll lie like a rug."

They said their goodbyes, and as they walked out the doors Violet said, "Mr. Patterson? What was the prank?"

"He was a patient, this old guy who liked to drop his drawers. David finagled it so I did his intake physical, and when I walked into the room, the guy was wearing the gown open in the front, and he was buck naked beneath." Andre chuckled. "More importantly, why didn't you tell me you volunteered here?"

"I didn't?"

"No. You said you still worked with kids, and you were working on a sculpture, and working with Joni, but you never mentioned the hospital."

"Oh, well, that's all true. What were you doing there?"

He took her hand as they crossed the parking lot toward her bike. "Visiting with David. He's a family friend. I've known him forever. By the way, you're having lunch with me and my parents next weekend. Don't you know how proud I am to have you as my girlfriend? Had I known you were volunteering here, I would have invited you to come along to meet him."

"Wait...*what*? I'm meeting your *parents*?"

"Yeah, next weekend for lunch. We'll take the ferry into Boston and—"

"Maybe you should *ask* me to meet them?"

"Why? So you can make up an excuse not to? It's easier this way, babe. Trust me. But can I ask you something else?"

"Apparently it's easier not to ask me anything." She smiled and said, "Go for it."

"This morning when the girls said something about your *mysterious* outings, why didn't you just say you were coming here to volunteer?" He had a feeling she was keeping this a secret like she kept the coffeehouse, her other group of friends, and her sculpting secret.

"It's none of their business."

"Do they *know* you volunteer at the hospital?"

She stopped by her bike and crossed her arms. "Why so many questions? Does it bother you that I volunteer, or are you so possessive that you need to know where I am twenty-four-seven?"

"That's hardly fair. You know I don't need that. I'm thrilled you're still working with kids, but I'm curious whether your friends know. Does Desiree? Justin?"

Her jaw tightened. After a long stretch of tense silence, she said, "I don't volunteer so I can go out and brag about it. I do it because I enjoy it, and I like helping children. What's the big deal?"

"I'm just trying to understand why you have to appear so mysterious to everyone. You're doing something wonderful, and it sounded like you're doing good things with Joni, too. But you have friends who love you and who don't know about either of those things."

She looked away.

"Babe, sharing what you do with the people who love you most, sharing the good *and* the bad parts of your life, is what relationships are all about. It isn't bragging; it's letting them *in*." He stepped closer, unfolded her arms, and held her hands. "You deserve to *shine*, babe. To be proud of what you do and let others be proud of you, too."

"I *am* proud of it, but I don't need *them* to be."

His heart hurt for her, because he had a feeling he knew why she was doing it. What he was going to say next might upset her, but he didn't know how else to get his point across. "Babe, we all do what we're taught, what we *know*. I think you might have learned from Lizza to hide the best parts of yourself. This might sound harsh, but in Lizza's case, I think she'd rather let you and Desiree believe she's *selfish* when maybe she's not. I don't know, babe. Maybe you like your sister and friends thinking you're up to rebellious things? It just seems like you might be patterning yourself after Lizza, which isn't necessarily bad."

She yanked her hands free and said, "Fuck that. I am *not* like her."

"Vi, please hear me out. I could be way off base, but just listen to why I'm asking. Lizza told you she was leaving early so Desiree could go on her honeymoon. But she told Desiree it was so you and I could finally find the answers we've been searching for."

Violet blinked several times, shaking her head. "What...?"

"I know it sounds bizarre, but it's true. And think about it. You and Desiree hadn't had a real relationship until she tricked you both into coming here—and gave you reasons to stay."

"Lizza hurts people," she said angrily. "I don't *ever* try to hurt people unless they deserve it."

"I know you don't. I don't think Lizza *tries* to hurt you or Desiree, either. It seems like she's trying to make amends the only way she knows how. Or maybe the only way she's able to handle doing it, by taking the goodness out of the equation. She takes the focus off what she's offering, or trying to facilitate, and in doing so, she hurts yours and Desiree's feelings. But the end result is that she opened doors for you two to be happy even *without* her."

"What are you saying? We should be *thankful* to her after she dragged me halfway around the world, away from the only family I'd ever known?"

"No, babe. I'm showing you the way she does things and saying that *maybe* by keeping your sister, and your friends, in the dark about these other parts of your life, *good* parts, *happy* parts, you might be unintentionally hurting them. They *know* you have other things you do, but it's all a big secret, which might make them feel like they're not worthy of being included."

Her lips parted as if she might say something, and then she closed her mouth and sadness rose in her eyes.

"Babe, I'm not trying to hurt you. I worry that you're hurting yourself by going to great lengths to keep so many sides of yourself, of your *life*, from intersecting. You don't allow yourself to take credit for the good things you do, and that doesn't let *anyone* fully know or appreciate you."

"I don't *need* to be appreciated."

"But you *deserve* to be," he said strongly. "It feels good to be happy for someone you love. Desiree adores you, and she doesn't even know the generous things you do. When we first met, you told me you'd worked with children for as long as you could remember. Desiree was a preschool teacher, and Rick told me she teaches art to kids during the school year. Does she have any idea that you two have that in common?"

Her eyes filled with tears and she looked away again. He reached for her and she stepped back and said, "I know what opening yourself up like that does. I did it when I was a kid, and look how far that got me."

He gathered her in his arms, despite her initial struggle, wanting to take away the hurt and fear in her voice. "They're *not* going to abandon you. Haven't they proven that to you already? You've only shown them about a third of who you really are, and it was enough for them to love you unconditionally."

Tears slipped from her eyes. He kissed them away and said, "Babe, imagine if they got to know all of you."

Chapter Eleven

VIOLET'S HAND MOVED over empty sheets Saturday morning. She opened her eyes and found a daisy on Andre's pillow. She picked it up and twirled it between her finger and thumb, thinking about yesterday. They'd walked down to Wellfleet Pier for lunch and watched the boats in the harbor. Later they'd gone for a drive and stopped at Drake's music shop. Andre wanted to see where her other friends worked, and as they drove from place to place, she realized she'd never even been to Serena and Gavin's new office, or the assisted living facility where Chloe worked. They drove down to Ben and Jerry's for ice cream and then headed to the Earth House, one of her favorite stores, where they scoured music paraphernalia and hemp clothing. It was a beautiful fall day, and after tooling around several of the small towns, they'd ended up at the coffeehouse. It had been the most carefree, exhilarating day she'd *ever* had, full of kissing, holding hands, and doing all the sappy shit she'd thought she'd never want—or *have*—again, and she wanted *more* of it.

Cosmos hopped up on the bed and crawled on his belly to her. She reached out to pet him and brushed over a mop of sandy, wet hair. *Ugh.* Andre had gone running with the guys again, and she guessed Cosmos had, too. Cosmos licked her arm.

"Guess I'll be washing the sheets and *you*, huh?"

He licked her again. He'd been awfully needy lately, following them around and sleeping in their room. "You miss Desiree, don't you?"

The pup tilted his head and whimpered.

"Yeah, I do, too," she said, surprising herself. "She'll be back after her honeymoon, and then you can spread sand on *her* bed."

She hadn't been able to stop thinking about everything Andre had said Thursday afternoon at the hospital. The thought that she could have been inadvertently hurting Desiree was killing her. She didn't want to bother Desiree on her honeymoon, but she was anxious to hear from her. Last night, as if Violet had willed it to happen, Desiree had texted to say Rick had surprised her with the trip to Portugal. She'd sent pictures of the inn where they were staying and of a friend she'd made there, Paige Bentley, whose family owned the inn. Desiree had invited Paige to visit Summer House and had learned that she knew Daphne and Chloe from their online book club. Desiree's openness with strangers had underscored the differences between her and Violet and had driven home Andre's point.

Violet had never considered herself to be someone who *hid* from anything. She approached situations head-on and never hesitated to say what was on her mind. But she was starting to see herself through Andre's eyes, and she wondered if he was right and she *was* going to great lengths to hide certain parts of herself. Maybe she wasn't just trying to keep her groups of friends separate because of the emotions they triggered, even if it had started out that way.

Cosmos leaped from the bed and scampered toward the sounds coming from the kitchen. Violet was glad she'd told their friends to fend for themselves this morning so she and Andre could have a quiet morning alone before heading up to Herring Cove for the volunteer appreciation day to see Rowan and Joni.

Violet pulled on one of Andre's soft shirts, brushed her teeth, and carried the daisy into the kitchen to put it in water.

"Hey, beautiful." Andre reached for her, looking deliciously sexy in his boxer briefs.

"Mm." She nuzzled against his neck. "You smell good."

He pressed his lips to hers, caressing her bare butt as he said, "You were fast asleep when I got back, so I used the outdoor shower on the patio."

"And I missed it? I just might have to get you dirty again."

"I like the sound of that." He pressed several shivery kisses along her neck, causing goose bumps to rise all over her. "I was about to bring you breakfast in bed."

She followed his gaze to a tray on the counter filled with a plate of French toast, a bowl of fruit, and a cup of coffee. When she set the daisy on the tray, it looked like a scene from a romantic postcard. She wasn't a postcard-romance girl, but she was starting to wonder if she didn't know herself as well as she thought she did. "Thank you. That looks amazing. Did you eat?"

"No." He brushed his scruff over her cheek, and then he sealed his mouth over her neck, sucking hard, his arousal pressing insistently against her belly. His hot breath washed over her skin as he said, "How could I *eat* without you?"

He lowered his mouth to hers, kissing her so deeply that when his fingers slipped between her legs she was already wet.

Their kisses went on and on, and when his mouth blazed a path down her neck, she couldn't hold on to a single thought. He pulled up her shirt and his mouth covered her breast at the same time as he dipped his fingers inside her, drawing a loud moan from her lungs.

"Forget breakfast in bed." She stripped off her shirt.

He made a low, hungry sound, and then his mouth covered hers and he backed her up against the counter, groping her breasts with one hand as his fingers worked their magic between her legs. He kissed her savagely, and she thrust her hand down his briefs, taking hold of his cock. He moaned into their kiss, and that utterly male, fucking *hot* sound turned her on even more. She tore her mouth from his, and their eyes connected for one scorching second before she dropped to her knees and lowered her mouth over every blessed inch of his cock. He groaned and fisted his hand in her hair.

"Fuck, baby," he said between clenched teeth as she sucked and stroked, devouring him the way she'd wished for the courage to do when they were in Ghana.

He was so good to her, so patient, and unwilling to let her fuck them up, that he'd unshackled something deep inside her, allowing her to release her inner vixen and accept the softer, submissive side that existed only when she was with *him*. She stroked him with her hand, licking and sucking until his cock swelled and his body shook with restraint. She grabbed his ass, forcing him deeper, making him thrust faster. He tightened his fingers in her hair, tugging hard, sending a scintillating sting slicing through her.

"I'm going to come," he warned.

She slipped his cock from her mouth and licked slowly over and around the broad head, loving the way his breathing became harder and his stare became predatory.

"Then I guess you'll have to find another way to make me come afterward." She slicked her tongue over his balls, earning another enticing moan, and said, "*Twice.*"

She took him to the back of her throat, working him fast and tight. She held on for dear life as he took over, thrusting deep and pumping hard, his leg and arm muscles straining. It felt so damn good to be *free* with him, she succumbed to his forceful domination. And dominate he did, with exquisite perfection, fucking her mouth like he owned it. His body shook as he pounded into her, and then his hips jerked and he found his release.

"*Daisy,*" burst from his lungs full of love, lust, and pure male *satisfaction.*

When the last shock rolled through his body, she drew back and he stroked her face, running his fingers lovingly through her hair as she rose to her feet and slanted her mouth over his. Her body trembled with desire as he lifted her onto the counter.

He broke their connection, his dark eyes boring into her as he said, "I love you so damn much, but there's no way I'm going to make you come twice."

"The fuck you're not," she challenged.

He lowered his mouth to her breast and sucked so hard she felt it between her legs, and a greedy moan escaped. She curled her fingers around the edge of the counter. "Andre, please—"

When he released her breast, all the air rushed from her lungs. She tried to catch her breath as he rained kisses down her belly and over her thighs, but Andre's love made the world feel bottomless. Cool air swept over the wet trails from his open-mouthed kisses, causing her skin to prickle like live wires. When he grabbed her legs and spread them wide, she closed her eyes in anticipation of his talented mouth landing where she so desperately needed it. But his mouth pressed against hers in another soul-reaching kiss, sending her reeling once again.

When he tore his mouth away, leaving her lips burning for more, he growled, "Twice could never be enough."

She barely had time to process his words when his tongue slicked down the center of her sex, and then his mouth covered it completely. Blood pounded through her as her need grew to explosive proportions. His mouth was gifted, his tongue, a weapon of orgasmic pleasures. Her emotions whirled and skidded as he sent her gasping in sweet ecstasy all the way up to the clouds and held her there, over and over again.

LATER THAT MORNING, as they climbed off Andre's bike at Herring Cove, the sounds of children playing and adults mingling carried in the salty sea air.

"That's Rowan's pickup truck, with the breast cancer magnets all over it." Violet pointed to a truck parked a few spots away. "He's got them all over the food truck, too."

Andre had thought he'd known pain when Violet had left him in Ghana. But after falling even deeper in love with her, the idea of being separated not by distance, but by death, brought a whole new meaning to the word. He wasn't sure he could survive that.

He locked up the helmets and reached for her hand, feeling so full of love he was sure no one in the world had ever loved a person as much as he did right at that moment. But when Violet's eyes caught his, he knew he was wrong.

"Have you volunteered at the soup kitchen?" he asked.

"A few times."

"Would you have come to this appreciation day if you didn't need to catch up with Rowan?"

She was quiet for a moment before shaking her head.

"Because you don't want to be appreciated by others?"

"*Yes* is on the tip of my tongue," she said sharply. "But you make me want to figure out why my first instinct is to say yes. I think it's because when I was a kid there was no better feeling than having Ted tell me how much he appreciated things I did, like watching out for Desiree or helping set the table. I loved the positive reinforcement, and I wanted to earn his praise. But when Lizza took me away, it felt like all that stuff he said wasn't real. Because how can you love and appreciate someone but let them go?" She inhaled a ragged breath and blew it out slowly. "But I loved and appreciated *you*, and then *I* left. My feelings for you weren't fake. I'm beginning to understand that nothing is black-and-white and what I've always believed may not necessarily be true."

"Ted loves you, babe. Nobody could fake the look in his eyes or the pride in his voice when he talked about you."

"I hope that's true, but I'm still fucked up, because I wouldn't have come here for myself. But don't worry. I'm trying to figure out why."

He kissed her softly and said, "You can't imagine how happy that makes me. I want you to feel good about letting your bright light shine for all to see."

"There's something else I want you to know. I'm going to talk to Desiree when she gets back from her honeymoon and tell her everything—about volunteering, working with Joni, sculpting…"

Surprise rose in his eyes. "You are?"

"Yup. That gives me a few weeks to mentally prepare for our come-to-Jesus moment. You should be a therapist with all the shit you've got me spewing." She pulled him across the parking lot. "Now, let's go. I feel naked."

He chuckled.

"Keep laughing. I've got a store full of sex toys and I'm not afraid to use them."

"As long as they're not replacing me, I'm cool with that," he said heatedly.

"I meant use them on *you*."

He stopped walking.

She laughed and tugged him toward a sandy path that cut through the dunes to the beach. "You know that uncomfortable feeling you've got right now?" she said when they stopped to take off their boots at the edge of the path. "It's about half as uncomfortable as I feel every time you get me to think about stuff I don't want to think about."

"Shit, baby. I'm sorry."

"Nothing worth anything in this life comes easily, right?" As they crossed the dunes she said, "Isn't that what everyone says?"

A wicked grin lifted his lips. "I can make you come pretty easily, and that's *so* fucking worth it."

"Violet!"

They spun around and saw a little girl running toward them wearing a blue button-down shirt with a fluffy green tutu. Her skinny little arms were spread wide, her fine brown hair floating above her shoulders. A guy stood at the end of the path in shorts and a colorful striped Baja hoodie.

"Hold that thought," Violet said. "That's Joni and Rowan." She scooped up the excited little girl and twirled her around. "Hey, peanut butter."

Little-girl giggles filled the air. "Hey, jelly! Do you like my tutu?"

"That's a spectacular tutu," Violet exclaimed. "Did you get it from a gorilla at the bank?"

Joni buried her giggling face in Violet's neck and said, "No." Then her head popped up and she said, "I got it from the mermaid at the zoo!"

They all laughed. Joni was adorable, with crooked baby teeth, happy brown eyes, and so much love for Violet it radiated off her. He wished Violet would let everyone see this warmer, animated side of herself.

Violet said, "Joni, this is my very special friend, Andre."

"Hi!" Joni said. "Where did *you* get your shirt from?"

Andre leaned in close and lowered his voice as if he were sharing a secret as he said, "I got it from the giraffe in the park!"

Joni wiggled from Violet's arms, giggling. She reached for each of their hands and pulled them toward Rowan. "Come on! There's hamburgers and hot dogs and lizards and snakes…"

As Joni rattled off several types of animals, Violet said, "Joni's got the greatest imagination on the planet."

Joni let go of their hands and ran to Rowan. He was a big man, at least six four, with shaggy hair, a short beard, and kind eyes. He lifted Joni up and kissed her cheek. "Love you, Jojo."

He set her in the sand as she said, "Love you, too, Daddy."

"How's it going, sugar?" Rowan threw an arm over Violet's shoulder, hugging her against his side.

Sugar?

Rowan extended a hand and said, "Hi. I'm Rowan. It's *Andre*, right?"

"No, Daddy," Joni said. "His name is *pretzel!*"

Andre shook his hand and said, "She's right. My name *is*

pretzel, but you can call me Andre if you'd like."

Joni grabbed Violet's hand and said, "Can me and peanut butter go down by the water?"

"You know the rules." Rowan winked at his little girl.

Joni turned wide, hopeful eyes up at Violet and said, "Would you like to play by the water with me?"

Violet glanced at Andre. "Think you'll be okay for a few minutes?"

"Of course," he said.

"Yay!" Joni dragged Violet toward the water, where a few other children were putting their toes in the water and then running up the beach.

"She's a cutie," he said to Rowan.

"Violet or Joni?" Rowan smiled and said, "I'm kidding. She's a great kid, and Vi's pretty awesome, too. Let's go grab a drink."

They walked down the beach to where a group of people sat on chairs and blankets in a semicircle, talking and eating. There was a mix of twentysomethings and seniors. Parked by the dunes were three trucks with enormous tires, one with coolers in the back. Near the trucks there were two grills and a table covered with platters of burgers, hot dogs, salads, pasta dishes, cookies, and a host of other delicious-looking food.

Andre and Rowan grabbed sodas, and Rowan introduced him to some of the other volunteers. After chatting with the others for a while, they sat in the sand talking. Rowan was easygoing, smart, and he kept a keen eye on his daughter, who was busy building a sandcastle with Violet.

"So, who goes first?" Rowan asked.

"For...?"

"You know, the regular bullshit that we're avoiding but

probably should get out of the way." He sipped his soda.

"Ah, well, Violet's already filled me in on how you two met. She said you own a food truck and that you're raising Joni alone. I'm sorry about your wife."

"Carlotta was my girlfriend, not my wife, but thank you. Not a day goes by that I don't miss her. But you've got one up on me. Vi didn't tell me shit about you, other than your name."

"That doesn't really surprise me."

"Nah, it shouldn't if you know Vi as well as I think you do." Rowan set his soda can in the sand and looked over at Violet and Joni.

Joni was sitting in Violet's lap, playing with the ends of Violet's hair. Violet was rocking side to side, and she looked like she was singing. Andre had seen Violet with dozens of children in Ghana, and she'd been just as at ease with each and every one of them.

"To be honest," Rowan said, "Violet told me everything I needed to know by taking you to the coffeehouse. I saw Steph and Cory the other day, and they told me you'd been there a few times with her. But even if I hadn't known that, the way she looked at you before going off with Joni? That told me she totally digs and trusts you, because Vi doesn't look for approval from anyone."

"It's mutual." He told Rowan how he and Violet had met and about their time together overseas. And then he said the hardest thing of all. "She took off more than two years ago, and I had no idea where she was or how to find her."

Rowan stretched his long legs out and said, "She's just like my Carlo. Feisty, stubborn. Every time I got too close, Carlo pulled away. That's why we never got married. We'd been together for two years when she got pregnant with Jojo. The second I mentioned marriage"—he shook his head—"she was like a pup that had seen the wrong end of a newspaper too many times. Her parents had an awful marriage, and she wanted no part of that union. I'd bet my life we would have had a great marriage, but what's a piece of paper? Right?"

"I made that mistake, too. I proposed to Vi. It was one of the reasons she took off."

Rowan smiled and said, "Everyone says guys are afraid of commitment, and look at us. Two dudes who fell in love with probably the only two women around who aren't pining for a ring on their finger. But Carlo and Vi? They have something else in common—two of the biggest hearts I've ever known. Since the day Vi and I met, she's been like an aunt to Jojo. She's come over when Jojo was having fits and I had no idea what to do, and she's picked her up from school when I had the flu. She's so easy with her, like she totally gets her in ways that sometimes confound me."

They sat in silence, each lost in their own thoughts for a few minutes, and then Rowan said, "From the second Jojo was born, she was mine and Carlo's world. Nothing in this world matters more than that trusting little girl, but I think I'm fucking up pretty badly."

"She seems happy," Andre said.

"Most of the time. But she gets real panicky, and when that anxiety sets in, it's like she gets lost in it. I've talked to her doctors and therapists. Vi works with her, and that seems to help, but how do you help a little girl past anxiety and frustration that no one can explain?"

"I'm a pediatrician, and when I was practicing in the States I encountered that often with children, much more so than overseas. Anxiety can come from many directions and oftentimes from several at once. It sounds like you've had her evaluated by licensed professionals?"

Rowan nodded. "They said it might have to do with losing her mom and that lots of kids get anxious when they go to school. The docs don't think it's unusual, and they say she'll probably outgrow it."

"When did you first notice her anxieties?"

"About the third week of preschool, when she was four. She started pitching fits, not wanting to go. I talked to the teachers, and they said it was normal, but it didn't feel normal. Still, I'm a first-time father, so I tried taking their advice, letting her cry when I left. But that was too hard on both of us. She's my baby, and she relies on me to take care of her. After a few weeks of constant struggles, I took her out of that school. But kindergarten was the same way, except her anxiety started the first week. She's six now, and she *already* hates school. Can you imagine how rebellious she'll be as a teenager?"

"The two might not go hand in hand. How'd she do with hitting milestones? Did she have any trouble remembering nursery rhymes? Her alphabet?"

"Nursery rhymes?" He scoffed. "She hates them. Even at three and four she mixed them up. That's why she has such a great imagination. She's been making shit up for years."

Down the beach, Joni and Violet were running in and out of ankle-deep water. Andre hated to second-guess other physicians, but his gut told him Joni's doctors were seeing a different picture than he was. "I may be way off base, but has she been evaluated for dyslexia? Preschool is young to diagnose issues related to dyslexia, but depending on the teaching methods and expectations, it can cause anxiety. It should at least be considered."

"I assume so. The doctors don't really tell me what they've ruled out. They ask a lot of questions about when Carlo died and our lifestyle. Sometimes it feels like they're too focused on those things or they just think I'm an overly worried father. Of course she'll always miss having her mother around, and maybe I am worrying too much. Or maybe I messed her up by taking her out of preschool or by letting her pitch a fit when she's frustrated. But sometimes there's no calming her down. Kids should come with guidelines, because the only thing I can think to do is distract her, hold her, make sure she knows she's loved even if she hates school."

"Love goes a long way," he said, thinking of how much Violet would have given for a mother who had seen the trials and tribulations she'd gone through and put her daughter's happiness above all else. "My buddy is the chief of pediatrics at Hyannis Hospital. He knows the best doctors and specialists in the area. Why don't I make a few calls and hook you up with him? I obviously haven't evaluated Joni, but it doesn't sound like you're overreacting. David's a father and an excellent physician. He won't let you slip through the cracks."

The look of relief on Rowan's face was palpable. "That'd be great. Thank you." Rowan clapped a hand on his shoulder and said, "I'm not giving up on my beautiful girl."

Andre watched Joni and Violet heading toward them hand in hand and thought, *I'm not giving up on mine, either.*

Chapter Twelve

"HEY, HOT MAMA." Emery breezed into the office of the inn Monday afternoon wearing a bikini top and sweatpants and flopped into a chair across the desk from Violet. She crossed her legs, smacking her chewing gum, and tapped her finger on the arm of the chair. "I'm still buzzing from that orgasmic breakfast you and your man whipped up."

After joining Emery for couples yoga, Andre claimed he wanted to teach Violet how to make eggs Benedict and cranberry muffins. He'd taken full advantage of every second her hands were busy and had made her so hot and bothered by the time their friends arrived, she'd dragged him back to the cottage for a quickie before he started his part-time work at the clinic.

Violet looked up from the bills she was paying and said, "And you thought it was a good idea that I witness your post-orgasmic bliss?" She'd spent the morning responding to inquiries, handling inventory, and working through reservation schedules. When she'd first come to the inn, she had been completely opposed to anything even resembling a schedule. Now she had schedules for the inn, the gallery, the hospital…

Emery blew a bubble, then sucked it back into her mouth

and said, "It's cold in here."

"It's September and you're wearing a bikini top."

"Last-ditch effort to work on my tan, but it was too chilly." She smiled and said, "Now that the others aren't around, you can give me the real scoop on you and Dr. McHottie."

"Not happening." Violet went back to paying the bills.

"Oh, come on!" She smacked her hand on the arm of the chair. "This morning you two looked *hot* doing couples yoga. You were so in sync it was like you'd been doing yoga together for *years*. That doesn't come from a week of good sex."

We are hot. Violet smiled inwardly. Emery was right. It didn't come from a week of good sex. It came from three months of using couples yoga as a means to try to calm their passion until Violet had been ready to finally make love with Andre.

"*Vi-o-let!*" Emery hopped to her feet and leaned all the way across the desk, placing her elbows on the schedule Violet had prepared. She propped her chin in her hands and said, "Talk to me. That's what friends do."

Violet stared at her, thinking about what Andre had said about shutting out her friends from certain parts of her life. Okay, maybe she could give Emery something…But what? Definitely not anything about their sex life. The gossip girls would have a field day if they knew she sometimes totally disappeared into him, turning into a pile of mushy, romantic emotions. Or if they realized she and Andre had found a darker side of themselves and he'd taken her from behind in the shower yesterday morning.

"Why are you *blushing?*"

Fuck. Violet blurted out, "I'm meeting his parents."

"Oh my God! His *parents?*" Emery began pacing. "This is

serious. I was a nervous wreck meeting Dean's parents. We *have* to go shopping. What are they like? Where are you meeting them? Have you ever met a guy's parents? It's the worst experience you could ever imagine."

Violet dropped her pen and pushed to her feet. "Can you please try to control your giddy word vomit?"

Emery put her hands on her hips and said, "Nope. When are you going?"

"Saturday. Lunch. Boston." Great, now she was getting nervous again.

"Restaurant or their house?"

"No idea. Shit. Does that matter? Either way I'll feel like I'm under a microscope."

Emery crossed her arms and tapped her chin with her finger, squinting at Violet. "It's lunch, not dinner. So you can be casual, but it's a *first* meeting, so not too casual. Maybe slacks?"

"Not a chance."

"Skirt?" Emery asked hopefully.

"Unless it's leather and mini, *no.*"

Emery let out a disapproving sigh. "I think we can do something with skinny jeans and the black fringe boots you bought for Des's wedding."

"I have black skinny jeans."

"The ones with tears?" Emery sat on the edge of the desk.

She didn't own jeans without tears. "Yes."

"You can't meet his parents wearing torn jeans. We need to shop, or I can lend you a pair, but you should have some clothes that aren't black and…Oh my gosh! You're wearing a *maroon* shirt. Holy crap. How did I not notice that at breakfast?"

"Between Dean's kisses and your egg-gasms, is it any wonder you missed it?" Violet looked down at her shirt and said, "I dress for my moods. Can we please move on? I have no idea what his parents are like, but they're doctors."

"Oh, Vi." Compassion rose in Emery's eyes. "I know your tattoos are a big part of who you are, but what if his parents are super uptight and conservative? You don't want to be judged unfairly."

"I've been thinking the same thing, even though it goes against everything I have ever believed in," she confessed.

"Well, you don't *have* to cover them."

Violet paced, mulling it over.

"You could ask Andre what he thinks," Emery suggested.

"No. Then he'll be in a sucky position. Who wants to tell their girlfriend she should cover her ink? Fuck it." She threw her arms up and said, "I'll cover up. I'm going to be nervous enough. I don't need my tats becoming a *thing*."

"Okay. So…*shopping?*"

"Why do I feel like I'm going to regret this?"

Emery squealed and threw her arms around Violet. "Because the best girlfriend-time memories always carry a little regret! Although it's usually from too much tequila and a guy whose name you can't remember in the morning."

Violet pried her off. "Yeah, well, I wouldn't know about that. I don't do *girlfriend time*."

"You do now!" Emery dragged her out of the office. "I need to grab a shirt, and then it's girlfriend time!"

SEVERAL HOURS LATER, Violet and Emery sat in a café with shopping bags at their feet and a plate of nachos between them.

"Admit it," Emery said as she snagged a chip. "You had fun shopping with me."

"It wasn't the worst thing I've ever endured."

"Ha! You liked it!" She picked up another chip and waved it at her. "And I didn't make you buy a bunch of…What did you call it?"

Violet stifled a laugh. "Frilly shit."

She'd been stifling laughs all afternoon. She didn't usually tag along on the girls' shopping trips, although she'd shopped with Desiree before, and of course she'd gone wedding-dress shopping with Desiree and the girls. But Desiree and the others were always giggling, and Violet might be a lot of things, but she was *not* a giggler.

"Right. Although I think you'd look hot in a naughty-nurse outfit with a frilly little skirt." She waggled her brows.

"Where the hell was *that* suggestion when we were shopping?" *Andre would love that.* They had a naughty-nurse outfit in their adult toy shop, along with several other sexy options. *Hm…*

"Hey, do you blame me for shutting up? I was afraid for my life after I showed you the black blouse with the ruffled collar. No way was I going to suggest anything else with frills or ruffles." Emery sat back and tossed another chip in her mouth. "I wanted to talk to you about throwing a welcome-home party for Des and Rick. I was thinking of using the community center at the resort…"

As Emery went on about the party, Violet's thoughts turned to Andre. He was a brave man. Not many people would push her, and he'd only ever hesitated to push her with regard to one thing—making love for the very first time. She'd sensed then what she now knew to be true. They'd been so deeply connected from the start, he'd known *exactly* what she'd needed, and he'd put off his own desires to give it to her.

At least until that proposal had fallen from his lips.

His voice whispered through her mind. *I was crazy in love, and I didn't think through any of that. All I knew was that I wanted a life with you.* She smiled to herself. He'd loved her too much to hold back. She'd often wondered if she would have taken off had she not received Lizza's message, or if she'd stayed, would they have talked about it? Would he have understood that at that point in her life she couldn't imagine living the structured, stifled existence of a big-city wife? She didn't have the answers, but she was thankful he was so forgiving *and* so wise. She wanted to show him how important he was to her, and because of him, she wanted to figure out a way to show her friends how important they were to her, too.

"*Hello.*" Emery touched her arm. "I said, what do you think?"

Emery was looking at her expectantly, but she'd lost track of what Emery was saying.

"Vi! Geez, what is wrong with you? Are you in for the welcome-home party for Des and Rick the night they come back?"

"Um, sure, but they're going to be exhausted from the time difference."

"Shoot. I didn't think about that. But if we put it off, doesn't Harper come back the next week, and isn't that when Andre leaves?"

"Yeah. Thanks for the reminder," Violet said sarcastically.

"Let's do a joint party! A welcome home and send-off all in one."

"Sure," she said, puzzling out her own idea about how to show everyone they were important to her.

"Great! I'll have the girls help me plan. Do you want to help?"

"No. I have my own stuff to figure out." Violet pushed to her feet and grabbed her bags. "Can we go? I'm sorry, but Andre's going to be back from the clinic soon and I have a few things I want to get done before he gets home."

"Look at you, working your schedule around a guy. I don't even know who you are right now."

"Shut up and get your keys out. I have shit to do."

"*Aaaand* she's back."

AT CLOSING TIME, the waiting room of the Outer Cape Health Clinic was still packed. Andre texted Violet to let her know he was running late, and then he worked through stuffy noses, stomachaches, injured bones, and a host of other issues. Almost two hours later, he was finishing up his note about the last patient when Perry, the office administrator, poked her head into the room. Two metal barbells pierced her right eyebrow, a ring hung from her septum, and tattoos decorated her neck.

"Did we scare you off?" she asked as she stepped into the room and set a box on the floor. Perry was rail thin, with short jet-black hair sculpted into spiky points that darted out from her head at various angles. She was a professional and efficient administrator with a friendly, though take-charge, personality. She could probably pass for being in her early thirties, but the fine lines around her wise eyes—and her twentysomething daughter, Eliza—suggested she was probably closer to her forties. Eliza also worked at the clinic, overseeing the students from the work-study program with the local high school.

"Hardly," he said with a smile. "It was a great day. You run a tight ship, and your efficiency makes it easier to see more patients. I really enjoyed getting to know Eliza and the rest of the staff."

"We have a good group here, and a caring community." She reached into the box she'd brought in and lifted out a colorful face mask like the ones Violet had made for the clinic in Ghana. "We were so busy today, I forgot to show you these. A local artist makes them for us to use with the children."

"Are they donated anonymously?" he asked.

"No. Violet Vancroft makes them. She and her sister own the Summer House Inn on the bayside. You should see their place. It's gorgeous, and they have an art gallery, too."

"Vi's my girlfriend," he said.

"And you didn't know she made the masks? Well, I guess maybe you two don't do much *talking*."

He chuckled.

She held up a hand and said, "Hey, no judgments over here, but it's too bad you're heading overseas. We could use a doc like you during the summers."

"Not in the winter?" he asked.

"Not as much. Wellfleet and the surrounding areas are tourist towns, tripling in population over the summers. It stays busy until the end of September, but winters are pretty desolate around here."

"I don't see myself settling down to one location again anytime soon, but if I do, I'll certainly keep the clinic in mind." He and Violet hadn't talked about the future in any detail. He didn't want to rock the boat by bringing it up just yet, but he knew they'd have to broach the subject soon.

He was thinking about that as he drove home a little while

later.

Violet was sitting on the steps of the main house when he pulled in. She popped up to her feet with a bright smile and strutted across the lawn as he climbed off his bike.

"How was work?" she asked as he pulled off his helmet.

She went up on her toes to kiss him, and he held her tight, taking the kiss deeper. She made a low, appreciative sound that made him want to kiss her all night long.

"It was great, but not nearly as fantastic as that kiss." He pulled her into another kiss. "Damn, baby. I missed you and we were only apart for a few hours."

"Me too. Are you exhausted and starved?"

"Nope. I'm exhilarated, and I had a granola bar at the clinic, so I'm good for a while. How was your day? Did you get the scheduling and stuff done for the inn?"

"My day was *interesting*. I went shopping with Emery."

"Whoa, really?"

"Yeah. It was good. I enjoyed it, but don't start shoving me into the gossip girl group or anything."

He chuckled. "I wasn't going to, but I'm glad you went."

"I didn't get all my work done, but I will. I'm working with Joni Wednesday morning, and volunteering at the hospital that afternoon and Friday morning, so I have plenty of time to finish up."

"Good. Oh, I almost forgot. I spoke to David today and gave his number to Rowan. Maybe he'll have some news about Joni by the time you see her."

"Thanks for doing that. Since you're not hungry or tired, come with me, and bring your helmet." She took his arm, leading him toward her bike.

"Where are we going?"

"It's a surprise." She grabbed her helmet and climbed onto her bike. "Climb on or lose out."

"Does this involve you being naked?"

She smirked. "Possibly. But you'll never find out if you don't get your fine ass on my bike."

A little while later they were cruising down a narrow road, and a house came into view that reminded Andre of work by Frank Lloyd Wright. He didn't have long to admire the cantilevered rooms and decks before they turned down another driveway and parked in front of a cool old stone and glass building.

He pulled off his helmet and said, "Who lives here?"

As she unlocked the doors she said, "Justin lives in the house we passed. This is his studio. I realized that I told you *where* I sculpt, but I never told you *what* I sculpt. I wanted to show you before you see them around."

She pushed open the door and stepped to the side. His gaze swept over large slabs of stone, power tools, sculpting tools, mallets, and other paraphernalia littering the concrete floors and metal tables and shelves. Against the far wall were two large stainless-steel sinks, more work areas, and an enormous kiln. A canvas tarp covered something at least five feet tall a few feet from where they stood.

"That's mostly Justin's stuff and the sculpture he's working on," Violet said.

He turned, bringing more tables and sculpting supplies into view, along with art magazines, glazes, and paints. Plastic covered what he knew had to be one of Violet's sculptures, but his eyes caught on several drawings hanging on a wall behind the table. They were sketches of *him* sculpting, drawing, sitting cross-legged, lying down, and in various other positions. He recognized two pictures she'd drawn when he was first teaching her to draw the human form.

He glanced at Violet. She had a pensive look in her eyes. His gaze drifted over her shoulder to a life-size sculpture of a male torso. The shoulders were angled and the clavicle protruded, as if the model had been preparing to throw a ball. The arms stopped just above the biceps. The stomach was neither muscular nor overly soft, though clearly defined with a hint of ribs on the sides and a fold of skin just above the belly button, accentuating the slight twist of the body. The sculpture ended just above the knees. Nestled between thick thighs and a nest of pubic hair was a nominal penis. The definition was incredible.

He walked around the table and found the backside to be just as beautifully done. The shoulder blades and lats were flexed, as if caught in motion. The spine carved a slim river down the body to the curve of fleshy buttocks. But it was the rough patch on the left flank that had him breathing harder.

Violet came to his side and put her hand on the same spot on his back.

"You put my scar on another man's body?"

She shrugged one shoulder and said, "Lots of other men's bodies, actually. Every torso I make has your mark."

He was so deeply touched, he didn't know what to say. He looked around the studio and said, "Where are the others?"

"I don't know. Remember when I told you that no one but Justin knows that I sculpt? He delivers them to galleries and lists them for sale by an anonymous artist. They pay him, and we donate the money." She smiled and said, "I had no idea SHINE was yours. A lot of the money goes there. I'm donating this one, along with some pottery, to the suicide-awareness rally. Justin will drop it off so they won't know it's mine. They'll auction off all the donations, and the money will be used to help local schools with their suicide-awareness programs."

He put his arms around her and kissed her. "How long have you been doing this?"

"Since I came back. I hope you don't think it's creepy. It started as a way to feel closer to you. Eventually my skills got better, and I was no longer creating *you* with every piece, but putting *us* into them."

"Violet, this is a remarkable piece of art. Why are you keeping it a secret?"

"It feels private." She ran her fingers over the scar on the back of the statue. "You taught me how to do this, and I treasure those memories."

It was another hidden part of herself, but he couldn't say he blamed her. What they had then—and now—was definitely worth treasuring.

"So do I, babe." He lowered his lips to hers in a deep, loving kiss. "Is this Justin?" He cringed inwardly and said, "Don't answer that. I don't want to know."

"It's not Justin, but I have sculpted him. It's just a guy I met when I was out one night. Anonymous, remember? I can't sculpt the people I'm closest to."

"But you did. You sculpted Justin, and that's okay, Vi. I'm glad he was there for you so you didn't have to deal with everything on your own *all* the time."

"Is that what Brindle did for you? Helped you deal with it?" She lowered her gaze.

He lifted her chin and said, "Have you been worrying about her?"

"No. You said she was only a *friend*. I just wondered if she helped you in the same way Justin helped me."

"I never drew her naked or slept with her, if that's what you're asking," he said with a smile. "She's pregnant and wasn't sure how to handle it. I showed her around Paris, and we commiserated about our complicated love lives. You'd like her. She's impetuous, pushy, and stubborn as a mule, but she's also kind, funny, and honest."

"I'd like to meet her one day, to thank her for telling you to accept Lizza's offer."

She took his hand and led him to the other table. She began unwrapping the plastic from the other large piece he'd noticed and said, "I have something else I want to show you. This is the first piece I've made that isn't a male torso."

She gathered the plastic and set it aside, revealing a sculpture of a child sitting, leaning back on one hand, holding the other up. Though her hands and fingers weren't yet defined, her arms, legs, and feet were. Her hair was beautifully sculpted with adorable waves and ringlets that hung just past her shoulder. Her face was shaped, but there were no features.

"I'm afraid to do her face, and that bulk of clay by her leg will be her cat," Violet said. "She loved that cat so much. She's going to be holding a blue butterfly. I'm going to soak fabric in slip to create her dress." Slip was like liquid clay, and though the fabric would burn off in the kiln, the slip would retain the form.

He put his hand on her back and said, "Who is this?"

"Erin Wilk." Tears welled in her eyes. "I spent a lot of time with her at the hospital and at her house. She was Joni's age when she died last year from a brain tumor."

"Oh, baby, I'm sorry." He kissed her temple, holding her tight against his side.

"She was the sweetest little girl. She loved butterflies and her cat, Igor. She knew she was dying, and she had the most amazing outlook. She said after she went up to heaven she'd come back as a blue butterfly and visit me. It's so fucking unfair that kids suffer like that when there are assholes in the world who literally *deserve* to suffer and they get off scot-free."

He gathered her in his arms and held her as tears slipped from her eyes. She held on tight, eventually giving in to her grief. Her body shook, her tears soaking his shirt, as if she'd been holding them in since she'd lost her little friend.

"It's okay, babe. Let it out. I've got you."

He had no idea how long he held her, but it was long enough for the sun to disappear and the evening to spill in through the glass ceiling. He wanted to take away all her sadness and all her pain, and he needed to figure out a way that being together wouldn't cause her more. But soon he'd go away, and he could never ask her to leave her sister or the family they'd created with their friends. That worry was too big for tonight, and he pushed it down deep.

When her breathing finally calmed, he cradled her face between his hands and wiped her tears with his thumbs. "You loved Erin," he said softly, wanting her to know he understood.

She nodded. "Very much." She inhaled a shaky breath and blew it out slowly. Embarrassment washed over her, and she said, "I'm sorry. I didn't mean to…"

"Baby, don't be sorry for being sad over losing someone you love. With me you can always honor your feelings, whether they're sad, happy, pissed off…" He went for levity and added, "Playful, seductive…"

She smiled and blinked her eyes dry. "God, I love you, but if you tell anyone I cried I'll have to kill you."

"Gotcha, boss." He pressed his lips to hers and said, "Your secrets are always safe with me."

"Her parents are having a memorial for her in the spring, and I wanted to give them something special. I figured it'll take weeks to fully dry."

"They'll love it," he said, and then he remembered that no one knew she sculpted. "You're giving them the sculpture? Anonymously?"

She shook her head. "I'm giving it to them from me, as a gift."

His heart filled to near bursting. "That's wonderful."

"I know you brought your own art supplies to work with while you're here," she said. "But I was thinking that maybe you could help me and we could finish this together. I've never sculpted a face, and you're so talented…"

"I'd be honored to work with you." He kissed her again, tasting the remnants of her salty tears, and then he said, "I ship my art supplies everywhere I go. I thought I'd have a month of lonely nights to fill. I never imagined I'd have the chance to fill them with you."

Chapter Thirteen

SATURDAY MORNING, ANDRE went with Dean and Drake to pick up supplies for something Dean and Drake were doing at the resort, which was just as well. Violet was so nervous to meet Andre's parents, it would have been worse if he were there. She decided to get ready in her cottage, thinking it might ease her nerves.

But it didn't help.

She felt like she was in the wrong house. They'd been staying at Andre's cottage for almost two weeks. She hadn't made a concerted effort to bring her things to his place, but her own closet was looking sparse. That was how it had happened in Ghana, too. One day she'd woken up in Andre's tent surrounded by her own belongings. It had been a wonderful feeling then, and it was even better now, despite making her cottage feel strange.

But her stomach was still in knots.

She felt like an imposter in her black skinny jeans, black-and-white long-sleeve sweater, and fringed boots. Emery had said she looked *polished* and beautiful, but she felt overdressed and fake. The sweater covered the tattoos on her arm and chest and there were no tears in her jeans to expose the ink on her thighs, but still she felt more exposed than she did when she wore miniskirts and tank tops.

She turned away from the mirror, telling herself she would be fine. *They're only clothes, for shit's sake.* She'd worn a dress for Desiree; she could cover up for Andre. Besides, she'd have a big enough strike against her once his parents found out how she'd left the last time they were together. She didn't need to add fuel to the fire.

Oh God. Had he told them how she'd left in middle of the night?

She sank down to the edge of her bed, feeling dizzy.

She heard the front door open, and a second later Andre called out, "Babe?"

"In the bedroom." She stood up, breathing deeply.

He was smiling when he walked in, looking casually sexy in an army-green bomber jacket over a white T-shirt, jeans, and brown boots. The loving look in his eyes took her anxiety down a notch.

"Hey, beautiful." He leaned in for a kiss, smelling deliciously familiar. "Great sweater."

She looked down at her clothes. "Do I look okay?"

"You look gorgeous, but I don't think I've ever seen you all covered up."

"I thought it would be better not to let your parents see all my tats the first time they meet me."

His brow wrinkled. "*That's* why you're covered up?"

She nodded.

"Off with the sweater, babe." He started pulling it up, but she pushed it back down.

"I don't want my tats to be a *thing*, a stumbling block I have to overcome with your parents from day one. Let's first see if they like me."

His jaw clenched, and his eyes turned deadly serious. "First of all, I love who you are, and your tats are part of *you*, just like your green eyes and that smirk that tells people to fuck off. I love *all* of you, babe, and my parents will, too. Please give them a chance to get to know the real you. Don't hide anything about your beautiful self, and I know they will adore you as much as I do."

Her eyes teared up. "Damn it. I've been so nervous I felt like an imposter, and then you come in here and say really sweet, sappy shit, and I get all *teary-eyed*. I haven't cried so much in my entire life." She pulled her sweater off and threw it on the bed. "You make me feel *real*, and *seen*, and *appreciated*, and *stupidly* emotional. It's got to be nerves."

He gathered her in his arms and said, "It's got to be *love*, babe. Embrace it."

She groaned. "What if they hate who I am? Sometimes I curse and I don't mean to."

"Don't you think I know that about you? They curse, too."

She rolled her eyes. "I'm serious."

"So am I. Now, put on that slinky black halter top I love, grab your leather jacket because it'll be cold on the ferry, and let's get the hell out of here before I tear off that black lace bra and we miss lunch altogether."

An hour later they were on the ferry that ran from Province-town to Boston, something neither of them had done before. They stood on the deck despite the cold air, wanting to experience every second of their romantic adventure to the fullest. Andre wrapped his arms around her from behind, his body heat keeping her warm even as the brisk air burned her cheeks.

As Provincetown fell away, all she could see was water, reminding her of how adrift and lonely she'd felt without Andre. She had no idea how it was possible to feel those things while at the same time finding stability for the first time in her life with Desiree, but she'd felt it just the same.

When the Boston skyline came into view, another sensation came over her—one she'd been tamping down for a very long time. She missed experiencing even this little sense of adventure, of walking into the unknown. After a lifetime of not knowing what the next day would hold, how had she pushed her adventurous soul aside for so long? She tried to figure out what she was feeling. It wasn't regret. She was glad for all she'd found on the Cape with Desiree and her friends, but a deep sense of longing was forming inside her.

They took a cab to the Union Oyster House, and when they stepped onto the busy sidewalk, Violet's nerves went crazy again.

Andre put his arm around her and kissed her temple. "Breathe, sweet Daisy, it's going to be fun. I promise."

"Fun? I don't exactly have a good track record with my own parents. I'm not sure why yours would be any different."

"That's hardly fair to you. Your real father was clearly a selfish ass for not sticking around, and that sucks, but it's not in any way a reflection of you. And Ted may not be your biological father, but he and Lizza *do* love you, even if Lizza has a strange way of showing it. In fact," he said as they stepped inside the restaurant. "I think we should try to get reacquainted with Ted. Remember, babe, it was Lizza's decision to take you overseas. He could have fought like hell to keep you, but how can you ever know without asking?"

"Oh God, you're going to be the death of me," she mumbled.

"Bug!" A tall woman ran toward them with her arms outstretched, eyes dancing with excitement. She threw her arms around Andre and proceeded to smother his cheeks in kisses. She had the same wavy desert-sand hair as he did, only hers hung to the shoulders of her silk blouse, which she'd paired with jeans, giving her a youthful appearance. "I've missed you so much! Oh, Bug, you're as handsome as ever. It's been too long."

Bug?

"Mom..." Andre said a little sheepishly as his mother looked him over with a smile that relayed her deep adoration for her son.

"Don't you *Mom* me. I've missed you, and if I had to sit at that table any longer I might have burst." She turned to Violet and said, "You're Violet, right? I can tell. You've got that spark of gumption in your eyes." She hugged Violet tight, then kissed both of her cheeks. "It's so nice to finally meet the woman who opened my son's eyes."

Before Violet could say a word, his mother took hers and Andre's arms and guided them through the restaurant as she said, "I'm sure Bug told you he takes after his father. My husband, Chuck, has always been the same way, too impetuous to hold back. He asked me to marry him on our first *date*! I didn't take off like you did, but I sure made him work for it."

Violet looked at Andre and mouthed, *You told them?*

Andre mouthed, *Sorry*, with an apologetic expression.

"I dated every man I could for the next six months, trying to get him out of my head," his mother said. "But Chuck was determined. He showed up at my house every single night, whether I'd gone out or not. He said he just wanted to make sure I got home safely. The little weasel didn't give me time or space to figure things out. He wasn't taking *any* chances."

"I…um…" Violet stammered as they neared a table in the back of the restaurant, where a man who looked like a younger, shaggier version of Harrison Ford was watching them with an amused expression.

"There were other things going on when I left," Violet tried to explain. "I thought my sister needed me."

His mother said, "Whatever the reason, you changed my boy's life for the better. Every woman should be so strong, so men can become even stronger."

Violet felt an unexpected rush of relief that almost knocked her off her feet. The worst thing she'd ever done in her life was out, and his mother didn't hate her for it or think she was out of her mind.

His mother released them, and Andre immediately came to Violet's side and said, "I'm sorry. I missed you so much, there was no hiding it."

"It's fine," she said softly. "I like her. She says what she thinks, like me."

His father dropped a kiss on his wife's cheek as he came around the table and said, "Kay was a little excited to see you two." He embraced Andre and said, "Missed you, Bug."

"Me too. Dad, this is Violet. Violet, this is my father, Chuck."

His father turned the same warm brown eyes as Andre's on her and said, "You look a little shell-shocked. Welcome to my world." As he wrapped her in his strong arms he said, "We're a crazy family, but Andre's a good man. Don't let us scare you off."

Violet didn't flinch during the embrace. Maybe it was because Kay had caught her off guard and stripped her of her worst fears, or it could have been because of his father's casual amusement and easy nature. Violet had a feeling it was because of both of those things, and underscored by Andre's complete and total support and love for who she was. And in that moment she knew she was exactly where she was meant to be.

When Andre reached for her jacket, she slipped it off, feeling only mildly nervous. His father's gaze swept over her shoulder, following the tattoos all the way down her arm, and she held her breath.

A playful smirk lifted the side of his father's mouth, and he said, "I'm glad to see the apple doesn't fall far from the tree. Shaw men have always fallen for women who aren't afraid to express themselves." He pointed his thumb at Andre's mother and said, "She's got ink."

"What?" Andre's eyes widened. "Mom has a tattoo?"

His mother laughed. "Honey, I've got several, but not anywhere I want my son looking."

THEY ORDERED DRINKS, and as they looked over the menu, Andre noticed his mother watching them with a tender look in her eyes. He glanced at his father, who was busy watching his mother. Andre couldn't remember a time when things hadn't been just like this—easy, happy, and *real*. He'd never had to worry whether his parents would stay together or what their future would look like as a family. As an adult, he realized how special that was, but it wasn't until he'd met Violet and learned of her family's history that he truly appreciated the value of his own.

During lunch, his parents peppered Violet with questions

about the inn, her artwork, volunteering, and her travels, carefully avoiding the topic of family. Andre had shared with them the basics of Violet's family history. He appreciated that his parents didn't put her in the uncomfortable position of trying to explain her mother's decisions. Violet talked animatedly, and when she cursed and covered her mouth, they all chuckled, and his father immediately went into a story about how Andre had trouble saying *truck* when he was young and would yell, *Look! A fire fuck*, leaving them all in hysterics.

They chatted long after they were done eating, and Andre caught his parents up on his visit with David and told them about his next trip into the field.

"Are you going to join him?" his mother asked Violet.

Violet looked down at her lap. Then she turned a thoughtful gaze to Andre and said, "We haven't really discussed it yet. Right now we're taking things one day at a time."

His father lifted his glass and said, "To new friends, reacquainted love, and taking things one day at a time."

They clinked glasses and sipped their drinks.

Violet set her glass down and said, "Who do I have to pay to hear the story behind the nickname *Bug*?"

They all laughed.

His mother smiled at Andre and said, "It all started with a little boy who loved playing in the dirt with bugs, until the day he started eating them…"

"I think that's our cue to leave." Andre flagged down the waitress and said, "Check please."

After narrowly escaping what Andre was sure would have been several more embarrassing stories, they said their goodbyes in front of the restaurant.

His father slung an arm over his shoulder, guiding him a

few feet away from the women, and said, "I'm happy for you, son."

"Thanks, Dad."

"I try not to stick my old nose into your business, but I want to tell you something, and you can decide what to take from it, if anything. Lord knows I spout garbage sometimes. Violet's obviously smart, strong, and she really likes your ugly ass, for some godforsaken reason." He laughed and patted Andre on the back.

"So far I'm not hearing any garbage."

"I'm getting to it. This is the part you'll hate. I can see how much you love her, but you said something to me before we met you for lunch that's got me thinking. You said she'd been at the Cape the whole time since she left you. For a woman who you described as someone who didn't know the meaning of roots, it sure seems like she's put some down."

Andre glanced over his shoulder at Violet chatting with his mother, who was listening intently to her every word. "She has," he said. "She reconnected with her sister and has a family of friends there now. A few families of friends, actually."

"Well, Bug, I know you want her with you, but tread carefully. You've had roots, and you chose to uproot them. She's just starting to grow her own. Like I said, I might be way off base, but my instincts tell me that you need to exercise caution there if you want her in your life."

"I know, Dad. Believe me, not a second goes by that I don't think about it."

His father said, "Okay. I'm here if you need me," and they headed back toward the women.

"I was just telling Violet that we still live in the same three-bedroom condo where we lived when we first moved to Boston, before Andre was born," his mother said.

"Too many happy memories to leave behind," his father said, reaching for his mother's hand. "It also afforded us the opportunity to travel as a family for a few weeks at a time without the stress of money issues or a large yard to deal with."

"In a society where people think bigger always equals better," Violet said, "that's fucki—*shit. Damn it. Oh my God!*" She covered her face and groaned, causing everyone to crack up. Then she lowered her hands and said, "*Awesome,* okay? It's *awesome!*"

Andre pulled her against his chest and kissed her. "I love you so much."

"I fucking love her, too," his mother said, causing them all to laugh again.

His parents hugged them too hard, his mother kissed them too much, and by the time his parents climbed into a cab, Andre couldn't have imagined the get-together going any better than it had.

"Your parents are amazing," Violet said as their cab drove off. "I didn't know parents could be like that. Everyone I know has fucked-up parents. Well, not *everyone,* but a lot of the people I know got ripped off in the parental department."

"They're pretty great. I'm glad you liked them."

"What's your parents' address?" she asked as he flagged down a cab.

He told her, and as they climbed into the cab, she repeated the address to the cabdriver. He hauled Violet across the seat, and she was smiling so big her cheeks had to hurt.

"Why are we going there?" he asked as the cab pulled into traffic. "They just said they were going to see friends. They won't be home."

"I know. I don't want to go inside, I just want to see where you grew up, the street, the building. I want to see the high school and that park where you used to go to draw."

"Why on earth do you want to see those boring places?"

"I spent my childhood wondering what it would have been like to have stayed in Oak Falls, to have the same bedroom until *I* decided to leave, to have the same friends, a *favorite spot* to do art. There's nothing boring about those things. I loved seeing different cultures and living in all those different places, but you know I longed for stability. I feel so close to you right now, and seeing those places will bring us even closer together."

He touched his forehead to hers and said, "God, baby, everything you do, everything you say, guts me."

"That sounds bad."

He kissed her softly and said, "No, *Dais*. It's the best feeling in the world."

They took a curbside tour of the 1900s brick condo building in which he'd grown up, the schools he'd attended, and the parks where he used to sit for hours and draw and where he played ball with his buddies. Violet got excited about each and every place, asking dozens of questions and commenting on how different it was from what she remembered about Oak Falls, which was apparently a town the size of a fist.

He gave the cabdriver another address and then he kissed Violet and said, "We have to get to the waterfront soon so we don't miss the last ferry, but first we need to get ice cream."

"I'm not going to argue with that. I just realized we'll be able to watch the sunset from the deck of the ferry. Remember how sunsets in Ghana sometimes looked like fire in the sky?"

"Yeah, and I remember how sexy you looked beneath them."

The cab stopped in front of the infamous forty-foot tall Hood Milk Bottle across from Fort Point Channel. As they climbed from the cab, Andre asked the driver to wait.

Violet shielded her eyes, looking up at the gigantic structure. "Holy cow. I had no idea this even existed."

"It's been here since 1930, when Arthur Gagner built it to sell homemade ice cream next to his store. When I was growing up, my mom took me here nearly every Tuesday afternoon for *Treat Tuesday*."

"It's not Tuesday. You sure we should be here?"

"Hell *yes*." He kissed her again and said, "Every day with you is a treat."

"I'm going to start calling you cheeseball if you don't stop the sappy shit."

They got ice cream, and on their way back to the cab Violet stopped in middle of the sidewalk and said, "Shit. How much time do we have before the ferry gets here?"

"Thirty minutes. Why?"

"Because we're in *Boston*, and if I don't bring Serena back Kane's Donuts, she'll give me hell for weeks. Do you think the cabdriver can find out where it is?"

He scoffed. "Babe, everyone here knows where Kane's Donuts is."

"I don't," she said as they settled into the cab.

On the way, she told him about Abby, the owner of the doughnut shop, and how she'd named the Perpetual Bliss doughnut after Serena and Drake.

They got a dozen Perpetual Bliss doughnuts and headed back to the ferry, making it onboard seconds before they closed the ramp.

Out of breath and pink cheeked from the chilly evening air,

Violet leaned against the railing and said, "I can't believe you tried to bribe Abby into naming a doughnut after us!"

"We're worth a hell of a lot more than a doughnut." He looked down at the doughnut box and said, "I'm not sure the doughnuts made it through our run."

She opened the box and peered inside. "Uh-oh. I think this doughnut has seen better days." She lifted it from the box. Half the chocolate frosting was smeared off, and all of the dark and white chocolate pearls were shoved to one side.

He suggested they eat the evidence.

Violet grinned and held the doughnut up for him to take a bite. Delicious Belgian cream filled his mouth. She went up on her toes, pressing several kisses to his lips. When she drew back and slicked her tongue along his lips, he shifted the box to his side and hauled her in for a deeper kiss. They kissed so long and passionately, he was sure they'd spark fire.

When their lips finally parted he said, "The doughnut was delicious, but those kisses make me want to toss the box in the water and find a dark corner where we can hunker down for the next hour and a half. *Naked.*"

Her eyes flamed, sending heat straight to his groin. She made a seductive show of licking the cream slowly from the doughnut and closed her eyes, emitting a raw, sexual sound.

He ground out, "*Fuck*," and crashed his mouth to hers, taking her in another fierce kiss. He wedged his knee between her legs, pressing against her center, and she pushed her fingers into the edge of his waistband, brushing over the head of his cock. Christ, she was *hot*. He didn't think, didn't seek approval, or even hesitate for a second, as he dragged her inside in search of someplace private.

Rows of seats blurred together as they passed, following the signs down a hallway and around the corner. He pinned her against the wall with his body, balancing the doughnut box against his side, unable to wait another second before devouring her again. She tasted sweet, sexy, and so damn ready, he threw the bathroom door open and hauled her inside. He dropped the box and locked the door without breaking their kiss. They tore at each other's clothes, sending shirts sailing into the air. Violet kicked her boots off, and they smacked into the wall. He shoved his jeans down to his ankles, taking her in another demanding kiss, and pushed his hand between her legs.

At the same time she said, "Fuck me," he said, "Fuck," and they both went wild.

He turned her around, and she grabbed the sides of the sink with both hands as he shoved her legs open wide with his foot and thrust into her slick heat.

"Christ, baby. You feel so fucking good."

He slammed into her, and she moaned loudly and reached back, clutching his hip with one hand, and said, "Harder!"

He grabbed her hair, turning her face so he could kiss her. Thank God the engines were loud, because with every thrust they both made hungry, lustful noises. He couldn't slow down. She felt too good. She was so tight, so hot, he nearly lost his mind. Their teeth gnashed as he drove into her, using his hand to pleasure her from the front and sending her body into a symphony of sensual sounds and thrusts. Her sex pulsed around his shaft so exquisitely he gritted his teeth, struggling to stave off his own release as he sent her soaring again. Her body trembled and quaked, drawing his orgasm to the surface. Electric shocks burned in his veins. His muscles flexed, his cock throbbed, and in the next breath heat seared down his spine, and he lost all control, coming in a series of powerful thrusts. Her fingers dug into his flesh until the last jerk of his hips.

He rested his forehead on her shoulder, his body shuddering with aftershocks. "I love you, baby." He kissed her shoulder. "I'm sorry we missed the sunset."

She leaned her back against his chest, and with a sated smile she said, "A double rainbow with you is better than ten thousand sunsets."

"You mesmerize me, the way you go from being vixenish Violet one minute to sweet-as-sugar Daisy the next." He turned her in his arms and said, "I couldn't love you more than I do right this second." He kissed her softly. "I was wrong. I love you even more now." He brushed his smiling lips over hers and said, "Just made a liar out of myself again. Another second, another level of love…"

Chapter Fourteen

VIOLET REACHED INTO the vat of slip and fished out the fabric she was going to use to create the dress on the sculpture of the little girl. She couldn't stop admiring the adorable face and the intricate detail on the cat she and Andre had created. Adding the clay-soaked fabric dress was the last element before they started the long drying process. It had been twelve sometimes-sappy, sometimes-erotic, always-*sensational* days since she'd met Andre's parents, during which time her life had also gone on as normal...*only better*. They went to work, hung out with their friends at the inn, and had even joined them for a bonfire on the beach. They ate ridiculously good breakfasts—*thanks to Andre*—and they'd gone to the coffeehouse to hang out. They'd also dropped off several pieces of pottery for the suicide-awareness rally and auction, which was taking place tonight.

"It looks pretty good, doesn't it?" Andre put his arm around her waist and kissed her cheek. "We make a great team, Dais—in the studio, on the beach, in the bedroom...*everywhere*."

Her pulse quickened, and she wondered if she would ever get so used to being with Andre that she'd lose that nervous edge. She sure hoped not.

"We always did," she said honestly. "Our timing just sucked."

"It doesn't suck now," he said as she gently squeezed the clay-soaked fabric. "And it doesn't have to suck ever again. Desiree comes back tomorrow. Are you still planning on talking with her?"

"Yes." Her stomach dipped. It was Thursday. She had one more day to prepare for that conversation. But she'd been avoiding any talk about the future, and she had a feeling that's where he was heading. "I'm going to tell her about volunteering and sculpting."

If Andre had his way, she'd tell Desiree about her friends at the coffeehouse, too. She didn't know why she was more nervous about revealing *that* part of her life, though she had a feeling it was because Andre was leaving in a week and a half and they hadn't discussed how they were going to handle it. If they decided to try a long-distance relationship, she might need the safety of that hideout and the comfort of those friends to make it through.

"Let's get this done," she said, trying to redirect the conversation. "I don't want to be late for the rally." She held the clay-soaked fabric in front of the sculpture and said, "I want it to look like she's in motion, lifting her hand as the butterfly lands, so we need to create the feel of the skirt of her dress shifting."

They'd made a beautiful clay butterfly in the girl's palm. Andre had helped her make Erin's hands look as soft and delicate as they had been in real life.

"Why don't I do one side and then you can do the other," she suggested. Andre had taught her how to sculpt, but she'd learned to use slip and add fabric to her sculptures on her own through trial and error.

"First we'll drape the thin area over one shoulder and bring it across the body," she said as she did it. "And then what I thought we'd do is create ripples like pleats, only softer like this." She manipulated the wet fabric, carefully lifting and shifting one-inch sections so they fell like soft pleats over the little girl's thighs. "Once we've done both sides, we'll put another strip of fabric around her waist and tie it in a bow in the back. I've been thinking about this piece for so long, I feel like I've already done this a hundred times."

As she placed the fabric in position she said, "I just realized—you can do the back while I do the front."

"Babe, I'll do you any way you'd like." He stepped behind her, pressing his hips to her ass, and groped her breasts.

When he began kissing her neck, her hands stilled and she closed her eyes. There was no better feeling than being loved by this man, and it didn't matter if they were taking a walk and holding hands or making out like they'd never get enough of each other. Every minute with him was magical. But if he kept this up, they'd never finish.

"Andre…"

He nipped at her earlobe and said, "*Violet…*"

"I *really* don't want to be late tonight," she said. "But I also *really* want to put my slimy hands all over you."

He chuckled, walked around the table, and began pleating the fabric.

"That's *it*?" she snapped. "You're not even going to try to get your way?"

"For now." He leaned in for a kiss, and she scowled at him.

"You're a tease."

"You ain't seen nothin' yet, babe. Teasing you is half the fun. I never know if I'll get Daisy or Violet when we get in bed.

Tonight I plan on having both. First I'll make love to you slow and sweet, drawing out each orgasm until you can barely breathe."

Her insides heated up. "Stop it."

"Then I'm going to take you hard and a little rough, just the way you like it," he said as he worked, his eyes flicking up to gauge her reaction every few seconds, which made his words even hotter. "I'll take you right up to the edge of ecstasy and hold you there as I withdraw slowly, leaving just the head of my—"

"How's it coming?" Justin asked as he came through the door, looking especially broody. His face was pinched and his brows were drawn tight.

Shit! Violet's hands were shaking, and she was sure her cheeks were flushed. She dipped her head so Justin couldn't see her and focused on the material as she tried to regain control.

Andre cocked a grin and said, "*Slow* and *steady*."

Violet glared at him.

Justin admired their work but didn't crack a smile. "Looks like you've got her nice and wet."

"That's the goal," Andre said, his gaze flicking up to hers. They both stifled a laugh.

"It has to be wet to shape the fabric," Violet said, trying to force her mind to think of the project rather than Andre's sexy promises. She peered over the sculpture, watching his hands move deftly as he created pleats in the fabric. There was something about watching her big, strong man creating something so delicate and beautiful that sucked her right in.

"Are you going to be done in time to go to the coffee-house?" Justin asked. He would be there with the rest of the Dark Knights to honor his cousin's memory.

"We wouldn't miss it. Are you okay?" She fished out another piece of fabric and placed it across the other shoulder, draping it diagonally down the body.

"Yeah, fine," Justin said. "Just dealing with some shit."

"Anything we can help with?" she asked.

He *almost* smiled and said, "No. It's cool. Thanks."

"I'm sorry about your cousin," Andre said.

"Yeah, we all are. She was a great girl." His eyes swept over the fabric again, and he said, "Looks like you've met your match, Vi. He's got talented hands."

You have no idea...

"I'm taking off," Justin said, heading for the door. "I want to spend time with Dwayne and his family before the rally."

The second he walked out the door, lust simmered in Andre's eyes and he said, "As I was saying—"

She leaned across the table and pressed her lips to his in a slow, sensual kiss.

"If you want to have any chance at mattress dancing with Daisy and banging your balls off with Violet, then focus on the work at hand," she said. "If we don't finish in time for the rally, the only action you'll be getting is the vibration of the bike between your legs."

He smirked, and damn it, that confidence made him even sexier.

"I'm a talented multitasker," he said huskily. "I can manipulate materials, turn you on, and get you off all without missing a beat."

She breathed deeply, preparing for his titillating assault.

THEY FINISHED THE sculpture and prepped it for the drying process, and Andre teased and *prepped* his girl for a special night. Sculpting with Violet had always been an incredibly sensual process. Andre had never felt that way when he was around other sculptors, but Violet was a passionate woman, and it carried over to every part of her life. He had no idea how other guys could keep from being lulled in by her innate sensuality. *Although,* he mused as they parked down the street from the coffeehouse later that evening, *you probably scare the shit out of most guys. Pussies.*

Motorcycles, trucks, Jeeps, and dozens of other vehicles lined the narrow road leading to Common Grounds Coffeehouse. They left their helmets on the bike, and he reached for Violet's hand. "Why do they hold the rally here? It's such a small place."

"Dwayne's family wanted to honor Ashley's memory in a place that accepted everyone, with no prejudices, so anyone, no matter how alone they feel, would know they were welcome. Can you think of a better place?"

"No, I guess not."

Children ran around on the grass beside the building with adults watching them from the perimeter. Music blared from the band playing on the patio, where people of all ages danced and mingled. A handful of guys in leather jackets stood out front smoking and talking.

Andre put his arm around Violet, holding her tighter. "How's it going?" he asked as they walked past the smokers.

"Good, man," one of them mumbled.

They walked inside, where it was standing room only. Burly bearded guys in leather jackets stood shoulder to shoulder along the wall, arms crossed, as if they were guarding the property.

Women and children gathered around a buffet table filling their plates, while waiters and waitresses rushed from table to table. Gabe waved from the corner of the room. Andre waved back, but she was already tending to another customer.

The line moved, and Elliott hollered over the music, "Violet! Andre!" He gave them high fives and said, "Steph saved you seats on the patio."

Violet put her hand on Elliott's shoulder and shouted, "How you holding up?"

"Okay. Thanks." He pushed his glasses up the bridge of his nose. "Are you taking the mic tonight after the rally?"

"Yeah, Vi. Are you going to take the mic tonight?" Andre asked.

She had yet to get up and say anything in front of the group, though Andre had asked her to every time they'd come. He was dying to get a peek into that side of her, and he had to admit that it stung knowing others had seen what he had not. Steph and Cory both told him that Violet would never get up and take the mic when asked. *She likes to do things at her own pace. She's got to feel the draw.*

Boy, did he know that.

"Don't hold your breath, you two," she said. "We'll catch you later, El." She grabbed a paper from in front of Elliott and shoved it in Andre's hand. "You'll need this later. Put it in your pocket."

He shoved it in his pocket as they moved through the crowd. Violet drew a lot of attention in her second-skin leather pants and leather jacket.

"Vi!" Steph waved them over when they stepped out onto the patio. She was sitting with Cory, Rowan, and Joni. A large pizza sat in middle of the table beside a tray of nachos and a bowl of breadsticks.

Joni jumped off her seat and ran over to them. She took their hands, grinning up at them as she said, "Hi, monkey! Hi, frog!"

Andre tousled her hair and said, "How's it going, chinchilla?"

Joni giggled and pulled them over to the table. She climbed onto Rowan's lap and said, "Daddy, what's a chilla?"

Rowan whispered something in her ear that sent her into a fit of giggles. He lifted his chin and said, "Hey, sugar," to Violet, then to Andre he said, "Hey, man, I can't thank you enough for hooking me up with Dr. Posillico. He got us in right away to see someone, and you were right; they didn't just blow us off."

"The doctor said I have dixia!" Joni announced. "'Cause I get frustrated with school stuff. They're going to help me learn better so maybe I won't hate school so much." She grabbed Rowan's face between her hands and put her nose right up against his as she said, "Can we dance now, peanut butter?"

"Sure, sugar." He set Joni on her feet and stood up. "Y'all should check out the cool sculpture they're auctioning off. If I had a few bucks, I'd snag it in a heartbeat."

"Daddy! It's *naked*!" Joni said as she led him into the crowd.

"It's a man's torso," Steph explained. "A little underendowed if you ask me."

Violet didn't flinch, look away, or give any other indication that she might be uncomfortable listening to them talk about her anonymous artwork. They'd been together again for almost a month, and he was starting to see the beauty in her artistic anonymity. There was something romantic about knowing she was putting pieces of them into the world without anyone else knowing it. He would always want her to be recognized for her talent, but maybe Violet was right to hold this piece so close to her chest, like their own secret.

Cory picked up a slice of pizza and said, "Because I ruined you for every other man."

Steph rolled her eyes. Her hair was cornrowed tonight, and she twisted the ends of a braid. "Seriously, though. I mean, someone had to pose for that, right? How does that guy feel knowing his less-than-impressive junk is being seen by hundreds of people? Someone should tell the artist to do the guy a solid and build him up."

They all chuckled.

"Steph, the dude obviously doesn't care or he wouldn't have modeled. Can we get off the *junk* talk now?" Cory slid the pizza tray closer to them. "You two hungry?" As Andre and Violet grabbed pieces, he said, "What are you guys doing November seventeenth?"

"Sorry, man. I'll be in Cambodia," Andre said.

"Dude, that's crazy," Cory said. "For how long?"

"I'm not really sure. Three or four months. Why? What's going on November seventeenth?"

Cory grinned and said, "I've got my first big gallery showing in Boston."

"That's awesome," Andre exclaimed. "You must be stoked."

"I'm beyond stoked. What about you, Vi?" Cory asked. "Can you make it?"

"Dwayne and Rowan and I are going," Steph said. "If you're around, we can go together."

Violet glanced nervously at Andre. He'd bet a buck her toe was turning in, too. He knew she loved him, but she'd changed the subject every time he'd gone anywhere near the topic of his leaving. If only she'd talk about it, at least then he'd know what she was thinking. He'd promised not to push, but waiting was killing him.

"I, um…" She looked down at her pizza, and then she sat up a little taller, looked at Cory, and said, "I don't know what I'm doing next week, much less in November. But that's incredible, and you know I'll be there if I can. Is this the gallery that architect buddy of yours was going to try to hook you up with?"

"Yeah. Drew really came through for me," Cory answered. "I've got to bust my ass to get ready for the show, though."

And just like that Violet was back to her confident self. His girl was a survivor.

Rowan and Joni returned to the table, and Joni was full of energy, leading the conversation in ten different directions.

A little while later Violet pointed across the patio to Dwayne and Justin standing with five other tough-looking guys. They were eyeing a table full of women a few feet away. "Those are Justin's three brothers to the right, and Dwayne's are the two to the left. And see the jarheads over there?"

He followed her gaze to the edge of the patio, where a bunch of guys with military cuts, massive muscles, and serious faces were talking.

"Those are Dwayne's military buddies. They come each year for the event, along with the Dark Knights, and as you can see, most of the community."

"Why don't your other friends come?" he asked. "I know they don't hang out here, but we've been here a number of times, and I've never seen most of these other people either."

"Because we're in *Harwich*," she said, as if that should answer his question. Then she added, "And they rarely go past the rotary in Orleans."

"But they know Justin and his family. Wouldn't they want to support them?"

"They do," she said. "His family holds a smaller service in Wellfleet. This is a Dark Knights event. My friends up there aren't really into this crowd."

They were a much rougher-looking group than he'd seen around her friends in Wellfleet, but he had a feeling if she invited them, they'd come. If for no other reason than to support Violet.

"Peach!" Joni shook Violet's arm. "Can you and Pepper dance with me?"

Violet smirked at Andre and said, "Geez, even the little ladies think you're hot. Come on, *Pepper*. Let's cut a rug with the munchkin."

They danced with Joni, ate, visited the auction table, chatted with Gabe, Dwayne, and other friends, and then they danced some more. A couple hours later, Gabe announced the winners of the silent auction and the amount of money each item had sold for.

Andre watched Violet closely when they announced that her sculpture had gone for eight thousand dollars. Her beautiful lips curved up as everyone cheered, and when they announced that the winner had submitted the bid anonymously and was donating the sculpture to the coffeehouse, Violet turned her wise, knowing eyes to him.

He put his mouth beside her ear and said, "I'm proud of you, baby. You made that donation possible." He pressed a kiss to her cheek, and she turned, meeting his lips in a sizzling kiss.

"Thank you," she said for his ears only.

Dwayne's father gave a speech, thanking everyone for coming out. He spoke about the daughter he'd lost and about spreading hope for a more peaceful future. Then they allowed friends and family to say a few words. Violet held Andre's hand, squeezing it as each person spoke. Her eyes teared up, and he put his arm around her, holding her close. Justin got up to speak, drawing tears with a tale about his late cousin's fifteenth birthday party. Rowan was the only one from their table who spoke before the group. Holding Joni, he talked about how hard it was to lose someone and how he and Joni are proud to be included in the suicide-awareness efforts. Dwayne and his brothers each spoke. The burly bikers broke down, and ended up with their arms around each other's shoulders, letting their tears fall without shame. Stephanie walked right up to them, and Dwayne pulled her into the fold. The military guys spoke of brotherhood and solidarity, their thoughtful words aimed at their brother in arms.

The outpouring of emotion was as sad and touching as it was inspiring, the way people from all walks of life came together to try to make their community a better place. By the time everyone had said their piece, Violet was practically in Andre's lap, safely nestled within his arms, her side to his chest, her tears landing on his arm.

He kissed her cheek and whispered, "I love you."

She turned her face into the crook of his neck and said, "I didn't know her, but I know how it feels to be an outsider, and I wish I had known her. I would have kicked anyone's ass who made her feel bad."

Before he could respond, the band started playing, and the entire crowd began singing Bruno Mars's "Just the Way You Are." All around them, people belted out the lyrics. Violet reached into Andre's pocket as she sang and handed him the paper she'd given him earlier. He scanned the lyric sheet, but he didn't need it.

He pulled her into his arms, singing every word with her. He might have started out singing for the young woman they were there to honor, but when the last words left his lips and *his* beautiful girl's trusting green eyes gazed up at him, each and every word was meant for her.

By the time they got home, Andre was drunk on love. He knew the first thing Violet would do was go to the inn to get Cosmos and bring him to the cottage to sleep, so he let her guide him. They went in through the kitchen door, and Cosmos trotted out to greet them. When Violet crouched to pick him up, he darted down the hall.

"He's a pest," Violet said, following Cosmos.

He was a *perfect* little pest.

Violet peered into the dining room. "Cosmos?"

The pup yapped and she crossed the hall to the living room. She stood stock-still in the entryway, and Andre watched as she took in the mass of leafy plants surrounding the canvas tent, above which the guys had hung twinkling white lights criss-crossing the ceiling, just as he'd planned. The flaps of the tent were tied back, revealing colorful blankets and pillows, in the center of which Cosmos lay with his tongue out, panting happily. A small end table he'd found at a yard sale that looked a lot like the one that had been in his tent in Ghana was draped with one of Violet's beautiful batiks. Candles sat ready to be lit beside a bottle of wine and two glasses.

Andre wrapped his arms around her from behind, pressed a kiss to her cheek, and said, "Surprise, sweetheart."

She turned in his arms, happiness glimmering in her eyes. "How did you do all this?"

"With help from Dean and Drake. But we didn't tell the gossip girls. I was afraid they'd spill the beans." He pressed his lips to hers, and then he said, "It's the closest I could come to being out in the wilderness. I wanted to set this up outside beneath the stars, but I was afraid you'd freeze."

She wound her arms around his neck and said, "It wouldn't matter if we were in the rainforest, the desert, at the beach, or in Antarctica, as long as we're together it's perfect. I love every-thing—the tent, the lights, the plants. But mostly I love *you* for loving *us* enough to take us back to the place where we began."

Chapter Fifteen

VIOLET LAY SNUGGLED against Andre Friday morning, gazing up at the peak of the tent while trying desperately not to think about him leaving next weekend. They had eight more days together, and each one seemed like a step on a plank leading up to the hardest decision of her life. She wanted to take his hand and fly into their next adventure. Oh, how she missed it all—being in the field with Andre, traveling, waking to the noises of an unfamiliar village, helping people who didn't have the advantages they had in the States, and becoming one with nature in a way she couldn't in modern society.

But at the same time, she couldn't imagine leaving Desiree.

Thoughts of her sister brought more anxiety. They had a *lot* to talk about, and serious talks were like rabid dogs—Violet avoided them at all costs. She knew Desiree would be on cloud nine from her honeymoon. How could Violet break her heart by telling her she was thinking about leaving?

Violet closed her eyes, bathing in memories of the last few weeks. She didn't try to dodge the confusion, anger, or hurt of when she and Andre had first reconnected. That pain had helped them become stronger in the same way the missing years between her and Desiree had led them to their unexpected common ground.

Cosmos made a noise, and she glanced at him, sleeping soundly against the crook of Andre's body. The pup who had once driven her batty had become a reminder of what unconditional love was all about.

The same way Andre has.

Memories of the amazing night they'd first made love came rushing back—she could still feel their bodies as one, still see the powerful look of true love in his eyes and hear the intensity of his emotions as he'd said, *I can't imagine a single day without you in it. Come back to Boston and marry me, Daisy.* She'd been as elated as she'd been terrified. *Oh,* how she'd loved him. Never in her life had she dreamed of, much less experienced, a love so deep and real as the love they shared. But she'd tried to imagine what life with Andre would be like in Boston, and reality had hit like a freight train. No matter how in love they were, the idea of staying in one place, of being a proper *doctor's* wife, was suffocating.

But now he'd changed his world because of the things they'd talked about and maybe even because of the love they'd shared. Was it so much to ask for her to do the same?

But he *hadn't* asked her to come with him this time, and that brought another level of panic, despite her indecision.

I can't imagine a life without you, either.

She thought she had eight days to figure things out, but what if he didn't want her to go with him, but wanted to try a long-distance relationship? Could she live with that? Could he? Maybe it was time to face all her fears.

She looked at his peaceful face, silently hoping she wouldn't mess things up. She mustered all her courage and kissed Andre's lips.

"Mm." His arm slid down her back, holding her tighter. "How's my girl?"

"Well fucked and…" She cringed at how harsh that sounded, which was weird in a frighteningly good way. His eyes opened and she said, "Well *loved* and stressing out."

He lifted his other arm slowly, trying not to wake Cosmos, and threaded his fingers into the hair just above her ear, cradling her cheek. His warm brown eyes drifted over her face, and his lips curved up in a reassuring smile. "There's not much I love more than waking up to your sweet face. We're in our magical tent, babe. No stress allowed."

"It would be easy to let reality fall away, but I know the next week will fly by, and then we'll be standing on the edge of that awful plank with the world spread out before us." Words tumbled from her mouth faster than she could think. "And I can't stop imagining all that'll be left on solid ground. Desiree and the life we've built here. The family we've created. That stupid dog. And you haven't even asked me to go with you, so for all I know…" Tears filled her eyes. She couldn't even say that he didn't want her to go, because she knew that wasn't true. She lowered her face to his chest and held on tight, as if her words alone might catapult her into darkness.

He kissed the top of her head, and she felt his heart beating faster against her cheek.

"I didn't realize we were walking a plank." He brushed her hair away from her face and kissed her forehead. "Are you ready to talk about the future? Every time I try to bring it up you avoid it like the plague."

"I do not," she snapped, but that wasn't true. That was her stupid self-preservation kicking in. "I'm sorry. It's true. But do you blame me?" She tilted her face up and said, "I screwed us up once, and I don't want to do it again. I want to be with you, but I want to be here, too, and I know I can't have it all. I'm not asking you to fix it or figure it out. I just wish I knew what to do. Desiree is coming back, and all I can think of is how far we've come—her and me and you and me. My heart is yours. I hope you know that, but she's—"

"Shh, babe." He gathered her in his arms and held her. "Nobody wants you to choose."

"Oh, *right*," she said sarcastically. "Maybe I can pack everyone's shit and drag them across the world, too."

He gently rolled her onto her back and gazed down at her with a sexy smile.

"Sex isn't going to solve this," she said half-heartedly.

"I don't want to have sex. I want you to close your eyes and just *breathe*. Come on. Do it with me, just like you taught me to do. Remember?"

"How could I ever forget? When you finally closed your eyes and relaxed, I wanted to crawl into your lap and disappear."

"Even with my eyes closed I felt you watching me, and I knew then that if I were ever to get through all your beautiful layers, I'd never want to let you go."

She closed her eyes and felt the sting of tears again. "Stop. No sappy stuff right now. It's too hard."

He kissed her and said, "I want you to be with me always, but figuring out how to make that work takes *conversation*." He brushed his lips beside her ear and whispered, "It takes two, baby. This has never been a one-sided decision. I need to know what's in your heart."

"You," she said quickly. "And Desiree. I committed to running the inn with her. I can't just *abandon* her." Pain washed over his face.

"You think following your heart means abandoning the people you love, but it doesn't. You see gray areas of potential in everything around you, but you also have this belief that some parts of your life—the people you love, your relationships—can only exist as all or nothing. Maybe that comes from Lizza cutting ties with Ted and Desiree when you were young. Or maybe not. *Why* you believe it isn't as important as realizing that there is a world of possibility between all and nothing."

He was quiet for a long moment, his gaze drifting over her face again, as if the answers were written there. She hoped they were because the only thing going through her mind was, *Which side are you on, or where do you fall in between? Wherever it is, I want to be there, too.*

"What if you could have both?" he said softly. "What if we spent the time between clinic openings here with Desiree and your friends, and we worked our schedules to be here each summer to help with the inn?"

"I can't ask you to change your schedule for me—"

He silenced her with a kiss and said, "You don't have to."

Cosmos raised his head and raced out of the living room, barking as the girls barreled into the kitchen in a cacophony of conversation. Violet groaned, and he kissed her again, smiling against her lips.

"Come on, babe. Those are the friends you don't want to leave, remember?" He climbed off her, tossed her his T-shirt, and pulled on his jeans.

She put on his shirt and her leather pants from last night, and they headed to the kitchen. Serena had her nose in the fridge, Chloe's hand was stuffed in a box of cereal, and Daphne had just bitten into an apple. Gavin and Emery were standing by the coffee machine.

"Where the heck did you two come from?" Emery asked.

"Living room," Violet said, ignoring Gavin's raised brow.

Drake and Dean ran through the door. "Sorry!" they both said in unison.

"We thought we'd beat them here," Dean said.

"It's okay," Andre said.

"What's going on?" Emery asked. "Why were you trying to beat us?"

"Something wrong with your place, Vi?" Serena asked. "Oh no, did you guys have a fight? Is that why there's no breakfast?"

Andre chuckled.

Violet rolled her eyes. "We got you doughnuts last weekend. Maybe it's time you made *us* breakfast."

"You got *doughnuts*?" Emery handed Gavin and Dean cups of coffee. "Why didn't we get any doughnuts?"

"Nice, Serena," Gavin said as he sat at the table. "I'm your business partner, *and* I always make sure you have ample sugar in the office. Where's the reciprocation?"

Serena pulled out a chair and sat down with a container of yogurt. "She means the smushed doughnuts that we had to scrape off the sides of the box to eat. I told you about them." She tore off the top of the yogurt, eyeing Violet and Andre. "How did they get so mangled from a simple ferry ride, anyway?"

Chloe stuffed a handful of cereal into her mouth, looking at Violet and Andre expectantly.

Daphne sat at the table with her apple and said, "Maybe they didn't go on the ferry after all."

"Sex on the ferry is more like it," Serena said.

"I need coffee." Violet headed for the coffeemaker.

Drake sat beside Serena and said, "Stop picking on Vi, babe. We got more than our fair share of *perpetual bliss* that night, and from what I recall, you didn't complain when I was licking that scraped chocolate off your—"

"Stop!" Daphne and Chloe yelled.

"Aw, I want to hear about their nasty little doughnut tryst," Emery teased.

Serena pointed at Drake and said, "If you say one more word, you won't be getting any *bliss*, perpetual or otherwise, for a very long time."

Drake blinked innocently and said, "I was going to say *off your fingers*. Where was *your* mind going?"

"Is this where the party is?" Justin sauntered into the kitchen carrying a bag from Blue Willow Bakery. "I brought bagels and muffins."

The girls rushed at him, all talking at once.

"Thank goodness! I'm starved!" Daphne said.

Emery squealed. "Yay!"

"This makes you even hotter." Chloe snagged the bag from him.

Justin held his hands up, and Violet said, "Welcome to the madhouse."

"Pass me a muffin!" Serena hollered.

"Don't you feed these people?" Justin asked.

Dean grabbed Emery around the waist and said, "I fed my woman this morning."

"That kind of food only makes me hungrier." Emery gave him a bagel and a kiss.

Violet handed Justin a mug of coffee and said, "I was wondering when you were going to show up."

"Yeah, well, I don't usually spend my mornings *solo*," he

said with a cocky grin.

"Take a seat, Casanova," Violet teased. "If you're lucky they'll leave you a few crumbs."

Justin laughed and sat at the table. Violet got coffee for herself and Andre, then sat on Andre's lap as the gossip girls and their men devoured the food.

"Thanks for bringing breakfast," Chloe said, shoving the bag across the table to Andre and Violet. "We should have a system. You know how churches have prayer chains, where one person calls the next? We need breakfast alerts. Like"—she lowered her voice—"SOS. Bad night at the inn. Bring bagels."

"That works!" Daphne said. "But that means someone has to check things out first."

"Me!" Emery chimed in. "I'll send a text to Des. *Did you get it good, or are we scrounging this morning?*"

"Okay, on *that* insane note..." Violet reached for a change in subject. "Did you get the party figured out?"

Emery grinned. "Yes! In fact, Justin, you should come to our party next weekend. It's a welcome-home party for Des, Rick, and Harper, and a—"

"Harper?" Andre asked.

"She's a fictional blonde they wave in front of single guys to get them to stick around," Gavin said with a smirk. "I don't believe she really exists."

"She *does*, and she'll knock your socks off," Chloe said.

"You mean Harper Garner?" Justin asked.

"Yes!" the girls all said at once.

"Dude, she's real, and she's hot," Justin said.

"I'll believe it when I see it," Gavin said. "You've got to come, Justin. I might need a wingman, and all the guys around here are too *taken* to do a good job of it." He lowered his voice and said, "But I'm still not banking on there being a real *Harper*."

"Oh, shut up," Emery said. "Harper is hot, smart, and isn't here because she's working on a *movie* she *wrote*. The party is also going to be a send-off for Andre."

A pang pierced Violet's chest at the thought of leaving Desiree if they followed Andre's plans.

Justin glanced at Violet with a confused expression, and Andre held her a little tighter with a hopeful look in his eyes. Did he think she was going to tell everyone she might be going with him right this second? She hadn't even talked with Desiree yet. She forced herself to say, "Good idea. You should come, Justin."

Emery filled him in on the details.

"I've got to run." Drake gave Serena a quick kiss and said, "Babe, don't forget Hagen's spending the night tonight." He looked at the others and said, "We're practicing."

Serena choked on her food. "We are *not* practicing."

"Yeah, we are," Drake said as he walked out the door, sparking more laughter and snarky comments.

"Thanks for coming last night," Justin said to Violet and Andre.

"Last night?" Emery asked. "Where'd you guys go last night?"

"The suicide-awareness rally in Harwich," Justin said before Violet could respond.

"Lots of bikers," Violet said. "Not really your scene."

Daphne's jaw dropped. "Hot bikers and you didn't invite us? I see there's no love for the single ladies over here. *Sheesh.*"

"You have a baby. You don't need a biker," Chloe said, popping a piece of a muffin into her mouth. "You need someone like Gavin, or Dean's brother Jett. He's hot."

"Hey," Gavin interjected. "I'm sitting right here, thank you very much. I'm hotter than Jett."

"Keep your pants on. You're not banging Daphne," Violet said with a glare.

"Chloe, have you ever seen a big, protective biker holding a baby?" Daphne looked up at the ceiling with a dreamy expression.

"Justin's a biker," Serena pointed out.

Violet leaned down and whispered in Andre's ear, "Remind me again why I'd miss them."

Chapter Sixteen

AFTER VOLUNTEERING AT the hospital Friday afternoon, Violet stopped by Justin's studio to check on the sculpture. Justin was getting ready to leave the studio when she arrived. He was covered in stone dust.

She tossed her keys on the table and said, "Hey. You and your goodies were a big hit this morning."

"That was an interesting breakfast. Is it like that every day?"

"That depends. Do you mean that *loud*? That *presumptive*? That—"

"Fun." He shrugged and said, "It was loud, and yeah, they seem to be all up in each other's shit, but you have to admit they're entertaining."

"That's one way to put it."

"Are we going to dance around the whole *Andre's leaving* thing?" Justin leaned his hip against the table as she inspected the sculpture.

She kept her eyes trained on the butterfly. "Do I look like I'm dancing?"

"Vi," he said softly. "Look at me. What's going on? Are you leaving with him?"

She huffed out a breath and crossed her arms. "I want to."

"But…?"

"I don't know. I need to talk to Des. She's back, but I've been at the hospital all afternoon."

"And now you're here, which means you're procrastinating."

Yup…

He frowned. "Okay, look. Maybe you just need a swift kick in the ass. You ran once. Don't fuck the guy over again."

"Way to have faith in me," she snapped. "I won't screw him over. I love him, Justin. I *want* to be with him. It's just that Des has been gone for weeks, and my leaving will crush her."

"She's always been your soft spot." His eyes warmed. "What can I do to help? Anything?"

She shook her head. "I could never repay you for all that you've already done for me over the years."

"Hey, you saved me from getting into drugs and shit when I was younger. We saved each other."

"Thanks, Jus."

"You know you never needed my help to figure things out, right? You wanted me there, and I'm glad for that. You're one of my best friends. But don't fool yourself into thinking you can't handle your own shit. You've always had a pretty clear picture of what you needed to do to survive." He put a hand on her back and said, "Want to talk it out?"

"No. I'll figure it out."

He winked and said, "You always do. I've got to go. Hit me up if you need anything."

She chewed on what he'd said long after she finished inspecting the sculpture. Maybe Justin was right and she'd always known what she needed to do to survive. But Andre had made her see her life much more clearly than she ever had before, and she no longer wanted to just *survive*, living every aspect of her life in a separate bubble. She was being offered a second chance at love, and she couldn't be the partner Andre deserved if she couldn't even be honest about who she was to her own sister.

She locked up the studio and headed back to the inn, determined to make things right.

She found Desiree in her bedroom folding clothes. Cosmos was asleep at her feet.

"Welcome home."

Desiree squealed and threw her arms around her, sending Cosmos into a flurry of barks. "Oh my gosh, I missed you! I have so much to tell you about our trip, and pictures to show you, and everything!"

How could her sister's happiness get her all choked up? "I missed you, too. Where's your new husband?"

Desiree sighed. Her skin was bronze, and her eyes twinkled with happiness. "My *husband*. Does that sound as nice as it feels?"

"It does."

"He's probably with Drake and Dean at the resort. It feels like we've been gone forever, but, Vi, we had the most *amazing* trip!"

"I want to hear all about it."

Desiree grabbed her phone and spent the next two hours catching Violet up on every moment of her honeymoon, sharing pictures and relaying stories about every place they went. Violet had never seen her sister so happy.

"Now I understand why you love traveling so much. Rick says I've caught the *traveling bug* because I want to plan another trip for next fall."

Bug made her think of Andre. Didn't he deserve to be that

happy, too? Didn't *she*?

"Listen to me going on like I'm the only one who matters," Desiree said. "I saw all the plants in the living room. Dean said Andre bought them and had him and Drake set up a tent, candles, lights on the ceiling, all in an effort to bring *Ghana* to you. That sounds *so* romantic. Does that mean you guys are serious?"

You could say that was on the tip of her tongue, but she stopped herself. She'd been hiding behind quippy comments for long enough. "We are."

Desiree squealed again. "That's great! I want to hear about *everything!*" In the next second the excitement drained from her face, and she put her hands in her lap and said, "I mean, whatever you're willing to share with me."

Jesus, I'm such a bitch. You just went from being elated to worried in the space of a breath because of how I've always treated you. That cut like a knife.

"I want to tell you everything," Violet said. "But first I need to explain a few things."

"Okay," Desiree said tentatively. "Did something bad happen?"

"Not bad, maybe just *unfair?*" She stood and paced. "You know how I take off sometimes and say I have to get shit done?"

"Yes."

"Well, sometimes I go to the hospital, where I volunteer."

Confusion rose in Desiree's eyes.

"Using art as a form of therapy, I help children deal with anxiety. We work with Play-Doh and clay mostly. It helped me when I was young, and—"

"Wait, Vi. That's great, but how long have you been volunteering?"

"Since my third week on the Cape."

Desiree's entire body seemed to deflate. "You've been volunteering this *whole* time?"

"Yes, and there's more. I help my friend Rowan's daughter, too."

"Rowan…? I don't know a Rowan."

Violet crossed her arms and said, "He's a friend of mine. His wife died and he's raising his little girl on his own. I've been helping her with anxiety, and she's just been diagnosed with dyslexia."

"You work with kids," Desiree said flatly.

"Yes."

"Why haven't you told me? I was a preschool teacher, for Pete's sake. I've been teaching art to children here at the Cape practically since we came here." Her voice escalated and she got up, worrying with her hands as she crossed in front of Violet. "How often do you go there? Is it just a once-a-month type of thing?"

Violet shook her head. "In the spring and fall I usually go four or five times a week for a few hours each day."

"Four or five times *a week*?" Desiree said angrily.

"Yes, and in the summers I cut back to two or three times a week, depending on our schedules here."

"Geez, Vi. I don't even know who you are, do I? And here I thought we'd grown close and we trusted each other."

"We have, and I do trust you, Des. *Explicitly.*"

Desiree's eyes filled with tears. "No, you don't. People who trust each other don't keep secrets or lie about where they're going."

"There are reasons," Violet started to explain, although she was so upset, words were evading her, making her appear hesitant.

"I don't *care* about your reasons. Do you know how much it hurts to know you've been hiding that from me for this long? I tell you *everything*! Everything about *me*, and *Rick*, and…oh my goodness. What *else* don't I know about you?"

Violet tried to speak past the emotions clogging her throat, but her voice came out strangled. "I sculpt at Justin's studio. I'm making a sculpture for the family of a little girl who passed away last year. Her name was Erin."

"Did you work with her, too?" she asked in a shaky, reluctantly empathetic tone.

The pain in Desiree's voice, the hurt in her eyes, made it almost impossible for Violet to think. She nodded, tears burning again.

"You lost a child you obviously loved, and I never knew?" Desiree sank down to the edge of the bed. "How does that even happen? How can my own sister, who I see every single day, have that much of a secret life? Do you have any idea how much that hurts?"

"I never meant to hurt you. It's *my* shit, Des, not a reflection on you." Violet stepped toward her.

"*Don't*," Desiree snapped, holding her hand up to warn Violet off. "Please."

Oh God, what have I done? "I'm sorry…"

"You're *sorry*? We grew up with a mother who built her life on lies and whims, and she didn't give two cents about us. She had a whole life I never knew anything about. You *know* how much that hurt me. I guess I shouldn't be surprised, but I thought…" Sobs stole her voice and she covered her face. "Just *go*, please. I can't do this right now."

"Just let me explain."

Desiree lifted her tear-streaked face and glared at her. "I said I don't want to hear it. Not now. It hurts too much. Please just *go*."

"But—"

"Go!" Desiree yelled. "Now!"

ANDRE HAD BEEN on a high all day. After their magnificent night, and their conversation about the future, he was ninety-nine percent sure Violet was going to come with him to Cambodia. He was still buzzing as he turned onto the road that led to the inn on his way home from the clinic and could hardly believe it had been almost a month since he'd arrived. It seemed like forever ago that he'd first seen Violet standing in the hallway of the inn, looking gorgeous in that sexy black dress with the enticing zipper.

The roar of a motorcycle pulled him from his thoughts as Violet sped down the driveway and across the road, flying past him in the opposite direction. Her reckless entrance and the hunch of her shoulders and dip of her head sent his protective urges surging. He turned his bike around and raced after her, wondering what the hell had happened.

He spotted her turning off the road and kicked up his speed even more. Trees and houses blurred as they flew down a number of streets. She turned off the pavement and onto a narrow and bumpy dirt road, slowing just enough for him to catch up. He followed her for at least a mile down the woodsy road to a dead end. He cut the engine, ripped off his helmet, and ran to her, slayed by her puffy red eyes and tear-soaked face.

"Babe, what's wrong?"

He reached for her, and she twisted violently out of his hands, stalking toward a sandy path, her arms flailing. "I fuck up *everything*!" she shouted.

"No, you don't, babe. What happened?"

"I told Desiree everything! About the hospital, sculpting, *Erin*!" She stomped across the sand in her boots, tears falling like rivers down her cheeks. "Now she hates me. And you know what? I don't fucking blame her. You were right." She spun around, glaring at him with so much hurt in her eyes he had to reach for her again. "I'm all the bad parts of Lizza wrapped up in one fucking bitch of a person." She fell into his arms, sobbing.

"No, babe, that's not true. You don't have a bad bone in your body. This is my fault. I shouldn't have pushed you to talk to her."

"This isn't *your* fault! I should have been honest with her from the start. This is on *me*. I don't even deserve to be *around* her. She'd *never* hurt anyone the way I hurt her." She gasped a breath between sobs and said, "She's *good* and *sweet*."

"So are you, baby." He kissed her head, wishing he'd never urged her to tell Desiree the truth. He lifted her face, brushing her tears away with his thumbs, his chest constricting so tight it was hard to breathe. "You are a loving, kindhearted person. I'm not going to let you villainize yourself. You were hurting when you came to the Cape. You needed space to deal with it all, and you acted in the only way you knew how. The only way you'd ever been able to survive. Did you tell her that?"

She clung to him, shaking her head. "She wouldn't even let me explain."

"Then I'll talk to her. We'll make this right, babe. Desiree loves you, and she knows how much you love her."

Violet looked up at him with the most defeated expression and said, "I can't stand this. It hurts so bad…"

She collapsed, burying her face in his shirt, and they sank down to the sand right there in the middle of the path. Andre held her as the sun disappeared behind the dunes.

"We'll make this right, babe," he vowed.

He held her until she had no more tears to cry. And then he continued holding her, whispering his love for her as cold air swept over the dunes and night fell around them.

Chapter Seventeen

VIOLET SAT ON the edge of the bed Saturday morning, trying to shake the fearful images from her nightmares. She pulled up the hood of her sweatshirt and pushed her hands deep into her pockets as Andre came out of the bathroom with wet hair, a towel riding low on his hips. She'd gotten up before the sun and showered while he slept. It was only the second time since they'd reconnected that they'd showered separately, and she hated it.

He knelt before her, worry hovering in his eyes. "I missed you in there."

"Sorry." Her entire body ached with sadness, despite the loving way Andre had cared for her last night. He'd held her on the path to the beach until she'd begun trembling with cold. Once they'd gotten home, he'd drawn a warm bath and climbed in behind her, lovingly bathing her and holding her, making her feel safe and adored, but still she'd ached for the pain she'd caused Desiree. He'd wrapped her in his arms and held her all night in bed, whispering the sweetest memories about their time in Ghana, reassuring her that things would be okay with Desiree, and doing everything possible to make her feel better.

She'd finally fallen into a fitful sleep safely nestled in his arms. But when the nightmares hit, she'd woken up in a cold sweat, panicked, and she knew what she had to do.

"I have to talk to her," she said.

"Of course you do. I'll go with you."

"No. I have to do this alone." She put her hands on his face, struggling to stave off the tears that had plagued her on and off all night. "I love you so much." The words she needed to say dug deeper, refusing to come out, so she said, "I had nightmares about trying to talk to Desiree, but she hated me too much to give me a chance. She said she never wanted to see me again. And then it was like she just disappeared. I was searching for her at the inn, opening door after door, and she was *gone*." She pulled back, looking away as she said, "It brought back all the guilt about leaving you. I hope you know how sorry I am, and how much I regret—"

He pulled her against him and said, "Stop it, babe. We already forgave each other. Now it's time to forgive yourself." He lifted his head, smoothing her hair back from her face, and said, "None of those things are going to happen today. Desiree loves you just as much as you love her. She was just in shock."

She hoped that was true, but she didn't know if it was even possible for Desiree to forgive her. The only time she'd seen Desiree look so upset was when they found out Lizza had tricked them into coming to the Cape—and then had abandoned them again. The only thing she knew for sure was that she had to be honest with Andre.

She looked into his trusting eyes and forced the words to come. "I can't go with you if I don't fix this."

He exhaled a long breath, and then he lifted her hood from around her face and kissed her softly. "I know, and I understand."

His acknowledgment sent a spear of loneliness through her.

"You're everything to me, Vi, but you were Desiree's sister before you became my soul mate. I know how important she is to you. We'll be okay, even across thousands of miles." He held her hand over his heart and said, "You're always with me here, and I know you feel the same. We're unbreakable, babe."

"I love you so much. But I have to go see her." She pressed her lips to his, and then she forced herself to stand up and walk out of the room before she could give in to the screaming voice in her head telling her to take it back.

When she left the cottage, everything felt wrong. The air was too cold, her hoodie was too bulky, and the walk to the inn seemed a million miles long. She pulled her hood up over her head, hunkering down with her hands in her pockets again. When she stepped inside the inn and closed the door behind her, it felt like all the air had been sucked from her lungs. She could run back to the cottage, ask Andre if they could pack up and leave today. *Like a hit-and-run.*

Like Lizza.

Rick came down the stairs, and she froze, afraid to meet his eyes. He walked right up to her, silence burgeoning between them.

"Hey, Vi. You okay?"

She shook her head, still unable to look at him. Tears welled in her eyes.

"We all deal with hurt in different ways. I hid from it until Des helped me see that I could face it." Rick's father had been lost at sea during a sudden storm. Rick and Drake had been on the deck of their family's boat when he'd gone overboard, and Rick had been so consumed with guilt, as soon as he was old enough, he'd left the Cape.

She forced herself to meet his pained, serious gaze and said, "I never meant to hurt her."

"If anyone understands that, it's me," he said kindly. "You're both hurting right now. Go up and talk to her."

It took her legs a minute to find their strength, but she managed to walk past him and up the wide staircase. She inhaled a deep breath and knocked on their bedroom door. She thought she heard Desiree say to come in, but it was so soft she couldn't be sure. She pushed open the door and found Desiree lying on her back across the width of the bed in a pair of pink pajamas. She glanced at Violet, then stared blankly up at the ceiling.

Violet walked tentatively into the room. Her heart was beating so fast it was hard to breathe. She stood by the bed, not knowing what to do. Her legs weakened, and she sank down to the edge of the mattress, staring at the open door, feeling like a caged bird who needed to fly. But she couldn't fly. She could barely even walk.

She lowered herself to the bed, lying beside Desiree and fisting her hand in the blanket. Silence pressed in on them, swelling in the tight space between them like a living, breathing being.

"I'm sorry—" they said in unison, and then they both turned their heads. Desiree's eyes were puffy and red. Dark crescents underscored her sadness, drawing instant tears from Violet.

"I'm so sorry," Violet said. "I should have told you what I was doing and where I was going."

Tears slid down Desiree's cheeks. "All I *ever* wanted was to be part of your life. I spent my whole childhood waiting for summertime so I could see you again, and you'd go off and do your own thing. I thought we got over that when we came here. I thought I'd finally gotten the chance to know you. But it wasn't real. Why didn't you trust me?"

"It was real. It *is* real," Violet pleaded. "And I do trust you."

"Then *why* did you hide everything from me?"

"Because I was a mess. I desperately wanted a relationship with you, too, and suddenly there you were, my sweet, smart, organized, capable, and *stable* sister, willing to stick around with me and *try*. But I didn't even know *how* to have a real relationship, and if you don't believe me, look at my history. I had just walked away from the only man I have ever loved and I didn't even have the guts to say goodbye to him." She inhaled one shaky breath after another and looked up at the ceiling. It was too hard seeing the pain she'd caused. "My childhood was spent as the new kid in foreign places where half the time I didn't even speak the language. Just when I'd find a friend, Lizza would drag me to someplace new, and I'd have to start all over. It was easier to try *not* to connect with people. I still have no idea how Andre got through to me, but he was like the fire in a kiln, refusing to stop until he'd infiltrated every iota of my being. And even then I hid parts of myself, parts of my *life*, from him by running away."

"I *thought* I got through to you," Desiree said. "That's why it hurts so bad."

"You did get through. I have never had to answer to anyone. When I was growing up Lizza would disappear for hours. By the time I was nine, sometimes she'd be gone from morning until night." She turned toward Desiree again and said, "I love you. But that's terrifying, too, and as much as I love being here with you, it has always been a double-edged sword. Coming here gave me an excuse to leave Andre and his proposal behind."

"I still can't believe you did that."

"Neither can I. I was so stupid. And as much as being here with you, and building a family with you and our friends, is the greatest feeling in the world, it has always reminded me of who and what I left behind. I needed an *escape*, someplace where no one knew about Lizza, or our crazy past, or Andre. So I found places to go where I didn't have those constant reminders."

"But what about Justin? When we first came here, and his father and Zeke and Zander came to renovate the house, you acted like you didn't even know them."

"No, I didn't. Don't you remember Zander *winking* at me?"

"Yes, but you scowled at him. You didn't say you knew him or his father."

"I scowled at him because he was trying to get in my pants, and he knows Justin would beat the living daylights out of him if he saw him do it. What did you want me to do? I hadn't seen him in years, and I barely knew any of Justin's brothers. I met Justin when I was twelve, and I saw him over the summers on the beach here and there, but I never knew his parents. And his brothers were just kids on the beach. They'd come looking for Justin and tell him he had to go home, or whatever. It's not like I hung out with them. I never really *knew* his family until we moved here."

"Oh..." Desiree's brow furrowed. "I thought you knew them better. But you were sleeping with Justin and you kept *him* a secret."

"I only slept with Justin *once* since moving to the Cape, and I told you about it."

"He was the one you tried to..." Desiree's cheeks pinked up. "*Eff* Andre out of your system with?"

Violet nodded, smiling at her sister's innocence. "And never again."

"But Emery said he was long-dong naked man."

"Yes, she saw him naked, but we didn't have sex. He's a good friend, and when I needed someone to hold me, he was there. When I needed a safe place to try to start over, he let me use his studio to sculpt."

"But that's another thing I don't understand. You have a studio here. Why would you hide the fact that you sculpt? How is that any different from pottery or the batik work you do?"

Violet told her about how Andre had taught her to sculpt and how their love of art had sparked what became the deepest connection she'd ever known. She even admitted that she'd only made love to him one night during their three months together.

Desiree's jaw dropped open. "But you pushed me to have sex with Rick after we'd only just met."

"Yeah, well, you needed it. And I didn't push you to have sex. I pushed you to make love, because loving Andre had taught me the difference. You knew the value of sex. It has always been sacred and special to you. But to me it was an outlet and not at all what it should have been. Until I met Andre. And, Des, before we even made love, he made me feel so much, so good, that I lost my edge. Like, *totally* lost it. I became...*you*. Soft and girlie. Not that that's a bad thing. You know I adore you, but it scared the hell out of me. For the first time in my *entire* life, I realized the difference between being with a guy and being intimately in love with a man. I knew making love with him would wreck me. Which it did. And then the bastard proposed, and you know the rest." She paused, feeling like a great weight had been lifted from her chest, and said, "But don't worry. We've more than made up for those three months."

Desiree smiled. "No details, please."

"I met his parents," Violet said. "They were kind and funny and accepting. They adore him so much, like Ted adores you. I have never met a couple that has been together that long and still has so much love and respect for each other. I didn't really think it was possible."

"But you believe in me and Rick, and Dean and Emery, and—"

"Hey, I never said I wasn't fucked up."

"You don't have to use the f-bomb," Desiree said.

"I kind of do sometimes," Violet said with a smile. "But there's more I need to share with you."

Desiree closed her eyes and took hold of Violet's hand between them on the bed. "Okay. I'm ready."

She told her about the coffeehouse and her friends there. "Like Justin's studio, it started as an escape, but Andre helped me see what I hadn't before. I think I created two separate worlds in case I lost one."

More tears slipped from Desiree's eyes. "That's so sad."

"Yeah, but what's worse is that I hurt you in the process. It would be easy to blame it on our past, but I take full responsibility. I fucked up, and I can only use Lizza's taking me away, and Ted's letting her, for so long."

Desiree turned onto her side and leaned on her elbow. "What do you mean *Ted's letting her?*"

"He let me go, but that's whatever it is. I don't want to get lost in the past. I really want to try to move forward."

Desiree bolted upright. "Is that what Lizza told you? That he just let you go?"

"No."

"Well, good, because he fought for you. He got lawyers and everything, but Lizza wouldn't relinquish her parental rights.

You were the one they *both* wanted. He just couldn't win the legal battle."

Violet sat up slowly, feeling dizzy. "How do you know that?"

"Because he was a mess after Lizza took you away from us. We both were. How could you think he'd do something like that?" Desiree crossed her arms, glaring at Violet. "Whenever Lizza breezed into town with you, our worlds stopped. He'd stay home from work and buy all sorts of art stuff and toys for you, and then she'd steal you away after a day or two and we'd both be left in tears."

Tears poured from Violet's eyes, and she felt herself smiling. "He wanted me?"

"Yes, and I have to admit, when I was little I was kind of mad at you for it."

"Oh shit, Des. I'm sorry. That was selfish of me to say it like that."

"No, it wasn't. Lizza was right when she said I was better off with him. She loves me, in her own way." Desiree flopped onto her back and said, "Rick and I better rethink the whole having a family thing. It's too complicated."

Violet lay beside her, still reeling from what Desiree had said about Ted wanting her. "You and Rick are solid. You didn't inherit any of Lizza's craziness."

Desiree took her hand again and said, "Neither did you. We have our own brand of crazy."

"I really am sorry, Des. I never meant to hurt you, and I know it'll take time before you trust me again. But I'm in a better place now, and I won't let you down again."

"Thank you. I love you, too." She wiped her eyes and said, "Andre is good for you."

"You have no idea how good," Violet said with a smirk.

"Violet! I didn't mean *that.*"

"Neither did I, but I love your reaction." She laughed. "He is good for me. He doesn't let me hide, and I have no idea why he even gave me the time of day when he came here, but I'm so fucking glad he did. I can't imagine my life without him in it."

"Is this when you tell me that you're going away with him?"

"No. I mean, I want to go with him, but I'd never abandon you like that, especially after all this."

"So you're just going to let him *leave?*" Desiree's brows knitted. "What is *wrong* with you?"

"I have roots for the first time, and it feels good. We have friends, the inn. Andre and I will be fine."

"Oh, really? Like I was *fine* when Rick went back to DC? Don't you remember what you said to me? You told me that I could live without you because I'd done it for years, but that I couldn't live without him. You were right. You're the reason I chased after him. You promised me that you were my blood and you'd be here for me no matter what."

"I remember." Desiree had been a mess without Rick.

"You're really good at getting everyone else to see what they need to do, and you're never afraid to tell it like it is. Now it's your turn, Vi. You *love* Andre, and by the looks of your sappy ass"—Desiree's cheeks pinked up with the curse—"you won't be okay without him." She scooted closer so they were nose to nose and fished the necklace Violet had given her from around her neck. "This is us. *Infinite strength, protection, and unity. The rings move freely but are forever connected. No matter where we are, we'll always have each other.*"

"I know, but I'm not sure I can leave."

"If you don't go with him, a huge piece of your heart will be thousands of miles away. Just because you put down roots doesn't mean it's where you are meant to stay forever. Sisters and friends move away all the time to start their lives, have families, travel. We've found each other, and I will *always* be here for you," Desiree assured her. "All of us will. No matter where life takes us, we'll always have each other."

"But the inn—"

"I'll hire someone to help run it, the same way you offered when I went after Rick. I know you're afraid that if you leave things will never be the same again, but you're wrong. We're not little girls anymore being torn apart by our mother. *We're solid.* So please get your tattooed, cursing ass out of my room and tell your man you'll go with him."

Violet laughed and pushed to her feet, pulling Desiree up with her. "You said *ass* twice today."

"See? You need to leave before you have me cursing like a sailor."

"Thank you for not hating me." Violet put her arms around Desiree, hugging her.

Desiree held her tighter. "You're hugging me! Are pigs flying? Have the cows come home?"

"Shut up." She pulled back and said, "I need your help with something."

"If you think I'm going to be the one to tell our friends about your secret life, you're nuts. They'll give you so much grief."

"Not that. Spend the day with me?"

"The *day*? You've never asked me to spend an entire day with you before."

"Put some clothes on before I change my mind."

"I had a hard night. I have to shower." Desiree opened a

drawer and pulled out a pair of jeans.

Violet grinned and said, "All sexed up despite our fight? Way to go, Rick."

"No! Geez." Desiree gathered the rest of her clothes. "What did Andre think of the sex shop? Wait. Don't tell me. I don't want to know."

"You know what? We never got around to going, but now that you mention it…"

"*Oh boy*. Should I warn the neighbors? Pass out earplugs?" Desiree headed for the bathroom. "And I'm *not* getting on your motorcycle."

"My *day*, my *rules*."

Desire smiled and said, "There's the stubborn sister I know and love."

Chapter Eighteen

ANDRE SAT AT a table in the back of Common Grounds at exactly seven o'clock that evening, wringing his hands and trying not to think the worst. He was thrilled that Violet had decided to spend the day with Desiree, but other than a text asking him to meet her at the coffeehouse at seven, he hadn't heard from her all day.

"What can I get you to drink, big guy?" Gabe handed him a menu, then tried to tame a few wild red tendrils that had escaped the elastic she'd secured them with at the base of her neck.

"I'll have a ginger chai, thanks."

"One *Violet Special* coming up." She winked and headed for the bar area.

There was a commotion at the door, and he looked over, hoping it was Violet, but it was Steph, Dwayne, and Cory, giving Elliot high fives as they came in. Elliott pointed to Andre. Andre waved, though he'd have liked at least a few minutes alone with Violet before being inundated with friends. Steph strode toward him, looking worried, twisting the ends of her hair, which was now streaked with bright blue. Cory followed her with an easy smile, and Dwayne hung back, talking to Elliott, then jogged to catch up.

"Hey, dude." Cory flicked his chin, and his bangs swung away from his eyes, then fell right back over them. "These seats taken? Vi texted and asked us to meet her here."

She did? "Uh, no. Have a seat."

"She said she needed us tonight," Steph explained. "I thought maybe you were leaving town early and she was bummed, but she said you're not leaving until next weekend."

"Engagement announcement?" Dwayne asked, taking the seat beside Cory. "Because if it is, I want to know what drugs you gave that woman to get her to agree."

Everyone except Andre laughed.

"No, definitely not that type of announcement. I have no idea why she asked you to come. She and her sister had a rough time yesterday, but I thought they made up today. They spent the day together. Maybe something went sour and she needs your support." If that were true, it would sting like hell. Wasn't supporting her *his* job?

Gabe brought his drink, and as she took orders from the others Andre watched the entrance, wishing Violet would show up. The sculpture she'd made sat on a table by the front door. Had she told Desiree about that particular part of her life, too?

Man, he hoped things hadn't gone bad between them.

He and Violet would be fine in a long-distance relationship, even if every day apart seemed like a year. But not being with Violet while she worked through a hard time with Desiree? Knowing she might be heartbroken or scared? *That* would be torture.

The front door opened and he watched hopefully, but Justin walked in. Elliott pointed him in Andre's direction. Rowan and Joni came in behind him. *Fuck.* Something was definitely wrong.

"What's up, dude?" Justin set a hand on Andre's shoulder and nodded to the others.

"Did Vi text you?" Dwayne asked.

"Yeah. Why? Did she text y'all, too?"

There was a collective "Yeah" from the group as Joni ran over with a beaming smile and said, "Hi, jelly beans!"

Everyone greeted her with silly comments as Rowan scooped her up and sat down with her on his lap.

Justin pulled out a chair beside Dwayne and said, "So, what's going on? Vi just said she needed me and to find Andre when I got here."

Andre splayed his hands. "I have no idea. She texted me and said to meet her here at seven. I didn't know she'd asked you guys to meet her, too."

There was more commotion by the front door and they all looked over. Desiree and Rick walked in, followed by Drake, Serena, Dean, and Emery. Rick spoke to Elliott, who called Rod over and pointed to Andre and the others. As Rod headed for them, Mira walked in, cradling baby Holly, followed by Matt, holding Hagen's hand. They all looked across the room toward Andre, who was completely baffled.

"Hey, can I get some help with this?" Rod said as he pushed another table toward theirs. "El said Vi wants you all together. Looks like we need to add a few more tables."

The guys helped him push several tables together, and he heard Justin say, "Gavin, Chloe, and Daphne just got here. And, dude, Daphne has a *baby*."

"Yeah, a little girl. *Hadley*." Andre looked up as Violet's *other* friends approached.

Desiree was smiling, but she was also nervously biting her

lower lip, while tucked safely beneath Rick's arm.

"Daddy! Who are all these people?" Joni asked loudly. Rowan whispered something to her and Joni said, "She has lots of friends!"

Andre stood to greet Desiree and said, "I thought you were with Vi?"

"We went our separate ways hours ago. She said she had stuff to do." Desiree leaned closer and said, "This is the place she told me about? Are those her other friends? Are they nice?"

Andre nodded. "They're great. But how are you and Vi? Are you okay? Do you know why she asked everyone to come?"

"We're more than okay, and I have no idea," Desiree said. "She texted us all separately."

"Dude, move over," Dwayne said to Justin. Then he waved to the open chairs between them and said, "Single women over here."

"That's us, Daph!" Chloe snagged the chair beside Justin.

Gavin pulled out a chair between Daphne and Steph and said, "How about single dudes? Does this work?"

"Hell yes." Steph grabbed his shirt and tugged him down beside her. She leaned closer and said, "I'm Steph, and you smell *amazing*."

Everyone began claiming seats and introducing themselves at once. Rod headed up to the stage and played his guitar. As the others settled in, Hagen entertained them with stories of his first few weeks of school. Gabe brought a high chair for Hadley, and then took everyone's orders.

"So you don't know why we're here either?" Desiree asked, looking around the café. "This looks like someplace Violet would enjoy. She told me about it, and her friends here. I can't believe she's had this whole other life for so long. She took me to meet some of the kids she works with at the hospital, and to see Justin's studio. I saw the beautiful sculpture you guys made for Erin's parents."

"I'm glad," Andre said. "I'm sorry it was so hard for both of you at first. Violet loves you. She loves all of you very much."

Desiree put her hand on his arm and said, "You don't have to explain. She told me everything. I'm glad she had this place, and I'm glad she has you."

"What else did you two do today?" *And why haven't I heard from her?*

Desiree's cheeks pinked up. She turned her back to the others at the table and pulled the neckline of her sweater to the side, exposing a heart tattoo that was half orange and half purple. "Violet has one over her heart, too. Orange is my favorite color, and well, the purple is for Vi, of course. I had the idea to get sister tattoos, but Violet suggested we get a tattoo that matched the one Lizza has."

That surprised Andre, but then again, he hadn't expected Violet to show Desiree the studio or take her to meet the children she worked with. As he looked around the table, he wondered what else she had up her sleeve.

Rick leaned back with pride in his eyes and said, "My wife's a badass."

"If you think about it," Desiree said, "it makes sense that we should honor Lizza, too. She might have made our lives harder, but how can we really know what they would have been like if she hadn't taken Vi away? Besides, Lizza is the reason we reconnected, and she brought Rick and me together. She closed the distance between you and Violet, too. She'll always be our mother, and despite her crazy antics, we love her. We just don't want to *become* her."

Gabe brought everyone's drinks and took their dinner orders. Andre wanted to ask Desiree if Violet had mentioned going away with him, but he had a feeling she would have already said something if she had.

After ordering, he asked Gabe if she'd heard from Violet. "I'm beginning to get a little worried that something might have happened to her."

Gabe smiled and said, "This is Violet, remember? Nobody's dumb enough to mess with her. She'll show up when she's good and ready."

As she said the words, Rod stopped strumming his guitar, and Andre glanced up just in time to see Violet strutting down the hall from the kitchen wearing a bright red leather miniskirt with a zipper running down the center of it from the waist to the hem. A low-cut black shirt hung off one of her shoulders and had the words *daughter, sister, friend, lover* listed in white down the front, with a bright red slash through each one, and below them, written in red, was BADASS BITCH. Her leather biker boots announced each step with a *thud*, and her sexy green eyes were locked on Andre as she strode up to the mic.

"Oh my God. She's wearing *red!*" Emery exclaimed. "Have you *ever* seen Violet wear red?"

As the others whispered about Violet's clothes, Andre's heart filled up anew. She had worn that same outfit early on in Ghana, and it had driven him out of his mind then, too. She put a hand on her jutted-out hip, with the defiance of a teenager, and the din of the others quieted.

"How's it going?" Violet said with the confidence of a fearless woman.

Everyone answered at once, and she nodded, her eyes sweeping over her friends. Then those gorgeous eyes narrowed and she said, "Thanks for coming."

She glanced at Elliott, who gave her a thumbs-up, and her expression softened. Her hand fell from her hip, and when she looked out over the tables, her left toe turned in. Andre's chest tightened. He wanted to go to her, to be her rock, her greatest supporter. But he knew that his strong, vulnerable, creative girl with the heart of gold needed the support of everyone sitting around that table, along with Gabe, Rod, and Elliott, just as much as she needed him. She might need them all in different ways, but they each owned a piece of her heart, and they'd helped her become the incredible woman she was. He'd never want to take that away from her.

Violet cleared her throat and said, "You know all that bull-shit about *love is patient, love is kind*? Well, growing up with Lizza Vancroft taught me something a little different. I was taught that love is meant to be spread around because children should inherently *know* they're loved. They shouldn't need their parents to prove it to them. And kindness? Well, that's not just for family members, is it? In fact, sometimes the people we love most are the ones we're least kind to. Kindness is meant to be tossed around like confetti, and if you're lucky, some of it might shower down around you. Those aren't bad lessons, even if a little hard to take as a kid."

She looked at Andre, and his stomach sank. She wasn't leaving with him. He saw it in her apologetic gaze. He inhaled deeply, telling himself it was okay. There was nothing they couldn't handle as long as he had her to come home to.

"But perhaps the biggest lesson I learned from my crazy-ass mother," Violet said, "is that sometimes those we love most get left behind." She looked at Desiree, who was clinging to Rick's hand. Violet touched the necklace hanging around her neck and smiled. Her beautiful eyes found Andre again, lingering only a second before they drifted over the others, and she said, "When I came here, I was broken, and I was brokenhearted. Other than Justin"—she smiled at him—"I'd never had a long-term friendship. Justin has always been there for me, giving me shit and straightening my ass out when I needed it." She looked at Desiree again and said, "But then my sister showed me that I had a friend in her all along. I just didn't know it. Des, you taught me what it meant to be loved unconditionally and, maybe more importantly, loved unconditionally by a family member."

Desiree's lower lip trembled, and tears slipped from her eyes.

Violet lifted her chin, visibly steeling herself against them. "I didn't call you all here for a pity party. Each of you have taught me what friendship is really about. Steph, we've cried and laughed about our families."

"She saw Violet *cry*?" Serena whispered.

"Shh." Emery glared at her.

"Yes, I *cry*," Violet said sarcastically. "I also work with kids and I sculpt, so yeah, there's that." Before the confused murmurs of her friends could take over, she said, "Rowan, you brought me into this amazing place, and Gabe, Rod, Elliott, and the rest of you welcomed my sorry ass and all my bitchiness with open arms. We've had some great times, and I've always known that if I needed anything, you had my back."

"Always, sugar," Rowan called out.

"Mira, you are the voice of reason, and in watching you with your children, your brothers Dean and Rick, and the gossip girls, I've learned what being a mother, a sister, and a friend should look like." Violet paused, swallowing hard. "Guys, you all know who you are." She shrugged, and a small smile lifted her lips. "You're the brothers I've never had. Em, Serena, Daphne, and Chloe, you drive me batty with your nosiness and your giggles, but I couldn't have survived these last couple years without each of you giving me a reason to drag my ass to breakfast and give you shit."

"*And* there she is," Serena said.

"We love you, Vi!" Emery hollered.

Violet touched the microphone stand, as if she needed something to stabilize her, and said, "I hope that you all know how much I love you. I'm not good at that shit, so I appreciate you forgiving my shortcomings. But I'm learning. Or trying to."

Her emotional gaze returned to Andre, and he readied himself against what he knew was coming. He pressed his fingers into his thighs beneath the table, gritting his teeth, vowing not to make this any harder for Violet than it already was.

"Getting back to those lessons about love that our parents are supposed to teach us," she said. "It wasn't until I met a certain man overseas that I learned what *loving* and being *loved* really meant." She looked down, nudging the floor with the toe of her boot during a long, silent pause. When she looked up again, her eyes met his with so much love, so much trust, he choked up. And then she said, "His love was so deep and true, it scared the fuck out of me. Sorry, Joni."

Joni giggled and said, "She always says that word," earning a rumble of low chuckles.

Violet smiled. "I was scared about what might happen if I brought you all together. Andre gave me the insight and the strength that I needed to see clearly. I thought my worlds colliding would leave me feeling alone again, which is insane, because how could I ever feel alone when I have so many great friends? Gabe was kind enough to close the coffeehouse for my private spewing of emotions. Thank you for that and too many other things to count. I can't think of a better place to do this."

Violet strode across the floor with a riveting, emotional stare aimed at Andre. He rose as she came to his side and slipped his arm around her waist.

"You don't have to say it, babe," he said softly.

"Yes, I do. *You* taught me that love *is* patient and love *is* kind. *You* loved me even after I left you behind. You aren't threatened by my love of my friends, and you understand my need to keep the roots I've finally planted alive. Perhaps the most important lesson I've learned from you, and Desiree, and the rest of our friends, is that even if those you love most get left behind, it doesn't mean they're forgotten or unloved." She smiled up at him with tears in her eyes and said, "That's why I've decided to go with you next weekend and, if you'll have me, on every future adventure. You are the only man I've ever loved and—"

"Thank Christ." He hauled her against him, crushing his mouth to hers as cheers and applause rang out around them. "I love you, Daisy. I always have, and I always will."

"Who the heck is *Daisy?*" Emery shouted. "Does he mean Vi? Oh my God! *Daisy!*" She burst into hysterics.

Violet tore her mouth away and glared at her. "Call me that and *die.*"

Everyone laughed, except Violet and Andre, who were too busy sealing their love, and their future, with kisses to care.

MUCH LATER, AFTER being called *Daisy* too many times to

count, eating too much pizza, and finally breathing again, Violet sat beside Andre, watching her worlds blend together. Gavin, Daphne, Chloe, Justin, Dwayne, and Cory hadn't stopped talking since dinner was served. Dean played Rod's guitar while Steph and Emery sang. Desiree sat with Joni on her lap, chatting with Rod, Gabe, Matt, and Mira, who was nursing Holly. Beside them, Hagen, Drake, and Rick were trying to convince Rowan to come fishing with them. Hadley sat stoically on Rowan's lap, pulling at his beard, but even he couldn't charm a smile out of her. Elliott moved from group to group, getting to know everyone.

Andre pressed his lips beside her ear in a tender kiss and whispered, "I can't believe you told everyone all your secrets."

"I didn't. I told them I sculpt, but I couldn't bring myself to tell Des or anyone else about the torsos. That still feels too private."

"Good," he said, kissing her again.

She whispered, "I have another secret. I just *might* have a naughty-nurse costume waiting for us at home."

"Damn, baby." His gorgeous eyes darkened. "Now I'll be hard all night."

He drew her face to his, taking her in a divinely delicious kiss.

"You know, babe, when Desiree said you'd gone off on your own several hours before they got here, I thought you had changed your mind about going away with me. I was sure you needed time alone to figure out how to tell me you were staying on the Cape."

"Oh shit! I almost forgot something." She popped up to her feet, then leaned down and said, "They're my friends, and they're important. But you're the love of my life, and I'll never make the mistake of leaving you again." She gave him a chaste kiss and said, "Be right back."

She grabbed Elliott and they headed for the kitchen.

"I was waiting for you to give me the signal," he said as they began placing blackberries on the five-layered heart-shaped puff pastries they'd spent the afternoon making. There was a layer of cream between each of the three layers of pastry, and they were topped with powdered sugar. They smelled heavenly.

"I'm sorry. I got so sidetracked I forgot. El, I can't thank you enough for taking so much time to help me make these. I kind of suck at cooking."

Elliott smiled and said, "I'm your friend. I'll always make time for you."

"Thank you. That means the world to me."

They finished garnishing the pastries, and Violet realized she'd be leaving soon and wouldn't see Elliott for a very long time. Like the rest of his family, he had a special way of seeing the best in people and, she liked to think, bringing that out in them, too. Suddenly overwhelmed with emotions, she said, "I think I need to hug you."

Elliott's eyes widened. "But you told me no hugs."

"I know, but that was when we first met, and I'm going away for a few months. I think I'm ready now." She opened her arms, and Elliott squeezed her so tight she choked out, "Okay, okay!"

"Sorry," he said sheepishly, still holding her tight. "You're moving away. I have to stock up."

Gabe walked in as he was releasing her and said, "Whoa! Was that a *hug*? I want in on that action." She pulled Violet into an embrace and said, "I'll miss you. You really are part of our family."

"I'll miss you guys, too." She choked up for the millionth time in the last month and cleared her throat to try to get a grip on her emotions. "All right, kiddo. Are you ready?"

"You bet!" Elliot reached for a tray. "Andre will be surprised!"

"I'll get the plates," Gabe said, following them out.

They set the treats on the table, and everyone gathered around to check them out.

"Oh my! Those look delicious." Serena reached for one.

Emery pushed closer, reaching around Serena to grab one. "Yum!"

Violet started to glare at them, wanting to give the first one to Andre, but she caught herself and let the girls grab their fill.

"They're like sharks," Elliott teased.

Violet laughed and said, "We call them vultures."

"Hey! We're prettier than vultures," Serena said. "We're…?"

Emery licked her fingers and said, "Forget it, Serena. We're *hot* vultures. Chloe, Daph! You have to taste these!"

"Count your fingers," Drake teased.

Daphne put a tiny piece of a pastry in Hadley's mouth, and her little girl smiled as she ate it. "Whoever made these needs to move in with me! You made Hadley smile!"

"Me and Violet made them," Elliott said. "But I'm not moving in with you."

Everyone looked at Violet, who was reaching between them for a pastry. "What? Elliott did most of the work. I just had the idea."

Gabe handed her a plate and said, "Don't let Violet fool you. She and Elliott spent hours making them together."

Andre reached for Violet as she came to his side, pulling her onto his lap. "You baked? And you're smiling."

"Yeah. I'll miss these crazy bitches." She set the plate on the table and put her arms around his neck, feeling luckier, and happier, than she ever had. "I baked for *you*. You might not have been able to convince Abby to name a doughnut after us, but you sure won me over. I call these delicious pastries Wandering Hearts."

There was a collective "Aw," and Violet realized everyone was watching them.

"They're just like Violet," Elliott announced. "Hard on the outside and sweet and soft on the inside!"

Everyone laughed—including Violet—until the loving look in Andre's eyes stole her voice and his words, "You're perfect, Daisy, inside and out," stole her heart.

Epilogue

ANDRE TRIED AGAIN to connect a FaceTime call to Desiree and their friends at Summer House. It was Christmastime, and he and Violet had been in Cambodia for two and half months. It hadn't taken her any time at all to readjust to life in the field. If anything, she'd been rejuvenated by the simplicity *and* the complexities of it. But she missed Desiree and their friends, and he was thankful for modern technology for that very reason. She was still nurturing those roots she'd discovered, and it was a beautiful thing, watching her blossoming in so many ways.

"I got it, Dais!" he called out as he crossed the yard to where she sat with three children making animals out of clay.

"There they are!" Desiree peered into the screen. "Hi, Andre! How are you?"

"Great. Hold on. I want you to have time with Vi in case we lose our connection." He turned the phone so Violet could see her, and the three boys got up to inspect the screen.

"Look at you!" Desiree squealed. "Who are those adorable boys?"

Violet touched each boy's shoulder as she introduced him. "Boran, Chann, and Davany. They like to hang out with us when we're not working."

Speaking to the boys in their native language of Khmer, she told them Desiree was her sister. The boys put their hands together in prayer position and bowed as they said hello, also in Khmer. Andre and Violet had been trying to learn the language, and thanks to a very patient translator, they knew just enough to get by.

Emery's and Serena's heads popped into view over Desiree's shoulder. And a second later Chloe and Daphne peered over *their* shoulders.

"Aw, they're so cute," Daphne said as the boys pointed at the phone, chattering so fast Andre couldn't make out a word of what they were saying.

"You look so relaxed," Emery said. "Are you still enjoying living there?"

Violet glanced at Andre and said, "I've never been happier."

It was dry, dusty, and warm, and their days were always busy, but with the exception of nights when there were medical emergencies, when they fell into each other's arms at night, the chaos fell away. Even when they made love ravenously, keeping the night animals awake, there was an underlying sense of peaceful, loving calm that engulfed them. They often lay beneath the stars as they had in Ghana, only this time it was better. There was no fear about what the future held, or how different their lives were, because even without being married, he knew they were forever intertwined.

"How are things there?" Violet asked. "Chloe's looking a little shaggy. I like it."

Chloe touched her hair and said, "I'm growing it out. I'm glad you like it."

"It looks edgy," Violet said. "What else is going on? Is Des pregnant yet?"

Desiree's cheeks pinked up. "Violet!"

"Not yet." Rick's deep voice floated in before his face appeared beside Desiree's, blocking out the others. "We haven't started trying yet, but we're having a hell of a lot of fun practicing."

The boys ran across the grass to join another group of kids, and Andre crouched beside Violet, holding the phone in front of them, and said, "I guess the girls can't complain about the quality of breakfasts anymore?"

Cheers rang out behind Desiree and Rick.

They talked for another minute with Rick, and then he said, "There are more people here who want to say hi. Love you guys. Be safe."

Rick stepped away, and Justin's face appeared, smiling warmly. "Hey, babe. Andre. How's it going?"

"Good. Things okay there?" Violet asked.

Justin nodded and said, "Yeah. Boy, you weren't kidding about the gossip around here. These chicks talk about *everything*."

Violet laughed. "No shit. Welcome to the *Real Housewives of Wellfleet*."

"Move over, wingman." Gavin's face appeared beside Justin's. "Andre, my man. Violet. Happy holidays!"

"Right back at you," Andre said. "How's it going?"

"Not bad. Especially since I finally have a single dude to hang with," Gavin said with a grin. "There's too much estrogen in this place…"

"Women of the Cape beware. Do I even want to know…?" Violet mumbled.

Justin smirked. "Trust me, you don't. But I still miss my favorite girl. It's lonely over here without your motorcycle roaring down my road every other night, and my studio feels empty, but you know…I'll get over it."

"It won't be empty for long," Gavin interjected. "But we aren't banking on that fictional blonde who supposedly got *hung up*"—he put air quotes around *hung up*—"in L.A., and isn't going to come out until spring or summer."

"Dude, for the millionth time, Harper is *real*," Justin said.

Harper hadn't made it back for their goodbye party, although Ted and Andre's parents had joined them, along with all the friends from the coffeehouse. Ted and Violet had been FaceTiming as well, and their relationship was growing stronger every time they talked.

"Where are the rest of the guys?" Andre asked.

Emery pushed the men out of the way and said, "Jett is home for the holidays. He's with Dean and Drake picking up a few things at the resort. I'll tell them you said hello." She leaned closer to the screen and spoke just above a whisper. "You should see Daphne drooling over Jett. It's hilarious. *And* look!" She thrust her left hand in front of the screen, showing off a beautiful gold wedding band. "We got married! We went to the courthouse. We just couldn't wait!"

Happiness rose in Violet's eyes. "Congratulations! I'm so happy for you."

"That's fantastic," Andre said. "We wish you both all the happiness in the world."

"Thank you," Emery said with a proud smile as she pulled her hand away from the screen.

Serena's head popped in next to Emery's. "And, Vi, my waistline thanks you *so* much for introducing us to everyone at the coffeehouse. I swear I have been there like a dozen times just for those delicious Wandering Hearts. Elliot is always making new creations for me to try, and I love hanging out with Steph and everyone. Oh my God, and Dwayne is a *riot*, the way he shamelessly flirts with Daph and Chloe."

Andre chuckled.

"Justin!" Violet hollered, and his face popped back into view. "You'd better watch out for those girls. I told you what'd happen if someone hurt them."

"Jesus, Vi. You're threating me from across the world?"

"Damn right I am," she snapped.

"Okay, you two," Desiree interrupted. "Can I please talk to my sister and her man?" She smiled at Violet and said, "I miss you both, and I love you. You'll be here in March, right?"

"Definitely. In time for Erin's memorial," Violet said. "But we're not sure yet about staying for the whole summer."

Andre had been working on their schedules, trying to arrange it so they could spend the summer at the Cape, but he wouldn't know for sure for a few more weeks. Perry was also waiting to hear if Andre would be back to help them out at the Outer Cape Health Clinic next summer.

"We'll know by March," he assured them.

"Steph said she and one of her friends might be able to help us out during the summer," Desiree said. "Just let us know. And, Vi, don't worry. I can handle everything."

"She's got plenty of backup," Rick said, and then he kissed Desiree's cheek.

The connection froze, and Violet said, "No!" She sighed and said, "I *hate* it when that happens." They waited for it to unfreeze, but after a minute they gave up and ended the call.

Andre set the phone on the blanket and pulled her into his arms. "I'm sorry, babe."

"It's okay," she said. "It was great seeing everyone. I was just thinking, when we were overseas before, I had no one to call, no one to go home to. I didn't even really know what *home* meant, or what it would feel like. And now I'm with the man I love every day, and I have a sister and more friends than I could have ever imagined possible just a FaceTime call away." She straddled his lap, her green eyes glittering with mischief. "Do you know what else I have?"

He grabbed her butt and said, "A fantastic ass?"

She smiled and pressed her lips to his.

"And an amazing mouth?" he said against her lips.

"Yours isn't too shabby either."

He nipped at her lower lip, and she laughed. The sweet, carefree sound filled him up inside. "What else do you have?"

"*Perspective*," she said softly. "I finally know the true meaning of *home*. It isn't about whether I spent my childhood there or how many years I've lived somewhere. It's a feeling of safety, and unconditional love, and as long as you're by my side, I'm always *home*."

Ready for More Bayside?

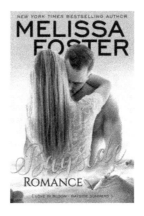

Gavin is about to find out that Harper really does exist—and she's going to knock his socks off! Find out why in Bayside Romance!

If you love Bayside, you'll adore the Seaside Summers series, featuring a group of fun, sexy, and emotional friends who gather each summer at their Cape Cod cottages. They're funny, flawed, and so hot you'll be begging to enter their circle of friends.

Start reading *FREE in digital format with
SEASIDE DREAMS!

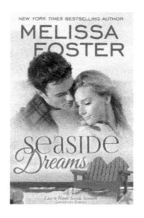

Bella Abbascia has returned to Seaside Cottages in Wellfleet, Massachusetts, as she does every summer. Only this year, Bella has more on her mind than sunbathing and skinny-dipping with her girlfriends. She's quit her job, put her house on the market, and sworn off relationships while she builds a new life in her favorite place on earth. That is, until good-time Bella's prank takes a bad turn and a sinfully sexy police officer appears on the scene.

Single father and police officer Caden Grant left Boston with his fourteen-year-old son, Evan, after his partner was killed in the line of duty. He hopes to find a safer life in the small resort town of Wellfleet, and when he meets Bella during a night patrol shift, he realizes he's found the one thing he'd never allowed himself to hope for—or even realized he was missing.

After fourteen years of focusing solely on his son, Caden cannot resist the intense attraction he feels toward beautiful Bella, and Bella's powerless to fight the heat of their budding romance. But starting over proves more difficult than either of them imagined, and when Evan gets mixed up with the wrong kids, Caden's loyalty is put to the test. Will he give up everything to protect his son—even Bella?

Have you met Tru Blue & the Whiskeys?

If you think you know everything about bearded, tattooed men, get ready to be surprised—and to fall hard for Truman Gritt.

He wore the skin of a killer and bore the heart of a lover

There's nothing Truman Gritt won't do to protect his family—including spending years in prison for a crime he didn't commit. When he's finally released, the life he knew is turned upside down by his mother's overdose, and Truman steps in to raise the children she's left behind. Truman's hard, he's secretive, and he's trying to save a brother who's even more broken than he is. He's never needed help in his life, and when beautiful Gemma Wright tries to step in, he's less than accepting. But Gemma has a way of slithering into people's lives, and eventually she pierces through his ironclad heart. When Truman's dark past collides with his future, his loyalties will be tested and he'll be faced with his toughest decision yet.

Fall in love with the fun, feisty Montgomerys!

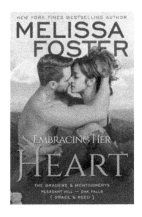

Welcome to Oak Falls, Virginia, home to horse farms, midnight rodeos, bookstores, coffee shops, and quaint restaurants where you're greeted like family and treated like treasured guests. Buckle up for a wild ride. Like any Southern girls worth their salt, the sweet-talking, sharp-tongued Montgomerys can take men to their knees with one seductive glance or a single sugarcoated sentence.

In EMBRACING HER HEART...

Leaving New York City and returning to her hometown to teach a screenplay writing class seems like just the break Grace Montgomery needs. Until her sisters wake her at four thirty in the morning to watch the hottest guys in town train wild horses and she realizes that escaping her sisters' drama-filled lives was a lot easier from hundreds of miles away. To make matters worse, she spots the one man she never wanted to see again—ruggedly handsome Reed Cross.

Reed was one of Michigan's leading historical preservation experts, but on the heels of catching his girlfriend in bed with his business partner, his uncle suffers a heart attack. Reed cuts all ties and returns home to Oak Falls to run his uncle's business. A chance encounter with Grace, his first love, brings back memories he's spent years trying to escape.

Grace is bound and determined not to fall under Reed's spell again—and Reed wants more than another taste of the woman he's never forgotten. When a midnight party brings them together, passion ignites and old wounds are reopened. Grace sets down the ground rules for the next three weeks. No touching, no kissing, and if she has it her way, no breathing, because every breath he takes steals her ability to think. But Reed has other ideas...

Love in Bloom FREE Reader Goodies

If you loved this story, be sure to check out the rest of the Love in Bloom big-family romance collection, and download your free reader goodies, including publication schedules, series checklists, family trees, and more!
www.MelissaFoster.com/RG

Remember to check my sales and freebies page for periodic first-in-series free and other great offers!
www.MelissaFoster.com/LIBFree

More Books By Melissa Foster

LOVE IN BLOOM SERIES

SNOW SISTERS
Sisters in Love
Sisters in Bloom
Sisters in White

THE BRADENS at Weston
Lovers at Heart, Reimagined
Destined for Love
Friendship on Fire
Sea of Love
Bursting with Love
Hearts at Play

THE BRADENS at Trusty
Taken by Love
Fated for Love
Romancing My Love
Flirting with Love
Dreaming of Love
Crashing into Love

THE BRADENS at Peaceful Harbor
Healed by Love
Surrender My Love
River of Love
Crushing on Love
Whisper of Love
Thrill of Love

THE BRADENS & MONTGOMERYS at Pleasant Hill – Oak Falls

Embracing Her Heart
Anything For Love
Trails of Love
Wild, Crazy Hearts
Making You Mine

THE BRADEN NOVELLAS

Promise My Love
Our New Love
Daring Her Love
Story of Love
Love at Last

THE REMINGTONS

Game of Love
Stroke of Love
Flames of Love
Slope of Love
Read, Write, Love
Touched by Love

SEASIDE SUMMERS

Seaside Dreams
Seaside Hearts
Seaside Sunsets
Seaside Secrets
Seaside Nights
Seaside Embrace
Seaside Lovers
Seaside Whispers

BAYSIDE SUMMERS

Bayside Desires
Bayside Passions
Bayside Heat
Bayside Escape
Bayside Romance

More Books by Melissa

Chasing Amanda (mystery/suspense)
Come Back to Me (mystery/suspense)
Have No Shame (historical fiction/romance)
Love, Lies & Mystery (3-book bundle)
Megan's Way (literary fiction)
Traces of Kara (psychological thriller)
Where Petals Fall (suspense)

Acknowledgments

I hope you loved learning more about Violet. While researching her craft, I had the pleasure of speaking with Tiffany Carmouche, an amazing sculptor and speaker. Thank you, Tiffany, for answering my endless questions with patience and professionalism. I have taken creative liberties in the story, and any crafting errors are my own, not a reflection of Tiffany's expertise. You can find out more about Tiffany on her website, www.TiffanyCarmouche.com.

Nothing excites me more than hearing from my fans and knowing you love my stories as much as I enjoy writing them. If you haven't joined my fan club, what are you waiting for? We have loads of fun, chat about books, and members get special sneak peeks of upcoming publications. facebook.com/groups/MelissaFosterFans

As always, thank you to all of my friends and fans who have talked me off the ledge while writing Violet and Andre's story. Heaps of gratitude go out to my meticulous and talented editorial team. Thank you, Kristen, Penina, Juliette, Marlene, Lynn, Justinn, and Elaini for all you do for me and for our readers. And as always, I am forever grateful to my family and my own hunky hero, Les, who allows me the time to create our wonderful worlds.

Meet Melissa

www.MelissaFoster.com

Melissa Foster is a *New York Times* and *USA Today* bestselling and award-winning author. Her books have been recommended by *USA Today's* book blog, *Hagerstown* magazine, *The Patriot*, and several other print venues. Melissa has painted and donated several murals to the Hospital for Sick Children in Washington, DC.

Visit Melissa on her website or chat with her on social media. Melissa enjoys discussing her books with book clubs and reader groups and welcomes an invitation to your event. Melissa's books are available through most online retailers in paperback, digital, and audio formats.

CPSIA information can be obtained
at www.ICGtesting.com
Printed in the USA
LVHW092129011019
632855LV00003BB/646/P